Bonus Kisses

USA TODAY BESTSELLING AUTHOR

FREYA BARKER

Bonus Kisses

ISBN: 9781988733562
Cover Design: Freya Barker
Editing: Karen Hrdlicka
Proofreading: Joanne Thompson

Author's Note

I wrote this story a little over a year after my mother passed away.

I had the privilege of looking after her in her home in Holland the final three months of her life.

Mom was the matriarch of our family in the truest meaning of the word. She was strong, she was kind, and she was loving. She showed that love in many different ways, but was not particularly liberal in expressing her affection. She tried, but growing up herself in a household where kisses and hugs were few and far between, it didn't always come natural for her.

I've lived in Canada since 1989 and saw my mother maybe once a year, so when I arrived in Holland—after she had her heart attack—I would give her the occasional random kiss in passing. One day she asked me what the kiss was for. I told her it was a bonus kiss, because I'd missed out on so many over the years.

I did that a lot over the next months; I'd kiss her as I passed by her chair on my way to the kitchen, or when I helped her in or out of bed. Each time I'd whisper "bonus kiss" and she'd smile.

I kissed her often as she was lying in bed in front of the French doors, surrounded by her children for the thirty-two hours it took for her to leave this life.

And when we finally closed her casket—as she had asked us kids to do— I kissed the lid over her head with one last bonus kiss.

It took me a year to begin to process what were both the most difficult, as well as the most treasured months of my life.

It took me two months to write my emotions into words that became "Bonus Kisses."

Freya

This book is dedicated to Mama; the best woman I have ever known.
I love and miss you still…

bonus kiss

Chapter One

Taz

THE SUN IS ALMOST down when I spot the glimmer of the Congo River.

Another half hour or so in the dusty Land Rover and I can have a real shower, and roll in my cool sheets, for the first time in twelve days.

Bouncing around on oftentimes nothing more than a faint, dusty trail to get to some of the remote villages of the Democratic Republic of Congo gets old fast.

I remember when I first landed in Ghana, nine years ago. Then twenty-nine, everything had still been an adventure. Growing up in the tiny town of Eminence, in the Ozarks, I'd always hungered to see more of the world.

After getting my nursing degree at twenty-five—it took me a while to decide what I wanted to do—I'd first moved to Seattle, working as a triage nurse at the Northgate Kindred Hospital. I thought moving to the big city would broaden my horizons, but I was never able to get used to the noise and the crowds. I stuck it out for four years before the walls of my small apartment started closing in on me.

When my father was diagnosed with Parkinson's I went back home, thinking maybe I could find something more local, but was quickly reminded why I'd been so eager to get so far away from Eminence in the first place.

I was there barely a month when an opportunity came along to work as a nurse for Doctors Without Borders in Ghana, and I jumped all over it. It had been perfect timing, since things at home were already going downhill fast.

I loved it. Loved the almost nomad type lifestyle of those first years. Living out of my duffel bag, never knowing where the new day would take me, and experiencing things I never imagined I would get to see.

After Ghana came Nigeria, then a short stint in Ethiopia, before I finally ended up in the Congo. That was four years ago. I'd only been back to the US a handful of times, and only one of those times visited home. That had been a mistake.

"Ntámbo," Wilson, our driver, says in his native Lingala, pointing to the left where a pride of lions is having a drink at the river's edge. Not an unusual scene to bump into here, but it never fails to impress me. I twist my head to keep the group in sight as we continue our bumpy path back to our home base.

My stomach is growling when Wilson pulls on to the road leading to the compound. The main building is a simple one-story structure housing the clinic. Behind it, partially hidden in the tree line, the small thatched roof living quarters are visible. The four clay huts called tukuls

—three single and one double-occupancy—makes up staff lodging for the two physicians and three nurses with Doctors Without Borders stationed here.

This is a satellite clinic from where we service a large area, hundreds of miles of wilderness dotted with small villages depending on our medical care. The past week and a half consisted of delivering vaccinations to mostly women and children in the hard-to-reach areas, and dealing with whatever emergencies landed in our path.

I'm exhausted. Tired in a way that goes beyond twelve days of traveling under the harshest of conditions. I'm tired of the heat, of the constant dust and grime I seem to be covered with twenty-four seven. Tired of feeling like anything we do is merely a drop on a hot plate, the results barely visible. Too many children still dying of diseases almost eradicated in other parts of the world. Too many easy-to-fix injuries, which without proper medical care, end up in unnecessary and often devastating trauma.

Nine years of living under rough conditions has taken its toll, both mentally and physically.

I sigh when I see Paul walking out of the clinic, his eyes immediately drawn to our approach. Now there's another reason I suddenly feel the weight of my life here heavy on my shoulders. When the very talented French physician arrived here, a little over a year ago, he'd seemed like a breath of fresh air with his charm, his clean good looks, and his apparent attraction to me.

I had a few brief sexual entanglements over the years, the most memorable one with Sven, a Dutch nurse. Six foot three of gorgeous lean mass, topped with a messy mop of dirty blond hair, reminiscent of a man I've tried to eradicate from my memory banks for the past nine years, without much luck. The moment I realized I was using Sven to live out that particular fantasy of mine, I'd broken it off.

There hadn't been anyone since, until Paul Bonnaire joined our team. Just a scant few inches over my five five —dark-haired and smooth-tongued—he'd seemed like the perfect antithesis. Unfortunately, he also hadn't held my interest long, and after a handful of less than satisfying sexual gymnastics in his tukul, I'd had enough.

Paul hadn't.

He's been trying to work his way back into my pants, unable to take 'not a chance in hell' for an answer. That too is wearing me down.

"Taz!" he calls out, walking up to the Land Rover when we pull into a parking spot. He has my door open before I have a chance to react. *"Je vous ai manqué."*

Well, I didn't miss you. In fact, some time away had provided welcome relief from the uncomfortably persistent man.

"Hey, Paul," I mumble under my breath, as I try to squeeze by him—without touching—to grab my bag from the back of the vehicle.

"Let me get that for you," he says, taking my duffel in one hand while throwing his other arm over my shoulder, steering me to my hut.

Rather than struggling fruitlessly over my bag, I shrug off his arm and rush ahead but stop, turning to face him outside my door.

"I wish you would stop, Paul. You're not only making me uncomfortable, but the rest of the team as well. We're done." I wave my hand between us. "This is done. Let's call it an error in judgment and move on."

"Je ne comprends pas?"

I roll my eyes at his feigned ignorance and snag my duffel from his hand. "Please, you understand me well enough, but just to make sure—*c'est fini entre nous.*"

Noticing the flash of anger in his eyes, I'm relieved when Patti, one of the other nurses, comes jogging up the path.

"Did you give her the message?" she asks Paul when she reaches us.

"What message?" I ask, ignoring him and keeping my eyes on Patti, who suddenly looks too sympathetic for comfort. We have ways to stay in touch here at the clinic by phone and with spotty Internet, but once we leave the compound; we're quickly out of range.

"Your friend, Kathleen, called the day before yesterday. It's your sister."

Mention of Nicky is followed by the familiar ache right in the middle of my chest. Only two years between us, my sister and I had been close growing up. They say opposites attract, and that had been a true statement for us. We were the perfect contrast, her light against my dark. Veronica had been the quiet and responsible child, whereas I'd always had a wild streak a mile wide and lived to break every rule in the book. The perfect yin and yang, until I left.

My sister put a smile on my parents' faces when all I did was give them gray hair. I hardly think they miss me. Kathleen, my best friend, is the only person I have any contact with from back home.

"My sister?"

"I'm sorry," Patti says, putting a hand on my arm. "I'm afraid it's bad news."

Rafe

CHRIST.

The past week has been an absolute nightmare.

Nicky hadn't been feeling well over the weekend, claiming she was likely coming down with something. Last Monday morning, she'd apparently gotten worse and ended up heading back to bed after she saw the kids off to school.

I had no idea; I'd been called out of bed by Jeff Van Duren at four that morning and was elbow deep in his prize heifer. She'd had trouble calving her first, the calf having gotten stuck in the birth canal. It had taken most of my morning making sure both mom and newborn bull calf were okay. I'd been on my way back to the veterinary clinic when my assistant called, asking me why there was an ambulance outside next door.

A heart attack.

Who would've thought a forty-year-old, seemingly healthy woman could be struck with a massive heart attack? There'd been no obvious signs, which I've learned since is not unusual in women. Her complaints had been of a more general nature, nothing really indicating that the arteries around her heart had slowly been clogging up.

She underwent an angioplasty and had three stents placed to restore some blood flow. A few days later, after a battery of tests, the cardiologist informed us that unfortunately the damage to her heart had been much more extensive than initially thought. It looks like she may have had prior cardiac events that went unnoticed but weakened the muscle. Her heart is failing and other than medication to keep her as stable as possible; there is nothing they can do.

I glance over at Sarah, who hasn't left her daughter's bedside since she and Ed got here. She looks exhausted.

"Why don't you join Ed and go lie down for a bit?" I suggest, but quickly clamp my mouth shut when I take in the fierce look she shoots me.

"Mom," Nicky pleads, her voice weak as she turns to her mother. "Get some rest, please."

Sarah's eyes fill with tears; not the first ones she's spilled since receiving the devastating news. "But I…"

"You're ready to collapse, Mom. Where would we be if that happened? Rafe will call if anything happens," she assures her mother.

"I promise," I add.

Sarah glances at me, and turns back to Nicky, before bending down to kiss her daughter's cheek. She turns and walks to the door, her shoulders slumped under the weight resting on them.

The moment the door falls shut behind her, Nicky grabs my hand.

"We need to talk."

I stroke my thumb over the back of her hand, feeling more connected to her than I have in a long time. "The kids," I offer gently.

Spencer and Sofie are back in Eminence being looked after by Nicky's friend, Kathleen. They'd only seen their mother briefly once, five days ago. Kathleen brought them to the hospital, but at five and eight years old, seeing their mother hooked up to tubes in a strange place had scared them. We decided we wouldn't put them through that again and instead had called them every night before bed.

"Yes," she whispers. "I want to go home, Rafe."

I automatically shake my head. "Sweetheart, you're better off here should anything happen."

"Like what? Dying? That will happen soon enough, whether I'm here or not."

I pull my hand free and run it through my hair. "Jesus."

"I want to be with my kids, in my house. I don't want to die here, hooked up to machines in a hospital bed, with strangers coming in every five minutes to check if I'm still breathing."

"But the kids…" I start, unable to finish.

"What is worse, Rafe? That you come home sometime in the next days or weeks, announcing their mother is gone, or having them able to ask questions, share fears, prepare them gently with the kind of love only parents can give? I don't want their last memory of me to be lying in a strange hospital bed, in an alien and scary place."

Fuck.

My own eyes well up when I hear the tears in hers.

"Please," she begs, and I drop my head on the bed beside her. Her fingers ruffle lightly through my hair. "I don't have much time to make good memories. For me or for them. Please give me a chance to do that."

"I'm sorry," I blurt out, my voice muffled by the bedding.

"You don't have anything to be sorry for."

"You deserved better than me."

"You're rewriting history, Rafe. It was me who stepped out on you."

She had. She confessed as much almost a year ago, but since then I've had a lot of time to think about cause and effect.

The truth is we never should've been more than friends. I'm the one who pushed for marriage when she got pregnant, so in love with the fantasy of settling down in a small town with a wife and two point one kids, I never took real feelings—mine or anyone else's—into account. Had I done that, my life would've looked much different. Instead 'fake it until you make it' had been my mantra, and I can't complain too much; my beautiful children are the reward.

Granting Nicky her last wish is the absolute least I can do.

"Okay, I'll bring you home." I lift my head and find her tired eyes. "I'll need to make a few phone calls, see if I can get home care organized."

"S'okay," she mumbles, her eyes already drifting shut. "Is taken care of…"

Before I can ask what she means she's asleep, something she's been doing a lot of. I let her rest and step out into the hallway, looking for her nurse. I find her at the desk down the hallway.

"Excuse me, Brenda?"

"Is everything okay?" she immediately asks, her eyes darting to Nicky's room.

"She's sleeping." Not quite sure how to approach this, I use the straightforward approach. "My wife wants to go home. I need to know what kinds of arrangements I should make for her comfort there."

She doesn't look at all shocked, but instead nods thoughtfully. "She mentioned something this morning. Let me get you the numbers for palliative home care, and I'll warn Dr. Abawi. He'll probably pop in to talk to all of you." She copies a few numbers from a Rolodex on the desk to a notepad. "Why don't you make your calls in the waiting room? There's no one in there right now. I'll keep an eye on Mrs. Thomas."

"Thank you." I take the piece of paper from her hand and slip into the empty room, closing the door behind me.

Forty minutes later I have twenty-four-hour care organized starting tomorrow afternoon, and Lisa is looking into getting a hospital bed installed in the living room on short notice.

I walk into Nicky's room with a plan in hand, but come to a dead standstill when I see some stranger with a head full of dreadlocks bend over her bed.

"Hey!" I call out, and the person whips up and swings around. *"Fuck me,"* I whisper when I recognize the face that is burned in my memory.

Last time I saw it was right before Spencer was born.

"I asked her to come," Nicky says from the bed, her eyes on me, but her hand clasping her sister's tightly.

Chapter Two

Taz

THAT VOICE.

Goosebumps break out over my skin as I swing around at the sound. The softly whispered *fuck me* when he recognizes me almost has me running.

The thirty-eight hours and four airplanes it took me to get here—from the small airstrip by the clinic to the international airport in Kinshasa, via Paris to New York, and finally Springfield—left me too much time to think. I'd reconsidered the wisdom of the split second it took me to make a promise I hadn't really thought through all the way.

The man who has my hair stand on end was one of the main reasons I almost changed my mind.

Damn, he looks good. A little gray in his whiskers and a few more lines in his face, but otherwise he's still the same Rafe I first met nine years ago in my parents' kitchen. The same deep blue eyes pin me in place.

All I can hear is the blood rushing through me, but I realize Nicky must've said something when his gaze flits to the bed behind me. I turn around. Shame instantly floods me when I see the mere shadow of my perfect sister lying in the hospital bed.

"You've got to be kidding me," Rafe finally says. "Need I remind you of the last time she decided to show her face? You were a mess for months."

I wince at his description of my last visit home five years ago. Nicky catches it and shoots me an apologetic smile. I instantly realize she hasn't told him the reason why I left in such a hurry and never returned.

"Well, I don't have months now. Besides, that was not Taz's fault," she defends me, but Rafe won't hear it.

"For the life of me I don't understand how you can stand up for her. You forget I lived through the aftermath."

"You don't know everything." Nicky's voice is weak and her eyes tired. "I need her. I can't do this without her." Her hand finds mine and she grabs on as the first tears I've shed in years start rolling down my cheeks "Please, Rafe," she pleads. "I need you to back me on this."

His eyes soften on her, before turning to me with suspicion and concern. It fucking hurts, but I lift my chin and stare him down, my sister's fragile hand in mine strengthening me.

Rafe's only answer is a curt nod.

The reason why a united front is necessary becomes clear when, half an hour later, Mom walks in the room pushing my father in a wheelchair, a sight that shocks me.

She stops right inside the door, clutching a fist to her chest when her eyes land on me.

"Out," she growls, and the single syllable is like a dagger in my back. My gaze darts to my father whose face has gone slack.

"Mom…"

Nicky's plea goes unheard as my mother narrows her eyes on me. "How dare you show up out of the blue. You broke your father's heart."

Not even my sister's surprisingly firm hold on my hand can give me the strength I need for this face-off. I've been traveling for days with little to no sleep, endured barbs from the one man who has the power to injure me, and haven't even begun to process that my sister is dying. There is no way I can handle my mother's anger or my dad's disappointment.

"That's enough," Rafe barks unexpectedly at my mother, shocking her as much as it shocks me. Then he adds a bit more gently, "Taz is here because Nicky called for her."

Using the brief silence that follows as my mother struggles to understand, I bend over my sister, my face close to hers, effectively shutting everyone else out. "I'm going to step out, but I'll be back."

"Promise?"

"I need a coffee and some fresh air, I promise I won't be long."

I kiss her papery cheek and without looking at Mom or Dad, slip by them and out of the room.

In the hospital lobby, I pick up a much-needed cup of coffee and head outside into the Missouri spring chill. Sinking down on a bench right outside the doors, I take a deep tug of the warm brew.

I wasn't kidding, I need some air and a little space to come to terms with the request Nicky dropped on me, right before my parents showed up. My sister wants to die at home and she wants me to help make that possible.

The brutal reality tears through me and I stuff my fist in my mouth, stifling a sob.

My sister, my first and best friend throughout childhood, is dying. The many years wasted sit like a stone in my chest now that time is slipping away. Regret is an evil bitch.

I guess I always assumed we'd have time to sort through our issues. Not only with Nicky, but Mom and Dad as well. Instead, I'd hidden out on a different continent, convincing myself I could do more good there than back home, where I seemed to do everything wrong.

Stupid. I should've known it eventually would bite me in the ass. With his diagnosis of Parkinson's, I'd always figured Dad would be the one to bring me home. I never thought it would be my perfect and much too young sister I'd come to say goodbye to.

Pulling out my phone, I dial the New York number for the US headquarters of Doctors Without Borders. There's no choice, really. Of course I'm going to stay and look after Nicky. After having given nine years of my life to the organization—when others generally sign up for one, maybe two years—I don't encounter any resistance when I tell them I will need an indefinite leave of absence and may not be returning to the Congo.

A few tears escape when I think of the people I'll miss, the friends I've made, and I bend my head to wipe under my eyes.

I know I've done the right thing, but it won't be easy.

"Taz?"

I look up to find Rafe standing a few feet away, looking at me curiously. "Hey."

"Nicky asked me to get you. The cardiologist is with her, he'd like a word."

I shoot to my feet, toss the half-empty coffee cup in the garbage and wipe my palms on my jeans. "Everything okay?"

"I think he wants to make sure you know what you're doing."

"Hardly," I mumble, heading for the entrance, Rafe falling in step beside me.

Rafe

TALK ABOUT CONFLICTED FEELINGS.

I almost hadn't recognized Taz with her now long, multi-colored hair twisted into dreadlocks, but when she'd turned around—those deep brown eyes wide open—the air sucked out of the room. Emotions instantly swirled before anger firmly settled in place. It was the safest option to go with.

It's mostly gone now. After some very difficult discussions these past few hours, I just feel intensely sad.

Nicky's parents—her mother in particular—had been pretty vocal in their disapproval of the plans for their daughter to die at home. I suspect they're still in denial and

I can't say I blame them. Sticking your head in the sand is a heck of a lot easier than dealing with the pain reality brings.

It didn't help that Nicky insisted having their younger prodigal daughter be the one to look after her. Aside from the lack of medical training, Sarah has her hands full with her husband whose Parkinson's is quite progressed. Taking on the care for Nicky would've been too much.

In the end they agreed, when a surprising vote of support came from Dr. Abawi, who emphasized the focus should be on quality—not quantity—of life at this point. The cardiologist took Taz aside to go over medications and a plan of care, with Sarah observing the interaction from a distance.

Even with everyone on one page—more or less—the situation remains a challenge.

"What about the kids?" Sarah asks the moment Taz disappears down the hall.

She finally headed to the hotel across the street to grab some shut-eye, unable to stay standing from exhaustion. With plans in place to move Nicky home early tomorrow morning, Taz should grab rest while she can.

"I talked to Kathleen. She's dropping them off tomorrow after school, once we've had a chance to settle in."

"That's not what I mean," she says. "They don't even know Natasha. She's a stranger to them."

"That's enough, Sarah," Ed unexpectedly pipes up. His soft raspy voice doesn't hide the steel underneath. The man doesn't assert himself often and it startles his wife. "She's their aunt, their mother's sister, our *daughter*. The kids will take their cue from us." He underlines his words with a sharp look. "It'll be hard enough without the adults in their life shooting barbs at each other."

Sarah looks duly chastised and I feel the same. Ed is right; Sofie especially is very sensitive to moods and atmospheres. Too perceptive for her age, she picked up on the growing distance between her mother and me this past year. Five-year-old Spencer simply follows along with whatever vibe his sister puts out there.

The kids' welfare has precedence over any family squabbles or grievances.

Not soon after, my in-laws say their goodbyes and leave. They're heading back to Eminence tonight, so someone is at the house when the hospital bed is delivered first thing tomorrow morning.

"Tough day."

I snort at Nicky's softly whispered comment and turn to look at her. "That's gotta be the understatement of the century."

She smiles before her face turns serious. "I love my sister."

I reach over and lace my fingers with hers. "I know you do. I'm just not sure she deserves it after the way she turned her back."

"Don't say that," she hisses, pulling her hand from mine. "She's not the only one who carries responsibility for that."

It's the second time, since Taz showed up, Nicky suggests there's more to her sister's years of absence. I shake my head, unable—or maybe unwilling—to deal with any more revelations or upheavals. For someone who is usually adept at suppressing emotions, I feel like I may come apart at the onslaught of the past few days.

"We should call the kids, and then you should have a rest," I offer. "You need your energy for tomorrow."

A cop-out. I know it and she does too, but she still nods her agreement and I pull out my phone.

"Hey, Kathleen, how are they?"

"Good, all things considered. I haven't talked to them about tomorrow yet, though. Figured you guys would want to tell them yourselves. They're just getting ready for bed, let me go get them."

"Hang on." I hand the phone to Nicky and see the moment the kids get on the line; her face lights up instantly.

"Hey, baby. How was school?" She smiles chatting with the kids, trying to inject as much normalcy in the chaos of their lives as she can.

This whole fucked-up situation suddenly hits me hard, and I dart into the restroom to try and get myself under control. I've never felt so goddamn raw in my life.

When I return to Nicky's bedside, after taking a breath and splashing some cold water on my face, she looks at me questioningly, but I merely shake my head. Moments later she hands me the phone.

"Hey, Pipsqueak."

"Hey, Daddy. Mommy says she's coming home tomorrow, is that true?"

"Yeah, honey. She'll be home when you come back from school."

"So she's all better?"

Jesus, this is torture.

I roll my eyes to the ceiling and take a shaky breath

before answering. "She's still pretty sick, Sofie, but she can't wait to get home and see you guys."

It's quiet on the other end of the line as my all-too-perceptive Sofie processes my response and the fist squeezing my chest goes a little tighter.

"Spencer wants to say hi," she finally says, her voice dejected.

"All right, honey. You sleep well, okay? I'll see you tomorrow. Let me talk to your brother."

"Okay. Love you, Daddy."

"Love you more."

By the time I end the call, after a brief chat with my sleepy youngest, I notice Nicky has drifted off, her face deeply lined, and teardrops shimmering on her pale cheeks.

Chapter Three

Taz

"YOU'RE NERVOUS."

I look up from the kitchen sink where I'm hand-washing the few dishes we used for lunch. Nicky, who'd fallen asleep on the couch earlier, is now watching me.

"A little."

I'd slept a restful ten hours sprawled out in the king-sized hotel bed last night. Not surprising, since I've spent most of the past almost decade on narrow cots and barely-there mattresses. It was tempting to simply stay in bed indefinitely, instead of facing my family again.

As luck would have it, my parents already went home last night, so there was a little less tension in the room when I walked in. Most of the morning was spent getting Nicky released and ready for the trip home, and sorting out her medication at the hospital pharmacy. The drive to

Eminence had been relatively quiet, something I was grateful for, since the increasingly familiar landscape of the Ozarks brought on a full range of memories for me. Good and not so good.

My parents had been waiting at the house I grew up in when we got there, but they didn't stay long. They moved to a small bungalow in town when Rafe bought the clinic, and with it the house, nine years ago. Shortly after Dad was diagnosed he retired, determined to get as much traveling in as his condition would allow.

Rafe didn't hang around long either. He had some work to do at the clinic before Kathleen dropped off the children. Nicky was visibly tired but wanted to stay on the couch, not ready to let me help her into the hospital bed set up in front of the bay window in the living room.

"They'll love you," she says, a soft smile on her face before worry replaced it. "But for the record, I'm nervous too. Now that I'm home, I'm second-guessing if this was such a good idea."

I drop the dishrag in the sink and wipe my hands before joining Nicky on the couch.

"I've learned that in most of Africa," I start, taking her hand in mine, "death is seen more as a transition than an ending. They don't look forward to the inevitable, but focus instead on the living that is left. Those who die continue to exist in a spiritual way as part of their family. They don't believe death is final, but rather an unending circle."

"I like that." Nicky sniffles, and I hand her the box of tissues off the table.

"Me too. I like the idea we don't stop being part of a family, simply because we're no longer there physically."

I don't realize the double meaning of my words until I feel my sister's hand squeezing my own.

"I like that even better," she whispers. "You may not have been here, but you were never gone from my heart, Taz."

I blink a few times when my nose prickles with the tears that want to come. No time for that with the kids on their way home.

"Ditto," I respond in a raw voice, before clearing my throat and changing the subject. "I'm not a parent, but maybe it would be easier to let the kids come with their own questions about what is happening. From my experience, kids are not stupid and often more tuned-in than we think. Let them indicate what they're ready to hear. We need to take their cues and be honest in our answers."

Nicky nods and opens her mouth to answer when the front door slams open and a tow-haired little boy comes barreling through.

"Mommy!"

My heart pounds in my ears as I watch the little Rafe replica advance on his mother, throwing his spindly arms around her neck. Pleasure and pain display in stark contrast on Nicky's face as she closes her arms around his small body. I have to swallow hard.

Not far behind, Kathleen guides in Spencer's more restrained big sister. Last time I saw Sofie she was a precocious toddler with a ready smile for everyone. There's no smile now, only suspicious eyes and a sullen look on her face.

"Oh my God, Taz." Kathleen lets go of the girl and I can barely get to my feet before she throws herself in my arms. "It's so good to see you," she sniffles in my neck, and I have a hard time keeping my own emotions in check.

Over the past years my friend has kept me informed on the welfare of my family. Pride had prevented me from reaching out myself, but that didn't mean I wasn't lapping up every little tidbit of information Kathleen shared with me.

She lets me go and takes a step back, her hand reaching up to tug on my dreadlocks. "When did you get these?" she wants to know, her fingers rubbing over the odd beads I had woven into my hair.

"Years ago. It was either this or shave my head. I wanted something with the least amount of daily fuss. One of my patients put them in."

Over Kathleen's shoulder I see Sofie finally approach her mother and sit beside her on the couch, her eyes still full of suspicion as she stares at me.

"Your hair looks funny," her brother points out. "Like rope."

Before I have a chance to answer, Kathleen does. "They're called dreads. They look like rope but are really soft, come feel." A smile plays around my sister's mouth as she releases him so he can reach out when I bend down. His little fist closes on my hair.

"How do you brush it?"

"I don't have to brush it. It stays exactly like this," I answer, smiling down at him.

His head whips around to his mom. "I want dreads too," he announces.

"You just don't want to brush your hair," his sister snaps, speaking up for the first time.

"So?" her brother fires back, but before the siblings can take the bickering any further, their mom jumps in.

"Guys, this is your aunt, Taz. Mommy's sister."

"Hi," Spencer says, looking at me with even more curiosity, but his sister stays silent.

"Sofie?" Nicky prompts.

"Yeah, hi."

My niece's brush-off response doesn't offend me in the least. I understand it. I see the awareness in her eyes and nothing she sees bodes well, and she knows it. My presence here is simply additional proof that things are not all right.

"You guys hungry?" I ask to break the tension.

As expected—he's male after all—Spencer is quick to confirm with enthusiastic nodding of his head.

"Come on then," I tell him, noting my sister's eyes are closing again. "Let's see what we can drum up." I take the boy by the hand and start walking out of the room. "Sofie?" I throw over my shoulder, purposely casual. "I think your mom is ready for a nap, want to see if you can help her into bed?"

I can see her hesitation as she looks from me to the hospital bed on the other side of the room, before her eyes settle on her mom. I catch Kathleen's eye, who seems to easily understand my silent communication.

"Come on, Sofie. Let's tuck your mom in," I hear her say, as I lead Spencer into the kitchen.

Fifteen minutes later Nicky is sleeping, Sofie snatched a banana and headed up to her room, Spencer is in front of the TV in the rec room downstairs, and Kathleen comes walking into the kitchen.

"Where is Rafe?"

I steel my shoulders, knowing a third-degree was coming. "Had to check on things at the clinic," I answer, feigning a casualness I don't feel.

But instead of the probing questions I was expecting, she mumbles, "Hiding already," and slips out the back door.

From the kitchen window I see her stalking over to the clinic next door.

Rafe

I'M A COWARD.

I saw Kathleen pull up and my kids get out of her van, but instead of heading home, I ducked my head and kept going over the notes Rick Moore, a colleague from neighboring Winona who'd looked after my practice, had left for me.

Not that I was really processing anything I read, my mind still trying to come to grips with the upsets of this past week. Hiding out in the clinic had become a habit I'd grown into over the past year already and is a safe place to slip back to with life throwing a bunch of curves.

I plan. That's what I do.

From when I was first placed with my foster parents at nine years old, I started plotting what my view of a perfect life should look like, since up to that point mine had been far from it. My foster parents—both since deceased—were kind enough, but being older and without kids of their own, remained detached during the ten years I lived with them. I craved the sense of family but realized early on I would have to rely on myself to create it.

I had it all worked out in my head. When I came to Eminence and met the Borans for the first time, I thought I'd found it. The town and the clinic were exactly what I'd hoped for, and the family it came with seemed perfect—as did their daughter.

Then I met Taz: younger than her sister by a couple of years and as different as the sun is from the moon. Opinionated, stubborn, irreverent, and uncontrolled, she was like turbulence on a smooth flight. Disruptive and jarring, but at the same time brightly exciting in an almost forbidden way.

Alive and effortlessly tempting. Like a moth to the light, I couldn't help but be drawn in by her and it terrified me.

I was almost relieved when Nicky ended up pregnant. Even though unexpected, it was something I was able to fit into the future I'd always envisioned.

Look at me now. Oh, the irony. My marriage a contrived farce, the mother of my children dying—and to top it off—the one woman who can make my heart beat out of my chest with just one of her crooked smiles shows up out of the blue.

I've lost all control.

The door to my office flies open.

"How long are you gonna hide in here?"

Kathleen has never been a big fan of mine. She'd been a friend to Taz long before she became one to Nicky, and neither of those roles has won me any favors. Whether intending to or not, in one way or another I've hurt both sisters and she knows it. She probably knows more than I do.

"It's work, Kathleen. I'm hardly hiding," I lie.

"Right," she scoffs, clearly not buying it. "Well then, when you're done *working* you may want to go check in on your kids, instead of leaving them to someone who's a stranger to them."

"You're the one who asked her to come," I fire back, realizing instantly I'm acting like a two-year-old.

"Yeah, I did, because Nicky asked me to, and because —whether you like it or not—your family needs her. That doesn't absolve you, though."

I know she's right. Like I said, I'm a coward.

I drop my head and run my hands over my face. "Let me check in with Lisa. I'll be right over."

"Okay." Her voice is suddenly much softer. "I'll just say my goodbyes and be on my way. My kids are waiting at home."

"Thanks, Kathleen," I mumble, looking up at her.

"Sure thing. Any time you need a swift kick in the ass, I'm your girl."

"WHY IS SHE HERE?"

I sit on the edge of Sofie's bed, nudging her hip. "Scoot over, Pipsqueak." When she does, I stretch out beside her, tucking her close. "I assume you're talking about your mom's sister? She's here because your mom loves her very much. She needs someone to help her, and it so happens your aunt is a nurse."

"How come she never visits?"

I should've known it would be my daughter—with a natural inclination to challenge everything—who asks the hard questions. So much like the aunt she's grumbling about, it's almost painful.

"Not so easy when you're living in Africa, Sofie. You've heard of Doctors Without Borders, right?" I know she has, because I heard Nicky proudly talk about the work they do, not that long ago. She nods almost reluctantly. "Your aunt, Taz, works as a nurse for them. She's been in several countries in Africa, running clinics and looking after people who don't always have access to medical care."

Her reluctant interest is piqued. "What countries?"

"I know she just came from the Congo, and other than that I'm not sure, but I think she may have been in Ghana at some point too. You should ask her yourself."

Her answer to that is a shrug. "I still don't get why she has to come all the way from Africa to help Mom."

Now I recognize the fear in her voice and I tuck her even closer, resting my chin on her head.

I had a chance to check in with Nicky earlier, while the kids were getting ready for bed. She mentioned Taz's suggestion to let the kids guide when a good time to tell them would be. Sofie's comment indicates to me she knows the answer to her own question but is not ready to hear it. So I'm careful in my response

"Don't you think it's better to have family than a bunch of strangers in your house?"

She looks at me, the lashes framing her pretty brown eyes batting tears away.

"I guess so."

Chapter Four

Taz

"ARE you going to be back for dinner?"

I stop Rafe right before he slips out the kitchen door.

Every morning this past week, he's done the same thing; disappear as soon as the kids leave for school and come home just in time to put them to bed. Left me to deal with Nicky, the kids, and my parents.

Don't get me wrong; reconnecting with my sister has been a gift even under these circumstances. Dealing with the kids has been more of a challenge, especially Sofie who still regards me with a healthy dose of suspicion. There'd been a few difficult questions, most of which Nicky had dealt with, but early this morning I woke up to my niece sitting on the edge of the couch where I've been sleeping at night, her eyes on her sleeping mother on the other side of the room. She looked like she'd been crying for a while, but when I tried to comfort her; she shrugged me off and dismissed my offer to talk about it with a shake of her head before slipping back upstairs.

My parents had come by daily, my mother directing angry glares at me as if the current situation was one of my making. My dad looked lost and I had no clue how to make inroads with either of them.

Tonight they're supposed to come by with dinner to spend some time with the kids, and I know it'll be difficult because of what Nicky asked me this morning.

"I'll try," Rafe mumbles.

"Try harder," I snap.

His eyes narrow on me. "Is there something I should know?"

"You mean other than your wife dying?" I hiss, stepping closer in hopes Nicky won't overhear. "Because she is, you know. No matter how deep you choose to bury your head in the sand."

"I'm not—" he starts, but I cut him off with a wave of my hand.

"Give me a break," I scoff, before handing him a dose of reality. "She told me this morning she thinks after today she'll be ready for morphine, but doesn't want me to give it to her."

He looks confused. "Why?"

"Because she knows as well as you and I do what it means once we start with the morphine. She doesn't want to put that burden on me."

"Oh." Realization steals over his face.

Morphine brings relief, but only covers up the underlying cause of the pain and discomfort of fluid collecting around the major organs when a heart pumps ineffectively.

The inevitable side effect is unfortunately a slowing down of both breathing and heart rate. In short, morphine will speed up the dying process and my sister does not want me to carry the burden of administering it.

I brush impatiently at my eyes. "You need to call in palliative home care, and you need to be here when Mom and Dad show up for dinner."

I stiffen when he suddenly reaches out and pulls me against his chest, his arms banding around me. "I'll call and I'll be here. I'm sorry," he whispers.

Without conscious thought, my hands slip around him, grabbing onto the back of his shirt. I press my cheek against him and breathe in his scent. The comfort it provides painfully growing like a balloon in my chest.

Just like that I'm transported nine years back, the last time we stood like this. Me with hope in my eyes and my heart on my sleeve. His arms had felt safe then too, until my mother walked in and those same arms pushed me away. That hurt, but not as much as Mom's anger. She yelled, telling me, in no uncertain terms, how horrible I was for throwing myself at my sister's fiancé, especially with a baby on the way. That was the first I'd heard of the pregnancy. The information tore through me like a knife.

The memory still burns ugly.

Ashamed, I blow out a lungful of air through pursed lips and move my hands to his chest, pushing firmly. He releases me quickly and I step out of his hold.

"Taz..."

I ward off anything more he has to say with a raised hand. "Just be here, please. Okay?"

His answer is a sharp nod before he walks out the door. I press my eyes shut and deeply inhale through my nose.

"Taz?" I hear my sister's voice calling from the living room.

I plaster a smile on my face as I walk in. "Hungry?"

It strikes me how much her appearance has changed, even in the past week. The lines and angles of her face stand out in stark contrast against the graying tinge of her skin. Her eyes are even more sunken and it's almost like I can see death creeping in.

"Not really," she says with an attempt at a smile. "I think I'll save my appetite for dinner tonight. With a bit of luck, Mom's making her macaroni and cheese."

My mouth waters at the mention of our mother's mac and cheese. She makes it from scratch with cream, three or four different cheeses, ham and bacon bits, and tops it with breadcrumbs for a crispy crust. At least fifteen thousand calories per serving, but tastier than any other I've ever had, bar none.

"Sounds like a plan," I tell her, approaching the bed. "I'll put some water on for tea as soon as I help you get dressed."

"Let me rest a little longer. I wouldn't mind that tea, though." But before I can move, she reaches for my hand and grabs on tight. "Thank you for being here. It means everything."

"Don't." I shake my head. "There isn't a place on the face of the earth I'd rather be." I bend over her bed and press a kiss to her forehead. "Bonus kiss," I tell her. "Making up for all the ones we've missed."

I put the kettle on in the kitchen, struggling to keep my

emotions in check. I thought I knew what it was like to have your emotions worn raw, but nothing compares to this. When I have two mugs ready with teabags I feel a little more in control, something I desperately need for my upcoming conversation with Mom. I grab the phone and dial.

"Everything okay?" My mother sounds almost breathless as she answers the phone.

"She's okay," I quickly reassure her.

"Oh. Natasha." Her voice is immediately flat when she hears it's me and I roll my eyes to the ceiling. *God, give me strength.*

"Yeah, it's me, Mom. Listen, I'm not sure what you had planned for tonight's dinner, but do you think you could make your mac and cheese?"

It's silent on the other side for a moment when I hear her derisive snort. "I'm making a rib roast. Nicky needs the iron to keep her strength up and it's Rafe's favorite. I'm not about to change my plans because you suddenly have a hankering for my cooking."

Yikes. Shot to the heart. She can't seem to help herself. This time it's me who needs a minute to rein in the need to lash back. This is not the time.

"It's not for me, Mom," I say deceptively calmly. "It's for Nicky. She says she's saving her appetite, hoping for your mac and cheese."

"She needs to eat—"

"Mom…"

"—Or she'll get too weak. You're a nurse, you know her body needs fuel."

"Mom," I repeat, shaking my head. "She's tired. I'm

not going to force her to do anything she doesn't feel up to, including eating something she doesn't want, and she doesn't want to eat anything but your mac and cheese casserole."

Another silence before she finally responds. "Fine. I'll bring mac and cheese."

The next thing I hear is dead air. She's hung up.

Christ.

Rafe

"GRAPES CAN BE VERY dangerous for Charlton, Mrs. Myers. Remember last time you fed him fruit salad and he was throwing up?"

I try to be gentle with the senior citizen, who brought in her overweight beagle because he was puking. Again.

"But aren't vegetables and fruits supposed to be healthy for you? You told me he had to lose weight."

"Yes, Mrs. Myers, but just because they're healthy for people doesn't make them healthy for dogs. Haven't you been feeding him the low calorie food I gave you a sample of last time you were here?"

She has two bright red spots on her cheeks as she mumbles something under her breath I don't quite catch.

"Sorry?"

"I said, that special food is three times as expensive as the regular stuff. How am I supposed to afford that on my tiny pension?"

I drop my head. We do this song and dance every time she comes in with the dog. Mrs. Myers is not suffering. Her husband, a local dentist who died five years ago, left her very well taken care of, but I don't have the heart to call her on it. I'm sure the woman is lonely, and I can't deny she loves her dog; I wish she'd look after him better.

"Lisa?" I call out and my assistant sticks her head in the door.

"Yes?"

"Can you give Mrs. Myers a large bag of the low cal Health Diet, please?"

"A large bag?" Lisa's eyebrows disappear into her hairline.

"Correct."

I catch my assistant's eye roll before she disappears into the back.

It takes another fifteen minutes before Mrs. Myers—my last appointment of the afternoon—drives off with a sixteen-pound bag of Health Diet in the trunk of her Honda Civic, and her beagle, Charlton, hanging out the passenger side window, his tongue lolling from his mouth.

"You do realize you're technically paying that woman for bringing her dog in at this rate, right?" Lisa comments from behind me.

"Hmmm," I mumble, neither confirming nor denying. My mind is already on what's waiting for me at home.

I slip by her and duck into my office where I quickly finish my notes on Charlton's file, shut down my computer, and turn off the lights. It's time to get my kids off the bus.

"Give her my love," Lisa says when I tell her I'm off.

"Will do. Just in case, would you give Rick a heads-up before you roll out? Things seem to be moving quickly."

"Oh no. I'm so sorry, Rafe."

Hearing the emotion in her words I avoid looking at her, having a hard enough time dealing with my own. "Me too," I mutter, as I pull open the door.

"What's wrong?" Sofie asks me the moment she steps off the bus and sees me, immediately suspicious.

"Nothing, Pipsqueak," I assure her, as I hoist Spencer up on my shoulders and grab for my girl's hand. "Was done early so I thought I'd wait for you at the stop. Grandma and Grandpa should be over soon. Grandma's bringing dinner." I ramble in an attempt to distract.

"Is Grandma making dessert?" Spencer asks above me.

"Probably," I tell him, glancing at his sister.

Her eyes are firmly focused on the house at the end of the driveway, her lips set in a straight line.

Fuck, I want to scoop her up too, take both my kids, and run as far as I can from the heartbreak I know is waiting inside.

"Hey, guys," Nicky says a tad too brightly when we walk in the door.

She's sitting in a corner of the couch, her feet up on the ottoman, covered with a quilt. It's at least seventy-five degrees outside, hardly the type of weather that requires an extra layer. The inability of her body to retain heat is another of the many signs her heart is failing. Another is the cough that seems to have developed these past two days, signaling fluid build up in her lungs.

Not that I needed additional signs, just looking at Nicky is evidence enough.

I leave the kids with her and stick my head into the kitchen, where I find Taz pulling chocolate milk from the fridge.

"Hey, how are things?"

When she turns around I note the strain in her face. "Tough. She spent most of the day in bed but insisted she needed to be up when the kids got home. It cost her though."

"I see that. I called palliative care. The nurse will be here at seven thirty tomorrow morning, but maybe I should see if someone can come in tonight? Get her some relief for the night?"

Taz shrugs her shoulders. "Not sure she'll go for that, not with Mom and Dad coming. I already tried to get her to let me give her only the first dose, but she refuses."

"Let me call," I insist. "If I can get them to pop in after nine, the kids will be in bed and we can make sure Mom and Dad have left."

Taz nods, setting the glasses and a plate with cheese, crackers, and grapes on a tray before carrying it inside, while I quickly call to arrange for a nurse to visit tonight.

"SHE HARDLY ATE AT ALL."

Sarah pins Taz, who's putting plates into the dishwasher, with a glare the moment she walks into the kitchen after putting the kids to bed.

From the moment Ed and Sarah showed, the tension had been thick enough to cut. Dinner had been a rather quiet affair, with Sarah and Spencer doing most of the talking. Sofie had been quietly observant, as had her grandpa. Nicky had a hard time keeping her eyes open, and Taz looked like she was trying hard to be invisible while keeping a close eye on her sister.

Some of the tension had lifted while Sarah took the children upstairs. With both Ed and Nicky dozing off side by side on the couch, I'd followed Taz in here to help clean up.

Taz quietly continues to load the dishwasher with Sarah's eyes boring a hole in her back.

"Mom," I quietly draw her attention. "Eating takes a lot of her energy. It's no use trying to force-feed her."

"Don't say that," she snaps, the eyes she turns on me fearful.

"Please, Mom," Taz pleads with her. "Don't waste precious time on things that don't matter."

Before Sarah has a chance to respond, Taz slips out of the kitchen.

"Come on." I put my arm around Sarah's slumped shoulders and guide her inside, where Taz perches on the armrest at her sister's side, kissing the top of her head before whispering something in her ear. A soft smile appears on Nicky's lips as she blinks her eyes open.

"How about a nightcap for the road?"

Ed's eyes shoot open at my offer. "You still have that Glenfiddich?"

"As much as you left in the bottle last time." I grin at him. "Mom? You want something? A glass of port?"

"Half," she says, sitting down in one of the club chairs, her eyes on her daughters.

"Taz? Baileys?" I offer, remembering that, like her older sister, she used to love the stuff over ice.

"If you have some, please."

By the time I have the drinks handed out and sit down, Ed is holding court, regaling old stories in his raspy voice even I have heard many times before. It doesn't matter, it feels familiar, and from the look on Nicky's face, it's clear she's enjoying the trips down memory lane.

"What are you doing?" Sarah's voice is suddenly sharp over her husband's mellow drone. She pushes out of her chair, her eyes on Taz who's lifting her glass to Nicky's lips. "She can't have alcohol with her medications." In two steps she covers the distance and reaches out, snatching the glass from Taz's hand. "Are you trying to kill her?"

A sharp gasp from Taz's lips is the only sound before a deadly silence falls in the room. Ed is the first one to break it.

"Uncalled for, Sarah," he snaps in a firmer tone than we're used to from him.

"Mom," Nicky manages, her hand seeking out Taz's empty one. "It doesn't matter."

"Of course it matters," her mother responds, agony twisting her features as she sets the glass on the table and wraps her arms around herself.

"Mom," Nicky repeats. "I'm dying. I can feel it, and I hate how hard this is for everyone. I'm gathering moments at this point. Sights, sounds, touches, and tastes, to take with me. It's all I'll be able to take when I leave soon."

Chapter Five

Taz

"ARE YOU AWAKE?"

I am. I haven't slept yet. It seems like every new day leaves more to process and my tired brain can't seem to stop churning on every word, thought, and feeling.

Nicky had fallen asleep soon after Chantal, the palliative care nurse, placed a subcutaneous cannula in her upper arm and administered her first dose of morphine. The port in her upper arm would stay there until no longer necessary.

"You okay?" I whisper into the dark room, reaching for the table lamp next to the couch.

"Yeah. Leave the light off?"

I pull my hand back and roll on my side to face her. I can see her eyes shimmer from the hospital bed. "Need me to get you something?" I hear a slight rustle as she shakes her head.

"I'm going to talk to him tomorrow," Nicky whispers. "I should've done it a long time ago."

I don't need to guess she's referring to the last blowout fight she and I had five years ago. Nicky had been eight months pregnant with Spencer at the time.

When Sofie was born three years prior, I'd missed it. In fact, I hadn't had any contact with my family until I came back from a vaccination run in Nigeria, when I received an email from Kathleen telling me I'd become an aunt. I may not have spoken with my family, but that doesn't mean I didn't love them. I've always loved them, regardless of our fucked-up dynamic. Kathleen had no problem providing me with any updates over the years. Eminence is a small town, anything of any significance happens and the whole town knows within twenty-four hours.

I started thinking—some time after Sofie was born—maybe I was cutting off my nose to spite my face. I'd been hiding out on the other side of the world, not giving my family a chance to bridge the gap. So when I heard from Kathleen my sister was pregnant again, I thought perhaps it was time to swallow my pride and take the first step.

My welcome then was only moderately warmer than the one I received this time, and I had to exercise a healthy dose of restraint when dealing with my mother. I mostly avoided her and Rafe, but was able to reconnect with my dad and my sister. It was short-lived.

Then one night—Rafe was out on a call—Nicky and I were hanging out watching a movie when she suddenly burst out crying. She'd been unhappy for a while and confessed she'd indulged in a brief fling with her chiropractor in Mountain View. She was afraid the baby could be his.

I lost it on her. She had the perfect life, the perfect husband, and she'd risked it all. Ugly words flew on both sides. She accused me of jealousy, which prompted me to fire back that she didn't deserve a man like Rafe. Of course that's all he heard when he walked in the door.

He was livid, but all I could see was the plea in my sister's eyes. He said some hurtful things before showing me the door, telling me to get the fuck out of their lives, and I went. I never even tried to defend myself, because it would've meant throwing my sister under the bus.

I never returned after that.

"Spencer is his spitting image," I tell her with a wistful smile.

"I know. I've always been the lucky one, haven't I? At least until now."

"Honey…" I slide out from under the quilt and make my way to the hospital bed. "Scoot over."

It's a tight fit, but I manage to crawl in beside her and pull her into my arms. Her hot tears seep through my nightshirt.

"I'm sorry," she sniffles.

"I know. I'm sorry too."

"In spite of everything, tell me you've been happy."

I stroke a hand over her limp hair and think about her question. "I've done work I'm proud of—am passionate about—I've seen places I used to dream of, met amazing people along the way, and I've learned so much. Yeah, I've been happy."

"Liar," she whispers. "You still love him."

My hand stops its stroking motion. "Nicky," I warn her. This is not a direction I want us to go in, but when my sister has her mind set on something she can be persistent.

"Look after them. The kids, Rafe, they need you. Even Mom and Dad. You're the strongest person I know, the only person I would trust. I know I'm asking a lot—again—but it would be so much easier to let go if I knew you…" Her breath is getting choppy and I tighten my arm around her.

"Shhh. Rest. I've got you. I'll be here as long as they need me. I promise."

I watch the early morning light start chasing some of the shadows from the room as I listen to her breath even out again. Upstairs I hear movement, a door closing and then the shower turn on. Rafe is up.

Nicky feels heavy in my arms and I assume she's fallen asleep, but when I try to slip out of the hospital bed, her hand on my stomach clenches into a fist.

"I'm scared, Taz."

"I know, honey. So am I," I admit quietly, pressing a kiss on her hair. "Bonus kiss," I whisper and settle back, holding my sister as she drifts off.

Rafe

ANOTHER RESTLESS NIGHT.

Sometime in the predawn hours, both my kids had found their way into my bed. In the last year, I had moved into the spare bedroom, but with Nicky downstairs in the living room, she'd asked I move back to the master. In part because of nights like this, when the kids blindly make the trek into the master suite, looking for comfort.

Spencer had been first, half asleep, looking for his mom. It didn't seem to faze him to find me instead and quickly fell back asleep. He's still so little; it's easy to think everything going on is well over his head, but I'm sure more than I'd like impacts him. He merely seems to process difficult information in his sleep.

Sofie is different. She absorbs everything. I'm pretty sure she heard some of the unfortunate scene last night when her grandmother blew up. God forbid she heard the gut-wrenching words of her mom right after, but I suspect that's what had her coming into the room barely five minutes after her brother.

The one good thing that came out of Sarah's outburst was Ed speaking up for Taz. I could tell that surprised not only his wife, but also their youngest daughter as well. Sarah apologized to Nicky, and to me on her way out, but not to the person who deserved the apology most. I'd been about to call her on it when I saw Taz give a sharp little shake of her head. I sucked back what I'd been about to say; it probably wasn't the right time.

I carefully roll out of bed, trying not to wake the kids, but when I pull open a drawer to grab clean clothes I hear rustling behind me.

"Dad?"

I turn around to find Sofie's eyes on me. "Yeah, Pipsqueak?" I whisper so we don't wake Spencer. It's way too early for a Saturday morning. I sit down on her side of the bed.

"She's not getting better, is she?"

I would've done anything to avoid this moment, and yet, I've known it was inevitable. I'm about to break my daughter's heart and it's killing me. The temptation to lie to her is great, but we agreed we'd be honest with the kids. "I'm sorry, baby, but she's not."

Her brown eyes quietly fill with tears as she nods in understanding. Taking it on the chin. It would almost be easier if she'd break down and plead for a different outcome. Seeing this kind of resignation in my little girl is tearing me apart.

"Then why didn't she stay in the hospital?"

"Because she wants to spend as much time as she can with the people she loves most." I hope I'm explaining it right. It's not like there's a handbook I can consult on how to deal with a situation like this.

"Does it hurt?"

"She gets medicine to help with that."

"Is she scared?"

Christ.

"I imagine so, but I think maybe we can make it a little less scary if we love her really hard." She nods with a serious face and pulls the covers up to her nose. I lean down and kiss her forehead. "Try and get a little more sleep."

I'm almost out of the room to grab my shower when I hear her.

"Dad?"

"Yes?"

"Can you make blueberry pancakes for breakfast?"

"Sure thing, baby," I answer with a lump in my throat.

Sofie hates blueberry pancakes, but they're Nicky's favorite.

THE CURTAINS ARE STILL CLOSED when I walk into the living room.

I've come to expect Taz to be up by the time I get downstairs. It takes my eyes a moment to adjust to the darkness to find her pillow and quilt crumpled on the couch, but no Taz.

My eyes immediately drift to the hospital bed where I find her gaze on me, a very still Nicky wrapped in her arms. I freeze at the sight, but Taz notices and quickly reassures me.

"She's sleeping," she whispers.

I nod, breathing in deeply to loosen the tight band around my chest. "I'll make us some coffee."

By the time I carry in a mug for Taz, she's managed to leave Nicky sleeping in bed and is putting away the bedding from the couch.

"Tough night?" I ask, handing her the coffee, keeping my eyes on her face.

"A little," she admits, groaning when she takes a sip of the hot brew. "Thanks. I needed that. What time is it?"

"Coming on six thirty."

"Shit. I should grab a quick shower. Chantal's going to be here at seven."

"Go," I tell her, taking a seat on the chair closest to Nicky's bed. "I've got her."

She shows me a little tired smile before she darts up the stairs and I force my eyes on my wife.

The two girls used to look alike; luxurious red-brown hair, olive skin, and large brown liquid eyes. You'd have to be blind not to see they were sisters.

They couldn't look more different now. Nicky's pallor is a sickly gray, her once luxurious hair a lank helmet around her head, and her skin almost translucent. In the past few weeks she's become a shadow of herself. Taz, with her colorful dreads, bright eyes, and tan complexion is almost the polar opposite. Alive and vibrant.

I take a sip of my coffee, listening to Nicky's labored breathing. Every so often a silence falls, and I anxiously wait for her next inhale. It's possible that one of these times the next breath never comes.

Leaning my head back I close my eyes, calming my own heart.

"I was wrong to let you be angry at her."

Her voice—so unexpected—startles me and I almost spill coffee over myself. "Sorry?"

"Taz. She didn't deserve the blame she carried."

Intrigued, I lean forward in my chair and listen.

Taz

"TAKE OVER."

The spatula is shoved in my hand the moment I step

into the kitchen, and in the next I watch Rafe's back disappear out the door.

What the hell?

I'd love to go after him, but the pancakes on the griddle need flipping, and I bumped into Sofie on the landing upstairs, so I know she'll be down any minute.

Between batches of pancakes, I sneak a peek into the living room to find my sister looking back over Sofie's head. I didn't hear her come down, but somehow she ended up in bed with Nicky. I shoot her a soft smile and duck back into the kitchen, not wanting to interrupt their moment.

I'm about to set the table when Chantal walks in the back door, Rafe right behind her.

"How was your night?" the nurse asks, walking toward the living room. I shove the plates I'm holding in Rafe's hands, and follow her inside.

Sofie shoots out of bed and bolts around us, into the sanctuary of the kitchen.

"I think I'll stick around," Chantal says, after she's given Nicky her next dose and she's drifted back to sleep. She had no interest in getting out of bed.

"Okay," I force out.

"I'm sorry," she says, putting a hand on my arm. "It could be days yet."

"Or it could be hours," I add.

"Yeah. I brought a bag. Is there anywhere for me to put my stuff? Somewhere I can retreat to and write my reports so I'm not in your way?"

"The spare bedroom upstairs. I've been sleeping on the couch anyway."

Once I've settled Chantal in upstairs, I head back to the kitchen to find the kids at the table, eating breakfast. Rafe is leaning against the counter watching me.

"You should eat something," he says softly when I get close.

"She's staying," I announce in the same tone of voice, ignoring his words.

"I figured. I'm sorry for earlier. I just..." He sneaks a glance at the kids before his eyes come back to me, "...I needed a minute. I just learned something that shook me."

I narrow my eyes on his face and notice the pale underneath his tan. He looks shaken.

"She told you," I conclude.

"About ripped my heart out."

Chapter Six

Taz

"Is that how people wear their hair in Africa?"

I try not to show my surprise at Sofie's unsolicited question.

Beyond finding her perched on the edge of the couch that one morning, I haven't had much interaction with my niece. Sure, she's spoken to me, mostly monosyllabic answers to mundane day-to-day questions—like what she wants to drink with dinner, or if she has any dirty laundry that needs washing—but little more than that.

"Not necessarily. Historically dreadlocks were worn in many cultures all over the world. I read somewhere, even the Vikings wore their hair in dreads. Every culture has their own reason behind them. For me it was just convenience. In my work, my long hair tended to get in the way, but I wasn't ready to cut it all off. A friend offered to twist my hair into dreadlocks." I hide a smile at seeing her interest piqued by my little history lesson. "Grab me the paper towels?"

She does as I ask and I dump the blueberries I've been rinsing under the tap on a few sheets on the counter.

"What are you making with those?"

"I'm going to freeze them. Did you know blueberries are your mom's favorite?" I sneak a glance and catch her nod. "She's is not very hungry with that medicine she gets. It also makes her mouth really dry. I thought if we froze the berries, she would at least get a taste of her favorite food and the cold would feel good in her mouth."

Sofie sidles up to me at the counter and helps me spread the berries onto a baking sheet. "I think she'll like it," she shares in a soft voice when I slide the tray in the freezer.

"I hope so."

I clean up the counter and wash my hands at the sink when Sofie speaks again.

"Why is grandma mad at you?"

From the mouths of babes.

My eyes are automatically drawn in the direction of the living room, where I know my parents are holding vigil by Nicky's bedside. They showed up after their weekly trek to the United Methodist Church in town. When Rafe took Spencer to get some groceries and Chantal headed upstairs to give everyone some space, I opted for the kitchen.

"That's not an easy question. First of all I think Grandma is upset because your mom is sick and she can't help her. I think we all feel like that. As to why she's upset with me: maybe because I haven't been home in a long time."

I stifle a relieved sigh when Sofie seems to accept my

answer without questioning further. I feel like I've just navigated a minefield. Parenting is apparently not for the weak of heart.

Before she has a chance to pelt me with the next difficult question, her dad and brother walk in the back door, loaded down with bags and bags of groceries.

"Did you guys leave anything on the shelves?"

Spencer giggles when I take the two heavy bags he dragged inside from his hands.

"We decided to stock up. Didn't we, buddy?" Rafe ruffles his son's hair and darts a grin in my direction. I almost drop the jar of peanut butter at the impact of it.

Mom walking in is for once a welcome distraction.

"Good Lord, what did you all get?" she asks.

"Enough so we won't run out for a while."

Any tension between Mom and Rafe after their run-in —over me—last night seems to have dissipated. I'm relieved. The last thing Nicky needs is more discontent at her bedside.

"What would you guys like for dinner?" Mom asks.

I'd planned to do soup and sandwiches for an easy meal, but I'm not about to stop my mother if she wants to do the cooking instead.

"Spaghetti and meatballs," Spencer announces at the same time his sister blurts out, "Pizza!"

"Why don't we do spaghetti tonight, and save the pizza for a day nobody feels like cooking," Mom diplomatically intervenes. "Maybe we can order from Nando's and get some of those cinnamon sticks they have for dessert?"

"Taz?" I look up to find Chantal sticking her head around the door. "I could use a hand."

"What's wrong?" I ask, following her out into the hallway.

"Your sister had an accident. If we do it together we can get her cleaned up in no time."

Dad's sitting on the edge of the couch, looking a little uncomfortable when we walk in.

"Hey, Dad, do you mind if I help you into the kitchen for a bit? Chantal wants to check on Nicky real quick."

His responding nod is almost grateful.

I grab his walker, help him up, and guide him down the hall. Rafe must've been watching the door because he moves quickly toward us. "Keep everyone here for bit?" I ask quietly. "We need to change the bed."

"Sure," he whispers before turning to my father. "Come on, Dad. Let's get you a drink. It's about that time."

I hear Mom asking what's going on, but I leave it to Rafe to answer.

"I'm sorry," Nicky apologizes when I walk in. "I was too late."

"Hush." I quickly take up position on the other side of her bed, and without wasting any more words, we quickly deal with her wet bedding and nightie.

"It's up to you," Chantal suggests when Nicky is cleaned up, "but I brought a catheter. It would take me two minutes to place and you wouldn't have to worry about any accidents. Or," she adds, "as an alternative, we can get you some adult diapers."

Exhausted, Nicky waves her hand. "Catheter."

Regardless of the fact my sister was naked as a jaybird a minute ago, I step away from the bed to leave Nicky with some dignity while I let Chantal take care of the catheter.

By the time she pulls the covers over my sister, Nicky looks asleep.

"I'll keep everyone out of here for a bit so she can sleep," I whisper to the nurse.

"Don't." The voice coming from the hospital bed is firm. My sister's eyes are open. "I like the sounds. It makes me feel part of life."

I make my way over to the bed and lean down, touching my forehead to hers. "You'll always be part of our life."

"I love you, Natasha," she mumbles her eyes fluttering shut again.

"I love you too, Veronica."

I swallow the lump in my throat and press a kiss on her cheek.

"Bonus kiss," I tell her, but she's already drifted off.

Rafe

TIME BECOMES tangible when every second carries more weight than the one before.

That's what it feels like.

Over the course of yesterday, Nicky drifted further and further away. Her moments of wakefulness becoming more infrequent and less lucid. Taz explained that was, in part, due to the morphine, but also the ever-waning energy as her body struggles to keep blood flowing.

Her extremities are so cold and the tips of her fingers and toes are turning blue with the lack of oxygen.

I helped Taz change the sheets in the master bedroom for Sarah and Ed. It was Taz who suggested they stay. I don't think they missed the implication. We can all see Nicky's close to the end.

Even Spencer, a normally energetic kid, is sensing it, and both he and his sister have taken turns quietly snuggling up to their mom in her bed.

We even watched a movie last night, trying hard to maintain some normalcy. I ended up carrying the kids to bed while Sarah and Taz helped Ed up the stairs.

For the past couple of hours, I've been listening to my wife's labored breathing, while Taz is dozing on the couch.

"Please…" The rasp of Nicky's voice holds an urgency that has Taz and me both rush to the side of the bed.

Taz takes one look at her sister and turns to me. "Get Chantal."

I don't argue, and rush upstairs to knock on her door. I don't wait around and hurry back downstairs to find Taz sitting on the edge of the bed. She has Nicky's hand clasped against her chest and her lips pressed to her sister's forehead.

"Nicky," Chantal's voice sounds behind me and I step out of her line of sight. "Do you want me to sedate you?"

"Yes." Her voice is surprisingly strong, even as her panicked eyes find mine. *"I'm sorry,"* she mouths, reaching out her free hand and I grab on.

"No more apologies." My voice sounds raw, which is pretty much how I feel.

Nicky looks from me to her sister and back again. "The kids…"

"I promise they will always carry you with them."

She briefly closes her eyes when Chantal administers the medication, only to open them wide searching for ours.

"Don't leave me alone."

"We'll be right by your side," Taz says firmly when I lose the ability to speak.

Holding each of our hands in hers, Nicky's eyes drift shut as the midazolam takes effect. I glance at the display on the TV receiver and note the time: three forty-seven.

Chantal disappears into the kitchen and within minutes I detect the smell of fresh coffee. Then I hear her footsteps going upstairs, a soft knock on the bedroom door, and the sound of muted voices as she wakes Nicky's parents.

Taz and I hold quiet vigil, feeling her hands go slack in ours.

At seven twenty-five, with her kids still asleep in their bedrooms upstairs, Nicky releases her last breath.

We never let go.

Chapter Seven

Rafe

"SHE WOULDN'T WANT THAT."

My head snaps up when I hear Taz voice what I am thinking.

The past twenty-four hours or so, things have been surprisingly calm. No conflicts at all, only a sad and subdued atmosphere while we all seemed focused on supporting the kids.

Sofie and Spencer are with Kathleen, who offered to look after them while the rest of us are at the funeral home to make arrangements.

I look at the ostentatious, heavy oak casket lined in pink satin Sarah wants for her daughter.

"How could you possibly know what your sister would want?" she snaps. "You've hardly been around enough. Suddenly you're an expert?"

I can almost visualize the punches landing by the way

Taz flinches at her mother's words. Still, she seems to steel herself and responds calmly.

"Not an expert, but Nicky brought up the subject of her funeral last week. She was clear about what was important to her. No visitation or viewing, and a biodegradable casket. She wanted us to remember her spirit instead of cry over the body she left behind. Her words, not mine," Taz quickly adds.

"I was part of that conversation," I interject, before Sarah has a chance to throw another barb. "She said since a funeral is for loved ones, we could make that into whatever we wanted, but that she should be able to decide what happened to her body."

"But it's pretty. My daughter deserves something pretty."

I lower my eyes at Sarah's plea and the depth of pain on her face.

"Sarah…" Ed, who's been very quiet, lays a shaking hand on his wife's arm. "Veronica deserves to have her wishes honored. She deserves us remembering her beautiful spirit, so let's focus on that."

The rest of the meeting, I'm happy to let Sarah take the lead. I lean against the doorjamb as the funeral director goes over the rest of the details with her.

I'm not religious, but on the rare occasion my wife wanted to take the kids to church, I went with them. I understand having a service for Nicky is important to her parents, and maybe to the kids as well, so I don't voice any objections.

"Are you okay with all this?" Taz whispers behind me.

She'd opted to stay outside in the hallway, probably not wanting to risk another possible scene.

I turn my head to the side and whisper back, "Yeah. They need this."

"I guess. Okay, well, unless you need me to jump in the fray for you, I'll be outside. I can't breathe in here."

I immediately feel the loss of her heat behind me, but resist turning around to watch her disappear down the hallway.

"READY TO GO?"

Taz is leaning against my truck when her parents and I walk out of the funeral home forty minutes later.

"Did you get it worked out?" she asks, looking at her mother.

"Friday. I need to find her something to wear and drop it off tomorrow." Sarah seems a little at a loss.

"Can I make a suggestion?" Taz's eyes dart to me. "I mean, if it's is okay with you, of course. I was going to suggest it might be nice to let Sofie pick clothes for her mom. Perhaps Spencer could pick some jewelry for her to wear."

I swallow hard, moved she thought of something that hadn't even occurred to me: giving the kids a chance to do one last special thing for their mother.

"Nicky would like that," I confirm before turning to her parents. "Mom? Dad?"

Ed nods, managing only the barest of smiles at his daughter as he battles his emotions.

"She would," Sarah says softly, glancing at Taz before she puts an arm around her husband and flashes a sad smile at me. "I should take Dad home. It's been a long morning."

It's silent in the truck when we head out to pick up the children. I occasionally glance over at Taz to gauge her mood, but she seems miles away. When I pull up alongside the curb in front of Kathleen and Brent's place, I reach over and put a hand on her arm.

"You okay?"

She blinks her eyes a few times before focusing them on me. "I'm not sure," she answers surprising me with her honesty. "I feel…hollow. Numb. I keep waiting for the moment it'll all hit me. It's like holding my breath in anticipation of a huge wave I know will crash over me, and there's nothing for me to hold onto. I'm afraid it'll drown me."

Before I can react, she's pulled away from me, has the door open, gets out of the truck, and starts walking toward the house. I scramble to catch up.

Kathleen, who must've seen us pull up, has the door open before we climb up her steps. She immediately pulls Taz into a hug.

"And?" she asks over Taz's shoulder, her red-rimmed eyes pinning me.

"Friday noon at the United Methodist. Interment immediately| after, and since there won't be visitation, Sarah suggested we do coffee and sandwiches in the church hall after to give people a chance to pay their respects."

"I can help with that," Kathleen offers, letting go of her friend before turning to me for a kiss on the cheek.

"Give Sarah a call," I suggest, noting Taz is quiet again.

"I will. Come in, the kids are watching cartoons."

Spencer is curled up in a corner of the couch, Kathleen's husky beside him with her big head on my son's leg. Sofie is on the other side, but jumps up when she sees us come in.

"Hey, Pipsqueak."

She wraps her arms around my hips and I lean down to kiss the top of her head. "Did you see her?"

"Not today. We get to say goodbye on Friday."

"Us too?" she asks, looking up at me.

I brush a strand of hair from her face and cup her cheek. She's the spitting image of her mother and my heart breaks to see her hurting.

"If you want."

Taz

SPENCER IS DONE in two seconds.

He picked a necklace that was hanging off the dressing table in the master bedroom. It looks like hand-painted pasta, enhanced with copious amounts of glitter. He proudly confirms he made it for his mom last Christmas.

I half expect Sofie to say something derogatory—if her expression was anything to go by—but she bites her tongue. She does however roll her eyes when her brother disappears downstairs to play.

"Now you," I encourage her. "Anything you want."

"I don't know," she mumbles, suddenly demure. "What if I get it wrong?"

I grab her hand and pull her down to sit beside me on the edge of the bed. "You couldn't even if you tried. There is no wrong choice. There are no wrong reasons. The only thing that matters is *you* pick something you feel would be right."

"Does it have to be a dress?" she asks.

"Nope. It can be anything. Something that reminds you of a fun time you guys had, something that looked really pretty on her, maybe something that still smells like her."

She gets up and hesitantly opens the door to the walk-in closet. A heavy weigh settles on my chest as she steps in, running her fingers along my sister's impressive collection.

She always liked pretty things, followed the latest fashion trends. Unlike me. My main criteria still is clothes have to be clean, comfortable, and durable. My entire wardrobe fits in my duffel bag, which still sits on the floor in the corner of the spare bedroom. In the morning I just grab in there blindly for something clean to wear.

I never give much thought to what I put on, something that used to drive my mother crazy. It probably still does.

Sofie comes out of the closet, carrying a pile of clothes in her arms and dumps them on the bed.

"It's hard," she announces, biting her lip.

"Do you want help?" Instead of answering, she nods. I spread the clothes out over the bed and step back, pointing at a navy, formfitted dress with three-quarter sleeves. The tag still attached. "What made you pick that?"

The girl shrugs. "Because she never had a chance to wear it and blue was her favorite color."

"Fair enough. How about that?" I point out the pale pink, floral summer dress.

"She looks pretty in that dress."

I note how my niece talks about her mother both in past and present tense. Something I've caught myself doing as well. "I can see that. It's a very pretty dress."

During our conversation, Sofie hasn't stopped stroking the last outfit on the bed. A pair of dark gray lounge pants, a black ribbed tank, and a matching gray, fuzzy hoodie.

"Can you tell me about that outfit?"

She picks up the sleeve of the hoodie and puts it to her nose, tears filling her eyes. "It smells like her. She'd wear it around the house, and I'd like to snuggle with her: the hoodie is really soft."

I reach over and pick up the sweater, rubbing the material against my cheek before giving it a good sniff. "You're right. It smells and feels like her." I try to smile at her through my own tears. "In which one do you think your mom would be happiest?"

"That one."

As I expected, she points at the hoodie I'm holding and I pull her into a hug. Nicky's sweater is caught in the middle, her scent drifting up around us.

"Perfect choice."

Rafe is at the bottom of the stairs when we come down and takes the garment bag for Nicky from my hands.

"I see you found something." He smiles at his daughter. "Good. Check in with your brother, he wanted to draw a picture for Mom. He's at the kitchen table. Maybe you'd like to do one too?" She doesn't answer but takes off for the kitchen. "I thought maybe they'd like to leave something with her," he says, his eyes on Sofie's retreating back.

"Good idea." His eyes come to me and I suddenly feel awkward, a little unsure. "I hope you don't mind, Sofie asked what she should wear for Friday, and I helped her pick something out."

"That's fine. I guess I haven't really thought that far."

"I hadn't either," I confess, thinking about Nicky's brand new blue dress. "I don't really have anything funeral appropriate." The corner of Rafe's mouth twitches as his gaze drifts down my length. It almost feels like a caress on my skin underneath the washed out Duran Duran concert T-shirt and ripped men's jeans I'm wearing.

"I can see that," he says, grinning now. "Suitable for a mosh pit, but maybe not church."

"*Anyway…*" I drawl, a little irritated being the subject of his amusement. "Sofie suggested I wear this never-worn dress Nicky bought recently, but I wanted to check with you first."

His face instantly blanks and he waves his hand dismissively. "Doesn't matter to me. Use whatever you want. I'm gonna run out and drop this at the funeral home."

"I DON'T KNOW if this is a good idea."

I look over at my mom, who's watching as the kids—each with a hand in one of Rafe's—approach the casket.

"It'll be okay." I lightly touch her arm. "They wanted to give her the drawings they made themselves."

Mom presses her lips together and leans against my

dad, who is flanking her on the other side. I don't even bother holding back my tears as we watch Rafe crouch down, putting an arm around each of his children. He lifts them simultaneously, stepping closer to my sister's casket.

"She's wearing my necklace," I hear Spencer stage-whisper.

"Why don't you put your drawings right by her hands." Rafe's low voice sounds rough as he leans forward so the kids can reach.

I suddenly have a moment of panic when a vision of one of the kids tumbling from Rafe's hold hits me, and breathe a sigh of relief when he straightens up.

"I love you, Mommy."

Sofie's tear-filled voice rips my heart right out of my chest, and I shove my fist against my mouth to stifle a sob.

"Daddy, I have to pee," her brother announces loudly, causing my father to chuckle. Rafe's head swings around, smiling through his tears.

"All right, kid. Let me get you guys to Kathleen, she can take you."

It had actually been Mom's idea to ask Kathleen to be here for the kids. She's in the hallway, waiting.

The moment the door closes behind Rafe and the kids, Mom and Dad make their way over to the casket. I stay right where I am.

"Couldn't you have suggested a dress?"

I squeeze my eyes shut at Mom's sharp comment when she sees Nicky. It's always been my mother's way, to lash out when she hurts, but I know inside she's torn up in pain. I ignore the comment, just as I ignore Dad's soft admonishment.

I hear the door open at the same time Mom hisses, "She's got sparkles all over herself, for cripes' sake. She'd be mortified"

A large hand presses in the small of my back as Rafe guides me closer to the casket.

"Actually, she wouldn't," he jumps in. "That sweater was her favorite, and she'd happily be covered in glitter if it meant it would make her kids happy. She looks perfect."

I lift my eyes and look at my sister. Except it's not her anymore; only the shell where she used to live.

Dad kisses his fingertips and presses them over her heart. "See you soon, sweetheart. I'll see you soon."

Mom reaches in and brushes a few sparkles off her cheek, before she turns to my father and buries her face in his chest.

Rafe stays where he is, but urges me to move closer. I straighten the two drawings the kids dropped in and take one last look at her before stepping back to let funeral home staff close the casket. When they start bolting down the lid, I instinctively lean into Rafe's strength and his arm settles around my shoulders.

"Wait," I call out as they start rolling her toward the door.

I hurry forward and bend down, pressing my lips against the cold wood covering her face.

"Bonus kiss," I whisper.

Chapter Eight

Rafe

IT'S BEEN a long ten days.

Nicky's absence had been glaringly obvious in the days following the funeral. Leading up to it, I'd had my hands full dealing with things, but the biggest challenge had been to try and get us into some semblance of a regular routine after.

I'd kept the kids home this past week so we could all catch our breath. I only took care of emergency calls and kept up with my farm visits, but I'd left the notice on the door for non-urgent care to contact Rick's clinic in Winona.

Having Taz around has been a mixed bag. As valuable as it is to have her help look after the kids and the house, it's also a challenge having her so close. In the last weeks of her life, Nicky had provided a natural boundary, but in the void she left behind; I find it more and more difficult to keep my distance.

It was almost a relief to drop the kids off at school for their first day back, and head straight to the clinic for my first scheduled appointment.

That relief is short-lived when I see my first appointment waiting in the reception area.

"Morning Mrs. Myers. Give me a chance to check in with Lisa and I'll be right with you." I indicate for my assistant to follow me to the back, out of earshot. "Please tell me she hasn't been feeding her dog crap again. I don't think I have the patience."

Lisa snorts and shakes her head. "It's better," she says, grinning. "Apparently the new food has poor Charlton's stomach upset. She says he's gassy."

I close my eyes and take a deep breath. "I hope to God we have a busy morning scheduled."

"We do. A lot of folks have been waiting for you to get back, rather than driving to Winona. Mrs. Myers gets only ten minutes of your time."

"Thank you. Give me five minutes to get caffeinated and then put her in exam one."

"Coffee in the pot," Lisa tosses over her shoulder, as she makes her way down the hall and I quickly duck into the small kitchen.

Fortified by Lisa's potent brew, I find my way to exam room one.

"Dr. Thomas, I'm so very sorry for your loss," Mrs. Myers blurts out before I even have a foot in the door. "You must be heartbroken. How are those precious little ones doing?"

"Thank you, Mrs. Myers. We're coping. Now what brings you in today?" I quickly redirect the conversation.

For a brief time it works as she recounts in painstaking detail the workings of Charlton's bowels in the past two weeks. While I examine the dog, however, she maneuvers her way back to what I'm sure is the real reason of her visit today. "I couldn't help but notice that sister of hers at the funeral. Natasha?" She makes a clucking sound as she shakes her head. "Good Lord, she looks a fright, doesn't she? So different from your lovely Veronica." She emits more disapproving sounds to broadcast her dislike. "Poor Sarah and Ed, they must be beside themselves having to bury their precious daughter. I can't imagine their shock when the other one showed up."

Malicious old biddy. At first I try to ignore her, but I can't stand by and have her feed what I assume is already a thriving, small-town gossip mill.

"Mrs. Myers," I snap sternly, lifting Charlton and setting him on the floor. "Not that it's any of your business, but Natasha has been here for weeks already. Her sister wanted her by her side in her final days, and she's been a lifesaver helping out with the children. I don't want to hear you speak ill of her."

She looks shocked, pressing her hand against her chest. "Of course. I would never…" she huffs before tilting her head to the side before she continues, "it's just…"

"Mrs. Myers, I'm sorry to cut you short, but my next appointment is waiting. Your dog is fine. Any change in diet always takes a bit of adjustment, I'm sure his bowels will settle down soon enough." I reach around her and pull the door open, revealing Lisa.

"I was about to let you know your next appointment is here," she announces, bulging her eyes at me.

"Send them in, please. Mrs. Myers is just leaving."

Lisa, hearing the tension in my voice, takes the older woman by the arm and guides her firmly down the hall.

Appointments keep me busy the rest of the morning and every single one starts with condolences. By the time noon comes around, I need some air. Maybe I'll pop home and check on things there. See how Taz is doing now the kids are back at school.

I tell myself it's out of concern for her.

"I'm going to grab some lunch."

Lisa is at the reception desk, the phone at her ear, and holding a finger up. "Hang on, he just finished his last appointment." She winces, shooting a silent apology with her eyes. "He can be there in ten."

"Where am I going?" I ask when she hangs up.

"Van Duren's farm. He found that new calf in a ditch, tangled up in barbed wire some idiot left out in the field. He says some of it has embedded deep."

A few choice expletives escape me as I quickly collect what I need and rush out to my truck.

It's not that these things never happen—they do—but that bull calf is special. Jeff Van Duren has a lot riding on that animal. It's the only calf left since two of his pregnant cows lost their calves earlier this year.

One of his hands is waiting at the gate when I drive up.

"They're on the far side, northwest corner, just left of those trees," he says, pointing, when I roll down the window.

"Can I drive the truck out there?"

"Yeah, stick to the trail along the fence line."

It's not looking good. By the time I reach Jeff he's

standing on the edge of the gully looking down, hands clasped behind his neck.

"Careful." He grabs my arm when I try to make my way down to the animal. "Every time I get close, dang thing struggles and hurts hisself more."

"Can't help him if I can't get to him," I point out.

"Ain't you got a dart gun?"

"That's not gonna work, Jeff. I have a better chance of keeping him calm if I can get my hands on him. Grab me that burlap sack from the back of the truck."

It takes me a while to ease my way down to the calf, but I'm finally able to drop the burlap over his head.

"Bring my bag," I call up, trying to get a grip on the animal without getting myself hurt. "Gonna need you to cut the wires while I hold him down."

Halfway down the slope, Jeff loses his footing and starts sliding, startling the terrified calf.

———

Taz

THE HOUSE IS SO QUIET.

I've tried to stay busy, ever since Rafe and the kids left this morning, but the silence is starting to get to me.

With the last load of laundry in the dryer, the house clean, and dinner prep done early, I've run out of things to do. Sort of. More like I've run out of excuses not to tackle Nicky's clothes.

Mom said something last week when she and Dad

dropped by. Then Rafe suggested over the weekend that maybe I'd want to go through her closet.

I don't. Not really. Touching her stuff, smelling her scent, feeling her absence—I'm not ready to leave this numb blanket I've covered myself under. I'm afraid if I even lift a corner, I'll get sucked into an emotional vortex I won't be able to find my way out of.

It's safer this way.

I had a weak moment yesterday when my parents dropped by after church. Mom seemed flat, only making an effort to be engaged with the kids, but barely speaking to Rafe or me. When they left, Dad unexpectedly pulled me into a hug, whispering to me to "give her some time."

It was more than I'd had from my parents since coming back, and it had me running up the stairs so I could deal with the wave of emotions it evoked in private. I didn't expect Rafe to follow me, but I suddenly found myself pressed against his chest. I'm ashamed to admit I clung to him, selfishly grabbing the comfort he offered with both hands.

Selfishly—yes—because even after the tears dried, I didn't make any effort to step away. I'm not sure how long we stood there, but Rafe ended up pulling my arms from around him and disappearing downstairs. It took me a while, but by the time I came down, I'd shoved all my emotions back under that heavy blanket of numbness.

It feels like we're all on shaky ground, moving cautiously around each other, trying hard not to be the one to upset the fragile balance.

Unable to help myself, I walk over to the bay window and check to see if Rafe's truck is there. I saw him leave a couple of hours ago, but apparently he hasn't returned yet. It's only two; it'll be another hour and a half before the kids get off the bus.

Maybe I can bake cookies or something for their snack. It'll give me something to do.

I check the pantry and pull out what ingredients I can find. Hope the kids like oatmeal raisin cookies, because the bag of chocolate chips only had five chips left. Looks like someone's been snacking.

I'm about to shove the first tray in the oven when I hear the front door and Rafe comes walking into the kitchen—covered in blood.

"Jesus! What happened to you?"

I drop the tray and rush over, my hands already doing a cursory exam of his body before he has a chance to respond.

"I'm fine," he says, trying to grab my hands but I brush his away. "It's not all mine."

I look up in his face and notice a pretty deep gash on the side of his forehead, in addition to a collection of smaller cuts and scrapes. "Wrestling feral cats today?" I mutter, pulling him over to the kitchen table and pushing him down in a chair. "Don't move."

He's still sitting where I left him when I return with the first aid kit. I set it on the table beside him and dig through to find some gauze pads and hydrogen peroxide. I notice him wince when I start cleaning the gash on his forehead.

"Sorry," I mumble.

"It was a calf."

I stop and look down into his blue eyes, realizing how close we are. "What?"

"I was wrestling a calf," he clarifies. "Except it was tangled in barbed wire."

"I see." My voice sounds breathless. "How is the calf?"

"He'll live."

Warning lights go off when his gaze drops down to my mouth and I force myself to focus on his injury. My hands shake slightly as I finish cleaning the wound and use butterfly bandages to close it.

"That could've done with a few stitches. It may leave a scar."

"Don't care about that."

He wouldn't. He's not particularly vain. Heck, I doubt he ever even uses a brush or a comb on that unruly mop.

"Anywhere else?" I ask, as I dig my fingers into his hair, probing his scalp for more injuries.

"I don't know." He sounds almost pained.

I drop my eyes to his face to find his closed. When I look down farther I see the front of his shirt is a mess. "Take off your shirt."

"What?" His eyes fly open.

"Some of the blood is wet. I think it's yours."

He looks down and pulls the shirt away from his skin. "Well, shit."

"Let me have a look."

I busy myself with the contents of the first aid kit as he reaches behind his back to pull the T-shirt off. I take in a deep breath, grab a wad of gauze in my hand, and drop down on my knees in front of him. Biting hard on my bottom lip to avoid groaning at the sight of his lightly dusted chest, I zoom in on the jagged tear above the left nipple oozing blood.

His skin is hot to the touch, and I mentally list every bone in the human body to resist the temptation to let my fingers explore. My hands work by rote, efficiently cleaning and closing that cut as well. Thank fuck for that, because the rest of me is in turmoil.

It's impossible not to notice his musky scent, the heavy muscles of his thighs framing me, or the rapid beat of his heart under my hands. So the moment I tape down the last bandage, I shoot to my feet. Pins and needles in my lower extremities have me stumble a step back and large hands grab me by the hips to stabilize me. I'm not sure if it's him or me, but one of us hisses at the touch and our eyes lock.

The loud beeping of my phone alarm startles me out of my trance and into action. Rafe's hands drop from my hips.

"I'll go get the kids from the bus stop, and you should grab a shower before you scare the crap out of them," I assign, stuffing supplies back in the zippered kit. "Just don't soak those cuts."

"Go." He gets up and stills my frantic hands with his. "I'll clean this up."

I don't need to be asked twice. I grab my phone off the counter, shove it in my pocket, and head for the front door, hoping like hell he doesn't notice my wobbly legs.

That was too close for comfort.

Chapter Nine

Rafe

"I DON'T WANT to go to school."

I glance over at my daughter, who has a familiar stubborn expression on her face.

"Come on, Sofie, get your stuff. You're gonna miss the bus," I try to coax her, but I can tell from the now quivering bottom lip we're heading for a meltdown.

"I don't care."

"But I do. Let's go, Pipsqueak." I get up from the kitchen table and collect the breakfast dishes, hoping my actions will prompt her. Instead, when I turn back from the sink I see she's dropped her head on her arms on the table.

"It's pizza day today." Spencer, already standing by the door toting his Spiderman backpack, tries to help.

My eyes dart to the calendar on the fridge. Sure enough, on today's date pizza day is marked in Nicky's tidy handwriting. So much for the lunches I packed them both. I should've checked the schedule.

Every last Friday of the month the elementary school—where Spencer is in kindergarten and Sofie in third grade—offers pizza lunch for the kids. Those are the kinds of things I've never really paid much attention to because Nicky had everything firmly in hand.

"Exactly," Sofie wails, shoving her chair back and storming out of the kitchen. I hear her feet stomping up the stairs.

Fuck. Not exactly how I want to start the busy day ahead. I take in a deep breath and move to follow her upstairs, when a hand on my arm holds me back.

I've tried extra hard to ignore Taz these past few days since I almost...

"I'll go," she says before I have a chance to finish that thought. "You take Spencer to the bus stop and I'll look after Sofie."

I want to object but I don't get a chance, she's already out of the kitchen.

Ten minutes later, just as the bus comes around the corner, I hear running footsteps behind me and my daughter's small body slams into me, her arms slipping around my hips.

"Hey, honey." I smile down at her blotchy face and run my hand over her hair, before throwing a questioning glance at Taz who mouths, *"Later."*

When the bus takes off—both kids on board—we start walking back to the house. I try not to notice Taz's energetic step beside me, her dreads bouncing around her shoulders.

"What was that all about?"

"Pizza lunch." She looks up at me and I notice the long lashes framing her expressive eyes. "Apparently, Nicky would always be at the school to volunteer."

"Ah."

It's messed up that I didn't know that. Then again, there was a lot about my wife's activities I was unaware of. First by design—hers—and then by choice—mine. I'd become adept at merely coexisting and naturally slipped back into that pattern with Taz, albeit for entirely different reasons.

My kids are hurting, though. Nicky may have wanted her sister here to look after them, but that doesn't absolve me. I need to be on the ball, and I haven't been, because I was too busy avoiding Taz.

"I promised Sofie I'd come to school to help out for lunch, but maybe you should call them first? There may be some list I need to be added to?"

It's on my lips to tell her I should be the one to help hand out pizza at lunch, but Lisa has my schedule packed today. "Okay," I agree instead.

"Good. Oh, that reminds me," she says, pushing open the front door and walking in ahead of me. "We're you planning on selling the SUV?"

"The CRV? Why?" I watch as she pours us fresh coffee from the pot and hands me my mug.

"I was wondering…I'm going to need some wheels. If you were going to get rid of it, I'd like to buy it off you."

I'm a little confused why she'd offer to buy her sister's ride when it's already sitting in the driveway. "It's outside, the keys are on the hook, just use it. Why would you need to buy anything in the first place?"

I recognize the stubborn set of her chin: I saw it this morning on Sofie's face.

"I pay my own way. Which brings me to another issue we haven't addressed yet: household expenses. I need to know what I owe you. I've been looking at rental places, but there isn't too much available around here at the moment, so until I find something I expect to carry my share."

"Rental places?" I know she said a whole lot more, but that's the one thing I hear. "Why? I don't get it. Why would you worry about wheels or a place to stay when you already have both?"

Abruptly she turns her back, focusing her attention on the window over the sink and I get the sense I said something wrong. Fuck if I know what.

"It's better that way."

I can hear she's hurting. It suddenly dawns on me that maybe it's simply too painful for her to live in this house. Her breath hitches and I put a comforting hand on her shoulder. "Look, I understand if staying here with these daily reminders your sister is gone is painful, but the house is big and you're more than welcome to make it yours."

I quickly withdraw my hand when she whirls around, those brown eyes, shiny with unshed tears, flashing unexpected anger.

"You're an idiot, you know that? It's not because of Nicky…it's because of *you*."

I'm still standing there slack-jawed well after I hear the door to her bedroom slam upstairs. I guess I *am* an idiot because I'm utterly clueless what just happened.

I dump the rest of my coffee in the sink, quickly call the school, and leave a note confirming she was already on the list of approved visitors for Taz, and dart out the back door.

Animals are a fuckofalot easier to understand even without the ability to talk.

Taz

I INWARDLY WINCE at the curious glances when I walk into the school. I'm sure most of these people were at Nicky's funeral, and this isn't the first time they've seen me, but I was preoccupied and didn't notice then.

I'm convinced it's partly because half the town is wondering where I was, while the other half wants to know what I'm doing back here. The dreads don't help either, I'm pretty sure I'm an oddity here in Eminence with this hairstyle.

An oddity, an interloper, a troublemaker, as I'd been before I left.

I felt like one too. Especially as an interloper. I'd been wanted—needed—when Nicky was still here, but in the weeks since her death, I've felt more and more out of place. I look after her kids, live in her house, drive her car; I've all but slipped into her life. I'm not fooling anyone, though, except maybe myself. If not for the promise I made her, and the love I have growing for her children, I wouldn't have stuck around.

Especially not after the almost embarrassing scene in the kitchen earlier this week. I'm not sure what I was thinking. Actually, I'm pretty sure I wasn't thinking at all. If that alarm on my phone hadn't gone off when it did, I'm afraid to think what might've happened.

It would've validated everything my mother holds over me. Home-wrecker would probably fit on the list as well. It's what she accused me of when she caught me in that same damn kitchen, throwing myself at my pregnant sister's boyfriend. At least that was her interpretation of the situation. She'd missed the difficult discussion which preceded that mostly innocent hug.

"I can't think straight when you look at me like that."

My breath sticks in my throat at his declaration. Since coming home a few weeks ago, I've tried hard to avoid him, but whenever he walks into a room my eyes lock on him. I can't get enough, registering every move, every gesture, every sound. It's been agony observing him with Nicky, and I didn't think he'd noticed me.

"Like what?"

"Like I'm ripping your heart out."

"You're not," I lie, and he looks at me like he knows it.

"Taz...If I'd met you—" he starts, and I rush to cut him off.

"But you didn't." I realize I've admitted to more with that simple statement than I'd intended to, but so had he. "She's perfect for you." I'm not sure who I'm trying to convince, but even as I say it, I know it's the truth. I don't want to stay in Eminence where I know I'll end up living the life my parents envision for me: with a suitable

husband, two-point-three kids, and a welcoming home. It's not that I don't want those things; it's just that it's not all I want from life.

"She is," he echoes, but I recognize regret in his eyes even as he pulls me into his arms.

"Taz!"

It takes me a moment to realize that it's not the memory of my mother's shocked voice calling my name, but Kathleen's from the other side of the gym. Of course she also draws the attention from the other three women helping out, who turn as one in my direction.

Kathleen meets me halfway and wraps me in a hug. "I've been meaning to call you, but the whole house was down with the flu this week. The kids are over it, but now Brent is home." She rolls her eyes dramatically. "He is the worst patient of them all, which is how I ended up here. Normally I wouldn't be found dead volunteering at the kids' school. Heck, I practically vibrated with glee when that damn school bus left this morning. Then that big galoot was whining and calling my name all morning."

I bite my lip trying to hold back the smile at her rambling. This is the Kathleen of old, the one whose mouth always ran a mile a minute, without the benefit of any filters. She's a little more reserved now she has kids, but clearly my old friend is still in there. "I'm sorry," I manage, sympathetically.

"Don't know how you do it; nursing. I don't have the patience for it. All these needy people." Kathleen isn't nearly as cold-hearted as she pretends to be. "Anyway, enough about me, what brings you here?"

"Pizza lunch." I indicate the cafeteria tables stacked with boxes, and notice the three women still watching.

"Ah, right. Come meet the girls." She drags me unceremoniously to where the three are still ogling me with curiosity. "Sheila, you remember Taz, don't you?"

I thought she looked familiar. Old feelings surge to the surface, but I plaster a smile on my face and hold out my hand. "Sheila Mantle, right? How have you been?"

"It's actually Sheila Quinn these days. I'm well, but you…you poor thing." She clasps my hand between hers and tilts her head, a fake look of sympathy on her face. "Such a horrible loss." I finally manage to get my hand back and resist the temptation to wipe it on my jeans. "We should do lunch soon," she titters on. "Catch up on old times."

Not a fucking chance in hell I'm going down memory lane with her. She was a snake in high school, and I get the feeling that hasn't changed much. I pointedly turn to the other two women and introduce myself.

"I need a job," I tell Kathleen forty-five minutes later when we walk onto the parking lot. "I need a job and a place to live."

"O-kay…" she drawls, looking at me quizzically. "I'm thinking I need a little more information than that."

I stop and turn to her. "I have some money set aside, but I haven't exactly been raking it in over my years in Africa, and I need to contribute to the household until I find a place of my own."

"Why?" Kathleen seems genuinely stunned. "I mean, I figured you'd live at the house. Easier with the kids and all that. Did Rafe say something?" Her tone turns fierce on that last question.

"No. It's not Rafe. At least, it's nothing he said. The kids are at school, Rafe works all day, and I'm wearing spots in the furniture because cleaning is all I do to keep me busy. I feel like a poor replica of the real thing, but I'm not Nicky. I need to feel useful."

"What does that have to do with the price of lemons? A poor replica? No one is expecting you to take Nicky's place, but have you considered maybe it's only you who thinks that? By all means get a job—nothing wrong with wanting to feel useful or paying your way—but why does that mean you have to move out? It just doesn't compute."

"It's complicated," I mutter, looking down at my toes.

"Uncomplicate it for me," she fires right back. "From where I stand, living in one place, working in another, and then looking after two young kids at a third location is what would complicate things." Suddenly she leans forward squinting her eyes. "Wait a minute…"

"Kathleen…" I try, but it's no use, she's like a terrier with a bone.

"It's Rafe, isn't it? He may not have said anything but he did something, didn't he?"

For some reason she has never been a fan of Rafe. I never told her I had feelings for my brother-in-law-to-be—too embarrassing—but that doesn't mean she didn't suspect. "He's done nothing. He's simply…Rafe." I shrug dismissively, but Kathleen has known me a long time. She's not easily fooled.

"Do you have feelings for him?" She rolls her eyes and slaps the palm of her hand to her forehead. "You do, you have feelings for him. Oh my God, Taz, your sister was right."

It's my turn to look stunned. "About what?"

"Oh, this is rich. Nicky once told me she suspected Rafe picked the wrong Boran sister."

Chapter Ten

Taz

"WHERE DO YOU WANT TO START?"

It had been Kathleen who suggested getting my mother involved in sorting through Nicky's things.

She and I talked a few times since she grilled me in the school parking lot. The most recent was this past week over coffee at her and Brent's place. This time it was me who broached the subject of Rafe. I told her everything starting from the first time I met him at my parents' house. I didn't leave anything out, and I felt relieved once I laid it all on the table. Everything that happened before I walked into my sister's hospital room, and everything after.

Kathleen had listened quietly—for which I was grateful —until I finally admitted my feelings for him were still strong, as well as utterly impossible. That's when she spoke up, and she wasn't shy about telling me I was an idiot for thinking I could ignore my feelings. Then and now. She further suggested I work on fixing my relationship with my parents before I hop in the sack with Rafe, a notion I reminded her would require two willing parties, to which she rolled her eyes.

I felt a lot lighter. I'd missed that, having someone to gab with about everything or nothing. Someone who knows your past and your present, who can listen patiently, but isn't afraid to give it to you straight when you need it. Amid the minefields I walk daily, with the kids, Rafe, and my parents, Kathleen's brand of honesty is a welcome relief.

When we were younger I used to share everything with her, but that stopped nine years ago, when I'd found myself falling fast for my sister's boyfriend. Shame, I suppose. It's not exactly the kind of information you'd proudly want to broadcast. Back then I never even explained why I ended up beelining it out of Eminence with barely a goodbye, but she knows now.

In fact, I've shared more about myself in my recent talk with Kathleen than I have with anyone in the past decade.

Still, I wasn't automatically on board when she proposed I ask Mom for her help. It was her comment that all it takes to move forward is for someone to take a step in the right direction. Her point hit home.

"I think the closet?" I answer Mom who nods.

"We'll need some garbage bags."

"There's a box in the pantry."

While she goes to grab bags, I pour us some coffee to take up. This is a task I've been avoiding for weeks, and I'm more than a little apprehensive about tackling it with my mother, with whom I've barely exchanged a civilized word in a long time. However, if there is any common ground between us, it would be our love for Nicky and our grief at her loss. Maybe doing this together will remind us of that.

We silently walk up the stairs to the master bedroom, where Mom drops the garbage bags on the bed and immediately heads for the walk-in closet.

"She always dressed well," Mom mumbles, as she pulls the first handful of hangers off the rail.

I bite my lip, trying hard not to hear her remark as veiled criticism. Reminding myself I may not be able to control what comes out of her mouth, but I can control my response to it.

"She does...did," I agree, and it's clear from the surprise on Mom's face she didn't expect that.

My acquiescence seems to have taken the wind from her sails because the next ten minutes we work almost in silence, emptying out the closet and piling everything on the bed.

"Before we start sorting things for garbage or Goodwill, we should probably see if there's anything we want to keep," Mom points out. "Maybe a few things for Sofie."

I nod and immediately reach for a pretty, colorful, silk scarf. "She might like this. They're her colors."

In turn Mom pulls out a sequined cocktail dress I've never seen before. "This one too. Sofie loved it when Nicky wore it two years ago for our fortieth wedding anniversary."

"It's pretty," I manage, my voice laced with regret.

I missed their anniversary, like I missed a lot of significant family events over the years. My sister's wedding, the births of my niece and nephew, Christmases, birthdays, I wasn't here for any of them. It would be easy to put that burden on my mother's shoulders, but it doesn't belong there. It belongs with me.

The realization has me sink on the edge of the bed, my knees suddenly weak. In the end, it doesn't matter who or what caused the breach; I'm the one who ran to the other side of the world and stayed there. I'm the one who created a divide that was impossible for anyone to cross. Except me.

God, all these years I've felt so justified in my choices, so righteous in my self-imposed martyrdom, I never considered I was the one preventing any chance of healing. Me.

I drop my head between my knees, fighting off the sudden wave of nausea.

"Natasha?" Concern is evident in my mother's voice. "Are you okay? Do you need a break?"

I shake my head, unable to speak, and keeping my eyes on the floor between my feet. I hear Mom move, then I hear the faucet turn on and off in the adjoining bathroom. Next thing I know, the heavy dreadlocks are lifted from my neck and something cold and damp is pressed against my skin.

I barely recall the last time my mother touched me with care. I reach back and cover her hand on my neck as my eyes burn.

"In through the nose and out through the mouth." Doing as she softly instructs, I manage to battle back both tears and nausea, finally lifting my head. "Better?" she asks, and I give her a small smile in response. She flashes a hint of one back before disappearing into the bathroom to discard the wet washcloth.

As if nothing happened, we return focus to the task of sorting through the piles of clothes, but it feels like the air is lighter.

With everything on the bed packed in the dozen or so bags lining the wall, Mom disappears back into the closet, coming out with a garment bag. Her turn to sink down on the edge of the mattress, the bag crushed in her arms.

"It's her wedding dress."

I sit down beside her, my eyes automatically drawn to the large frame hanging over the dresser. Even though I wasn't there for the event, I've seen enough pictures to know my sister was gorgeous on her wedding day. Still, none of them showed her radiance like the enlarged image on the wall, dancing by herself in the small orchard out back, her long skirt twirling around her legs.

"She was so beautiful," I whisper. "Sofie will look just like her when she's older."

"I know."

"We should save the dress for her."

"Yes, but that's not all that's in this bag," Mom says, standing up and laying the garment bag on the bed, pulling down the zipper. I get a glimpse of a deep turquoise material. "I think you should have this. It matches the beads in your hair." She pulls out a fifties-style dress with wide straps, a tight bodice, and full skirt. The material is a luxurious Shantung silk with large, dark green, tropical foliage and an occasional deep cherry flower on the turquoise background.

"It's beautiful."

It is. It's absolutely stunning, yet nothing at all I'd imagine my sister ever wearing.

"It's perfect," Mom confirms, her eyes meeting mine, but I don't see any of the anger and resentment I'm used to seeing there, only sadness. "And it's yours."

"Mom, I don't think—" I start, but she shakes her head and I snap my mouth shut.

"It was always yours; she had it made for you to wear on her wedding day."

Rafe

THE LAST THING I expect to find is Sarah and Ed's car in front of the house.

I've been out most of the day at a local dude ranch west of town, for my quarterly visit. Nothing too exciting, just routine exams of the horses and the small herd of cattle, and administering necessary vaccinations. It still takes up a whole day and the rest of the week I'm scheduled to visit the other farms in the area raising livestock.

My normal routine would be to stop at the clinic to update the ranch's files, but fueled by a sudden sense of urgency I aim straight for the house.

The first thing I hear when I walk in is the loud slamming of a door upstairs. Both the living room and kitchen are empty, so I take the stairs two a time. The door to the master is open and I can just see Sarah zipping up the garment bag I know holds Nicky's wedding dress. Overcome with a surge of anger, I burst into the room.

"What are you doing?"

Startled, her head snaps around, and I notice guilt behind the shine of tears in her eyes. "Rafe," she mutters.

"What did you say to her this time?" I pelt another question at her, but don't wait around for the answer. I turn on my heel and head down the hallway to the spare bedroom, only vaguely registering the large number of garbage bags against the wall.

"Taz?" I knock on the door and call her name again. There's no answer so I turn the knob and stick my head around the corner.

At first it looks like the room is empty, until I hear a soft rustle on the other side of the bed. When I walk into the room, I see her. She's sitting with her back to the wall between the window and the bed, her knees drawn up to her chest and her face buried between them.

"Leave me alone."

Ignoring her soft plea, I slide down on the floor beside her, lifting an arm around her and tucking her close. It takes only a minute for her rigid body to relax into mine and a hand comes up to my chest, fisting the material of my shirt. Belatedly I realize I probably reek of sweat, cow, horse, and manure, but it hardly seems to matter.

It would seem I'm unable to keep my distance when I know she's hurting. I sit there quietly, listening to my mother-in-law's soft footfalls going down the stairs, while absorbing Taz's grief until I feel her silent tears soaking my shirt to the skin.

"What did she say to you?" I finally ask softly, repeating my earlier question to Sarah.

She pulls her head back, and I involuntarily notice how pretty she is, even with her eyes swollen and nose running. "What?"

"Mom; what did she say to upset you?"

"It's not her. It's me."

"I don't understand." I brush aside one of her dreads stuck to her tear-streaked cheek.

"I asked her to come," she explains. I keep a straight face, even though I'm surprised as hell. "To help me go through Nicky's stuff. I've been procrastinating long enough, and I should get it done while I still have time. When I mentioned it to Kathleen this week, she suggested I ask Mom to give me a hand. I thought...well, I'm not sure what I thought, but it actually was a good thing. Cleansing in a way."

"So this is why you're sitting on the bedroom floor crying?"

She smirks at my doubtful tone—which I like—but then she sits back creating some distance between us, which I like less. "I'm not crying because of anything she said. Not this time. I'm upset because I'm starting to realize a few things about myself that aren't particularly flattering."

I lift my knees and rest my now empty arms on them. "I find that hard to believe." The words are out before I can check them.

"Believe it," she immediately replies, apparently oblivious to the meaning behind my statement. "It's me who has some soul-searching to do."

"You certainly aren't the only one," I admit, realizing I should probably apologize to Sarah for my earlier knee-jerk reaction. "Let me know if you want company. Maybe we can be each other's sounding board."

She doesn't answer, but she gives me a wobbly smile. Before I give into the temptation to kiss those full, smiling lips, I push myself to my feet. Bending down only to kiss the top of her head. "I have an apology to deliver," I announce, before walking out of her room.

I'm relieved to find Sarah in the kitchen, washing a few mugs by hand in the sink. I reach over her shoulder to pluck the rag from her fingers before turning her in my hold.

"I'm sorry, Mom. I jumped to conclusions I had no business jumping to."

For a brief moment, I feel her arms tightening around me before she lets go and steps out of my reach. "Forgiven," she says, before her face scrunches up. "But your stench is inexcusable. For the sake of humanity, go have a shower. I'll grab the kids from the bus and get them settled."

I don't bother arguing and do what she suggests. My thoughts started running the moment the warm water stream starts pelting my back, replaying the past half hour in my mind. Something Taz said keeps nagging at me. *"I should get it done while I still have time."*

Still has time? What does that mean?

I rush through my shower while anger starts building in my veins. With a towel around my hips, I slip into the bedroom to grab clean clothes and almost bump into Taz dragging a couple of garbage bags out into the hallway.

Ignoring her sharp intake of breath, I lean into her space.

"What exactly did you mean, you 'should get it done while you still have time'? Are you going somewhere?"

"What?" She takes a step back, but I simply close the distance.

"Is there something you forgot to tell me?"

Suddenly her hand is in the middle of my chest, burning my skin. I barely notice the force she tries to put behind it. "I have no idea what you're talking about, but you may wanna back up."

I take a step back, close my eyes, and suck in air through my nose, trying to calm myself down before I do or say something I'll regret. Again.

I'm normally a pretty cool and collected guy, but since Nicky ended up in the hospital and her sister showed up, I feel like I've been taken on an emotional rollercoaster ride, hanging on by the skin of my teeth.

"Earlier," I finally trust myself to say, "you mentioned you wanted to get Nicky's stuff sorted *'while you still have time.'* Time before what?"

Realization steals over her face and her eyes go big with understanding. Finally.

"Oh. I start my job on Monday."

"Job?"

She looks a little sheepish when she answers, "I got a position with Shannon County Home Health Care. Shit. I should've mentioned something."

"You think?"

"I'm just picking up a few shifts. Only during school hours," she quickly adds.

Her hand is still resting on my chest when I lean forward, gently butting my forehead to hers. "We really need to learn to communicate better," I whisper.

"I know." Her response is no more than a sigh.

"*Fuck*. I'm going to kiss you now."

My mouth is a breath away from hers when the front door slams open and the kids' voices fill the house.

The next moment Taz is gone, hurrying down the stairs.

Chapter Eleven

Taz

"Auntie Taz?"

"Yes, Spencer?"

"How come you don't have kids?"

I almost drop the knife I'm using to spread cream cheese on the bagel he wanted to take for lunch. Where on earth did that come from?

"Well…" I start, turning to the boy sitting at the kitchen table, "…I'm not married, and you need a mom and a dad to have a baby." I have no idea whether Spencer knows even the basic logistics of making a child, but I figure my response is safe enough.

He does not seem satisfied. His face scrunches up and he appears to be thinking hard. "But you don't really need a dad. Colin doesn't have a dad, he has two moms."

Oh boy.

I lick my upper lip when I feel beads of sweat pop up.

"It's possible. Sometimes, if a woman badly wants a baby, there are doctors who can help with that."

"So why don't you get a doctor to help you have a baby? Don't you want kids?"

I hear a muffled sound behind me. Throwing a glance over my shoulder I see Rafe leaning against the door opening, a grin on his face and one eyebrow raised high.

"I didn't say that." I focus back on Spencer and try to ignore his father behind me. "The truth is, I love kids, which is why I'm so lucky I get to help look after you two."

"All right, Son. Enough with the interrogation," Rafe finally speaks up behind me. "Are you almost done with your cereal? Sofie's already brushing her teeth. You may wanna hurry up or she'll beat you to the bus stop."

I press my lips together to hide my grin when Spencer shoves two huge spoonfuls in his mouth, leaps off the chair, and bolts past his father out of the kitchen and up the stairs.

"You're cultivating their competitive nature," I accuse him, turning around.

"Absolutely I am," he says unapologetically. "And I'll keep doing so as long as it serves me."

I turn back to the kids' lunches and snicker. "We'll talk again when they hit puberty and both of them run circles around you."

"Are you laughing at me?" Rafe leans his body against the counter beside me, and I try to ignore my body's now almost Pavlovian response to his proximity.

"No more than you laughing at me during your son's inquisition," I fire back, as I zip up the kids' lunch totes and reach for my coffee.

"Fair enough." He grabs the travel mug I've started

filling for him in the morning and takes a sip. "What does your day look like?"

I'm a little taken aback by the casual question. It feels almost…domestic. Something has shifted these last few days, since our run-in upstairs. Who am I kidding? Since our almost kiss in his bedroom. I may have run, but in my mind I've felt his lips on mine over and over again. I give a little shake to clear my head. "Uh, I'm picking up my uniform at the Shannon County Home Health Care office and meeting with my coordinator this morning, and after that I thought I'd finish clearing Nicky's stuff out of the dresser. That is, if you don't mind? I just figured—"

"Fine by me. Thank you for doing that, by the way. I realize it isn't an easy task."

I smile at him and shrug my shoulders. "It seems so final, getting rid of her things. It's a little invasive. At times it feels like I'm getting rid of her, but then I remind myself I'm merely cleaning up things that clutter her memory."

"Mmm, that's a good way to look at it.

The thunder of a pair of footsteps racing down the stairs has me stick my head out of the kitchen. "Guys, slow down. One of these days you'll be a pile of broken bones at the bottom of the stairs."

"I win!" Spencer announces proudly, clearly not having heard a single word I said. I cast an accusatory glance at Rafe who winks at me, apparently finding the situation amusing.

"Only because you skipped half your teeth brushing," Sofie stomps past me, snatching her lunch bag off the counter.

"Put a sweater on or something, it's still chilly in the

mornings," I call after them when I feel Rafe right behind me in the doorway.

"It's already almost sixty-eight degrees out," he whispers by my ear, his breath stroking my skin. "All those years in a tropical climate has thrown off your thermostat."

"Whatever," I mumble, but a shiver runs down my spine as his body brushes past me.

"I'm out on farm visits again today, but call my cell if you need me," he announces over his shoulder, as he herds the kids out the door.

This is also a recent development, the reminders to contact him. It's like he's heeding his own comment about better communication. Instead of keeping himself distant like he did before, he's now clearly placing himself in the middle of the household. He's making it hard to ignore him.

IT'S ALREADY lunchtime when I get home.

I struggle to get the door open and stumble inside; dropping half the load I'm trying to manage with one arm.

My meeting ran a little longer than I'd anticipated when Nathan, my new boss, asked a million questions about my work with Doctors Without Borders. He admitted, once upon a time, he'd fantasized about working in underdeveloped countries, but he'd met his wife and started a family, which effectively ended that dream.

He's a nice guy, a little older—I peg him at mid-forties —but with an obvious love for his job. When he went over my schedule with me, he briefly described each of the patients and informed me he'd be tagging along the first week to introduce me.

I was relieved to see the uniform: navy blue scrub pants, navy T-shirts with a logo, and a zip-up sweater in the same color. I'd been imagining something more hideous I'd be forced to wear. I'm not one for uniforms of any kind—never really had to wear one—but I can live with simple scrubs and a tee.

When I walked out of the office, I had a large bag of clothes and a big binder with details on the patients I'd be seeing. Something to familiarize myself with over the weekend.

I haul the bags into the kitchen, put away the groceries I picked up on the way home, and eat a quick sandwich while flipping through the binder. A glance at the clock tells me I barely have two hours left before the kids get off the bus, and I still have one task to finish.

Steeling myself, I dump my plate in the sink, grab the bag with my uniforms, and make my way upstairs.

The top drawer is underwear and socks, none of which I particularly care to keep or hand off to Goodwill. It would appear my sister had a taste for lace, which doesn't surprise me. She started ordering from Victoria's Secret when she got her first job at the grocery store in town. I don't share her love for lingerie and generally buy my cotton panties in bulk.

The whole thing ends up in the garbage pile.

The second drawer yields tops and T-shirts, some of which date back to our high school years. I smile when I come across a familiar concert tee.

I had a crush on the lead singer since I first saw the

local band play at a school function. I think I was about fifteen, which would've made Nicky seventeen. When I found out they would be playing an open-air concert in a park in Mountain View a few weeks later, I begged my sister to take me, knowing there was no way Mom and Dad would ever allow it. I would've asked Kathleen, but Mountain View is a forty-minute drive and neither of us had a driver's license. Nicky did.

She never would've agreed to it if I hadn't caught Andrew Fryer with his hand up her shirt behind the restrooms at the practice fields the week before. A little blackmail went a long way.

It hadn't been hard to sneak out, since my parents were usually in bed by nine thirty, ten o'clock. Unfortunately they were wide awake when we tried to sneak back in at two in the morning, giggling our asses off. Apparently Dad was getting ready to go out on an emergency call.

It hadn't been the first time—and would definitely not be the last—I dragged my sister into my adventures. It was, however, the first time my parents clued in, which is probably when I earned my label as troublemaker. We were grounded for a month, but at least we both had a concert T-shirt to show for it.

I put the shirt to the side. I'm keeping it.

The bottom drawer nets a stack of sweaters and some yoga pants. I may want to keep some of those. I don't have much in the way of cold-weather clothes. I sort through the stack, until I get to the last sweater, a gray zip-up hoodie. I lift it up to check for holes when a large manila envelope falls out.

It had been hidden inside.

Rafe

"Two more visits next week and then you're done," Lisa says when I hand her the updated files.

"Until September," I point out.

"Yeah, well, that's three months away. A whole summer. Which reminds me, do you want me to block off vacation time on the schedule?"

Vacation time? I can't remember the last time I took time off in the summer.

Not since that disastrous week when Sofie was maybe three, or four. She'd been an adventurous little thing, often bringing me critters—frogs, worms, and even small snakes —when she came in from spending time playing outside. It had been my idea to go camping at Table Rock State Park on the Arkansas border, about three hours away.

Sofie had taken to camping right away, but it didn't take long to conclude sleeping in a tent and cooking over an open fire was not Nicky's idea of a good time. Come to think of it, it may have been around then I started to sense perhaps we weren't as well suited as I convinced myself we were.

"I haven't thought about it."

"Maybe you should," Lisa insists. "The end of this month the kids will be home for the summer."

Well, shit. I haven't really thought about that either. I know the past two years Nicky had Sofie signed up for some kind of day camp for most of the summer, while she kept Spencer at home. That won't be possible with Taz starting her new job.

Jesus. Mark me down for another parent fail.

"I'll talk to Taz this weekend, figure it out. I'll let you know Monday."

I walk out of the clinic—waving a distracted goodbye when Lisa wishes me a good weekend—wondering if I should contact my alma mater to see if there are any third-year students looking for practicum placements during the summer months.

"We need to talk," I announce, walking in the back door to find Taz in the kitchen.

"We sure do," she snaps, surprising me with her tone. "After the kids are in bed."

During dinner Taz engages with the kids, but freezes me out completely. Very different from this morning, and I struggle to figure out what might have brought about the change.

Unfortunately, I have to sit through a Disney movie the kids wanted to watch, get them ready for bed after, and read Spencer a chapter from his book, before I turn off their lights and make my way downstairs.

Taz is sitting on the couch, clasping a manila envelope against her chest.

"Were you even planning to tell me you were divorcing my sister?"

I narrowly catch the envelope she tosses in my direction, but I don't need to see the contents to know what it holds.

"I hadn't really thought about it," I tell her honestly.

I've uttered that same line a few times today. Perhaps it's time I start thinking about stuff.

The divorce papers I handed Nicky four months ago hadn't even been on my radar, given how things turned out.

I'd filed the application, but only after a mutual agreement that our marriage was null and void. Heck, for the last year we'd been sleeping in separate rooms. For the sake of the kids we weren't obvious about it, but every night I'd do my thing in the master bath before heading down the hall to the spare bedroom. Sofie had questioned us once, and Nicky quickly covered by saying Daddy sometimes snores. I don't even know if that's true or not, but it seemed to satisfy Sofie for the moment.

I sink down in one of the club chairs and rest my elbows on my knees, my eyes on an obviously angry Taz.

"To be honest, I'm not sure I would've. It was a mutual decision to end things."

"Easy to say. She's not here to argue it."

That was a low blow, and I know she sees the impact it has on me when she briefly winces.

"Which is why I probably wouldn't have brought it up." I'm torn, on one hand I don't want to say anything bad about her sister, but I'm also the one insisting on better communication. Transparency would be a good start. "A year ago, I discovered Nicky was having an affair."

Taz's eyes grow big and she blurts out, "Again?"

"Right. I discovered about her prior indiscretion a few days before she died. Which is another discussion we should have, but let's stick with this one first. I've come to realize in this past year that her affair—although still not excusable—was not so much the cause of our differences, but rather a symptom."

"Puleeze…" Taz rolls her eyes for good measure and I bite down a grin at the dramatics. "I didn't get it the first time, I certainly don't get it now. Why make excuses for her? She had everything. Why would she throw that away?"

She had everything.

I let those words burrow under my skin, giving me courage.

"Because she never really had me."

Chapter Twelve

Taz

"*Spencer.*"

I think I must've imagined the whispered name until I feel a shift under the covers beside me. My eyes blink open, and I roll on my side, to find my nephew slipping from the bed and joining his father by the door. He hustles his son into the hallway, throws me a wink, and pulls the door shut, leaving me to get my bearings.

I'd been struck dumb after the bombshell Rafe dropped last night, and had simply sat there staring openmouthed until he finally filled the silence by talking about plans for the summer. It took me a few moments to catch up to what he was saying. Something about making plans for the kids' upcoming summer vacation, and possibly taking them camping for a week. He asked for my thoughts, but with my brain still scrambled, all I could do was tell him I'd sleep on it.

Well, I didn't exactly sleep, but lay in bed staring up at the ceiling, mulling over his words half the night. Then around three thirty my door opened and Spencer padded in, mumbling something about a nightmare. Before I could say anything, he'd crawled into bed, his little body curling into mine. I must've fallen asleep shortly after.

Now my mind is churning again until I finally flip back the covers and head for the bathroom. No way I'll be able to get back to sleep.

Half an hour later, with my dreads twisted in a towel on my head, I walk into the kitchen, expecting to find everyone there, but it's empty. My favorite mug is sitting on the counter with a note underneath.

Fresh coffee in pot. Don't eat. Bringing home breakfast.

x R

MY EYE GETS CAUGHT on the signature. More specifically, the X beside his initial. Is that a kiss? Is that his normal way of signing his name or is it intended for me? He probably signed that way by rote. I'm probably reading altogether too much into this.

Yet I'm still staring at the note when the kids barrel through the front door moments later. Rafe follows at a slower pace, carrying a familiar bag.

"You drove to Winona?" I bulge my eyes and smile up at him.

"We got donuts!" Spencer announces, quite unnecessarily.

There isn't a person able to hold down solid food that has ever lived in this area, who wouldn't know what that logo means. Bloedow Bakery has been around for almost a century and is legendary for making the best donuts.

"Grab some napkins, Sofie," Rafe orders his daughter, dropping the bag in the middle of the kitchen table before turning to the coffeepot.

"Can we eat in front of the TV?"

The question is almost whispered by Spencer, batting his eyelashes at me. I smell a rat and dart a glance at Rafe. "What does your father say?" I can tell from the crestfallen look on his face he'd already asked and been given an answer.

"No TV until after breakfast, Son," Rafe mutters, carrying his coffee to the table.

I wink at the disappointed boy. "Tell me you picked me out a blueberry donut."

Spencer nods with a serious face. "We always do. It's Mom's favorite, but I guess you can have it."

I'm suddenly overwhelmed with sadness and bend down to press a kiss on my nephew's forehead.

"What's that for?" he asks, and I can't help smiling as he wipes his sleeve over the spot.

"Bonus kiss. Only special people get those," I whisper, before giving him a little shove to the table. "Better hurry before all the good ones are gone."

"We only pick the good ones," Sofie informs me, her mouth already circled with powdered sugar.

I grab my cup and sit down across from Rafe, who looks at me as he puts the blueberry donut on a napkin and slides it to me across the table. Ignoring three pairs of eyes on me, I take a bite, and moan at the taste as my eyes close involuntarily.

"Is it good?" I hear Sofie ask and I turn to her.

"The best."

I'M TRYING to make my way to the checkout lane, with an overflowing cart on a wonky wheel, when my phone rings in my pocket. Rafe calling.

He said he would take the kids to see a litter of pups at one of the farms he visited earlier this week. I immediately have visions of one them upsetting the mom by getting too close. I've seen too many ugly injuries left by feral dogs in Central Africa.

"Are the kids okay?"

A brief silence follows before he responds, sounding amused. "Why wouldn't they be? We haven't even left yet."

"Oh." The air audibly deflates from my lungs.

"I wanted to give you a heads-up, I just got off the phone with Mom. They're planning to come by tomorrow. She says she'll bring dinner."

"I'll cook," I blurt out, not entirely sure where that came from.

"Are you sure?"

I don't need to think about it. I want to. "Positive. Can you let her know? I need to pick up a few more things."

The soft chuckle on the other side instantly warms me. "Sure thing. I'll do it before we go. We shouldn't be too long. See you in a bit."

"Okay. See you," I mumble distractedly before ending the call. My mind is already planning tomorrow's dinner.

I'm not sure what suddenly drives my need to cook for my family, but it seems important to make a good impression. Maybe it's because it's the one thing in which I take after Mom, my skills in the kitchen.

Growing up there was never room in the kitchen for anyone other than Mom, so neither Nicky nor I ever felt the need to learn. In college I mostly ate out, but there aren't any restaurants in the unpopulated areas of central Africa where I worked. If you wanted a decent meal, more often than not you had to prepare it yourself. Cooking was both a necessity and a hobby.

For some reason, I'm eager to show my mother that contrary to popular opinion, perhaps the apple doesn't fall too far from the tree in that respect.

Maybe I'll introduce them to Moambe Chicken, a Congolese national dish. If I don't make it too spicy, the kids will probably like it too. The biggest challenge will be to find the proper ingredients in the single grocery store in Eminence, Missouri.

"Excuse me," I approach a woman wearing a store smock with *Manager* embroidered on her chest.

She looks up and smiles. "Can I help you?"

"I hope so. By any chance do you carry palm butter?"

"I don't even know what that is," she says apologetically. "In aisle three you'll find peanut butter, almond butter, and even sunflower seed butter, but I doubt you'll find palm butter."

"I could probably use peanut butter," I mutter, more to myself than to her. "What about cassava leaves?"

She seems to study me, putting her hands on her hips and tilting her head to the side. "You're not from here, are you?"

I can't help it; I burst out laughing. "Actually, I am. Originally. Born and raised."

"You're shitting me." She leans a little closer and whispers conspiratorially, "I've lived here for four years and was convinced there weren't any interesting people living in Eminence. I can't tell you how happy I am to be wrong."

"Well, I guess…thank you?" I grin at her, sticking my hand out. "Natasha, but most people call me Taz."

"Meredith," she says, taking my hand. "Now tell me, what on earth are you cooking?"

When I walk out of the store half an hour later, with enough groceries to last us a month, I do it with a giant smile on my face.

It looks like I made a new friend. One who seems satisfied taking me at face value instead of judging me based on an old reputation or a different appearance.

It gives me hope that perhaps I will be able to make a life here.

Rafe

. . .

I T 's a lot later than I anticipated when I pull the truck in the spot beside the CRV.

A quick glance at the kids in the back seat puts a smile on my face, despite the niggling concern I may have jumped the gun.

It's not like me to make spontaneous decisions, but there'd been something about the way the kids had buried their unguarded smiling faces in the soft fur of the wiggling pups in their arms. The words had flown from my mouth before I realized perhaps I should've included Taz.

Too late now.

As usual, Spencer is first through the door, this time with Sofie close on his heels. My hands full of bags, I kick the door shut behind me and freeze at the sight of Taz on her back on the living room floor, giggling like a loon with the two puppies crawling all over her face and biting at her hair.

Any concern I had flies out the window.

"You're a pushover," she teases me when I drop the bags and sit down on the coffee table.

"I'm not the one on the floor covered in puppy spit."

She grins at my retort and the light in her eyes feels warm on my skin. I was concerned over nothing.

"Do they have names?" she asks the kids.

"Lilo and Stitch." Of course it's Spencer who's the first to answer, even though Sofie was the one to come up with the names. Given that was the title of the movie the kids watched last night, Spencer immediately agreed. "That's Stitch, he's a boy," my son quickly ads, pointing at the puppy sniffing a spot on the rug.

Shit. Before I can even react, Taz is up, scooping the pup up and running to the back door.

"Grab Lilo, Sofie. She may be ready for a pee too."

With the kids following the exploring pups around the yard, I sink down beside Taz on the steps.

"What are they?"

I shrug. "Who knows? I'm guessing some English Shepherd, maybe some beagle, it's hard to tell when they're this small."

"So barnyard mutts."

"Pretty much."

"They're adorable. I think they'll be good for the kids."

I turn my head and find her eyes on me. "I'm hoping. It's the happiest I've seen them in months."

"I get it. The love of a dog is unconditional, much like the love of a parent..." she seems to hesitate a moment before she adds, "...should be. No limitations or expectations."

It's not a stretch to know she's talking about her own experience, and my heart goes out to her. Things can't have been easy on her since she came back to Eminence. Not only for the obvious reasons, but also because of the way she was welcomed home, and I use that term lightly. It wasn't only by her parents but me as well, until Nicky set me straight a few days before she died.

"So you're okay with this?" I nudge her shoulder with mine. "I probably should've checked with you first. Especially since I'm pretty sure your sister wouldn't have approved. Sorry about that."

"They're your kids, it's your house; it should be your

decision. It just so happens I adore dogs, so you won't hear any complaints from me."

"Phew." She smiles when I wipe imaginary sweat off my forehead, and I have a hard time looking away, until I hear Spencer yelling.

"He's pooping!"

"Good," I call out. "Wait 'til he's done and then tell him what a good boy he is." I watch as my boy does exactly that. "That's great, Spencer. Now go inside and grab that box of little bags we bought at the store." When he hands me the box and starts walking away I stop him. "Hang on, Son." I rip open the box and hand him a baggie. "It's your dog, so your job to clean up after him."

"Ewww." His face is scrunched up, but he takes the bag from my hand.

Taz's amused eyes sparkle up at me. "Bet he didn't see that one coming," she mumbles under her breath. "But that does bring up a practical question. The kids are in school during the day, and I start work on Monday, so who's going to look after the puppies then?"

"I will. They can come with me to the clinic."

She looks at me dubiously. "You will? You mean Lisa will."

I figure best would probably be not to say anything to that, so I keep my mouth shut. Apparently Taz isn't done yet.

"And who gets up when they cry during the night?"

This I had not exactly thought all the way through, so I throw Taz a winning smile I hope will earn me some goodwill.

"I thought we could take turns?"

She tosses her hair back and bursts out laughing. The sound—like the woman—is carefree. She's gorgeous and I can't take my eyes off the silk column of her exposed neck I'd like to run my lips along.

Chapter Thirteen

Taz

IT WAS me who ended up sleeping on the couch last night.

After what had been an exciting day, with the addition of the new family members, the kids had been exhausted. While Rafe went up to put them to bed, I waited for him outside, finishing my glass of wine while keeping an eye on the pups.

An hour later he still hadn't surfaced. I went to look for him and found him fast asleep with both kids on the big king-sized bed in the master bedroom. I didn't have the heart to wake him so I backed out of the room, went to put my pj's on, grabbed a pillow and blanket from my bedroom, and curled up on the couch.

The dogs were up a few times during the night; whimpering and crying until I finally picked them up and let them cuddle on the couch with me. As far as puppy training goes, probably not the best idea, but at least I got some sleep.

The wiggling of a pair of small warm bodies curled up against my stomach wakes me up, and the first thing I see is Rafe crouched beside the couch, his blue eyes inches from mine.

"I was about to let them out."

"Okay," I mumble, stretching my body the moment he picks up the dogs. "I'll make us some coffee."

Padding into the kitchen, I catch a glimpse of Rafe bending over one of the dogs, probably praising it for doing its business. It isn't the first time I've noticed his firm ass, especially in those well-worn jeans, but what holds my attention is how low they ride on his hips. There's a wedge of pale skin visible instead of the customary waistband of his boxer briefs.

My body is instantly awake.

Jesus.

I blow out air between pursed lips and force myself to turn away from the window, but that doesn't stop the fantasy playing out in my mind.

By the time the coffee is brewing and the back door opens, my face is flushed.

"You okay?" Rafe says, clueless I've just mentally had my way with him.

"Yup."

I can feel him staring as I pull down our mugs, until the restless pups finally draw his attention, wanting food. Listening to him fill the dog bowls I keep my back turned, trying to force the blood to slow down in my veins. A hiss escapes me at a slight brush against my hip and I feel his heat as his arm reaches around me, grabbing his coffee from the counter. Just like that my body runs hot again.

"We need to talk."

Those words are like an ice bath, instantly cooling me down. "About what?" I turn to find him leaning against the kitchen island.

"We never finished our plans for the kids this summer. There's only two weeks of school left."

Right, I was supposed to give that some thought. "Well, I got my work schedule on Friday and I have shifts three days a week: Mondays, Wednesdays, and Fridays."

"Okay. I can ask Lisa to schedule me in on Saturdays, so I can have Sunday and Monday off."

"That leaves two days," I point out. "What about camps? You mentioned something about Sofie being in day camp last year?"

"I asked her about that last night," he says, a shadow sliding over his face. "It caused a bit of a meltdown."

"Oh, no." I instinctively cross the space separating us and touch his arm. "What happened?"

Rafe's blue eyes turn a dark indigo, and as if burned I immediately pull my hand back. I don't get far when his fingers snap firmly around my wrist, holding me in place.

For what seems like an eternity, we stare into each other's eyes. Rafe's face is impassive, but his eyes swirl with emotions I can't even begin to identify. Worried about what he might recognize in my own, I finally lower my gaze. Unfortunately that has me staring at the front of his jeans, where a substantial bulge is pressing against the fabric.

Holy shit.

I swing around, ripping out of his hold, and take two wobbly steps to brace my hands on the counter.

My *sister's* counter.

In my sister's kitchen.

In my sister's house with my sister's husband—my *dead* sister.

I drop my chin down and draw in a shaky breath through the pain ballooning in my chest. I'm going to hell.

"Taz…" His deep rumbly voice too close behind me skitters like a dose of voltage over my skin.

I shake my head sharply. "Summer camp," I grind out, determined to pull us back from what surely would be a disaster.

There's a long pause before I sense him stepping back. "She doesn't want to go. Sofie," he unnecessarily explains. "She was pretty adamant, even though she couldn't really explain why."

"It doesn't matter," I point out without turning around. "I'm sure she is feeling a lot of things she can't really explain. Grief is like that; attaching itself irrationally to random things or experiences without real rhyme or reason."

I know, because I just had a moment like that.

I squeeze my eyes shut at the realization that no matter what my body tells me—what my heart wants—it will always be stained with the grief of Nicky's loss.

"I'm going to grab a shower," Rafe says behind me before I feel a light tug on my dreads. "Don't worry, we'll figure it out."

I listen to his footsteps disappear down the hall and up

the stairs, wondering what exactly he proposes we figure out.

Rafe

THE HOUSE SMELLS incredible when I walk in the back door.

After my cold shower this morning, I was almost grateful to be called out for an emergency. Nothing sobers you instantly like a poor dog getting his leg caught in a poacher's trap. Unfortunately the leg couldn't be saved, but the dog will live.

There's no one in the kitchen, so I walk over to the stove to lift the lid off the heavy cast iron pot, and stick my nose in it.

"It's not ready." I almost drop the lid at the sound of Taz's voice behind me. She's smiling when I whip my head around, but her heart is not in it. "Give it another forty-five minutes and you can have a taste."

"What is it?"

"Moambe Chicken, I had to tweak the recipe because I couldn't get everything at the grocery store, but it's close enough."

I ease the lid back on the pan and turn fully to face her. "Where are the kids?"

"The four-legged ones are zonked out underneath the coffee table and the two-legged ones are at Kathleen and Brent's, playing in the pool."

"Good." It's perfect actually.

I reach for her hand and pull her along into the living room and down on the couch beside me. Lilo and Stitch barely seem to notice.

"What are you doing?"

"We need to talk."

"Again?" She pulls he hand from mine. "We talked this morning, before we went…off track."

"That's what we need to talk about." I reach for her again, determined to get us past this elephant in the room. "I know you haven't missed the way my body responds to you whenever you're near. I haven't missed yours."

Her mouth falls open in shock, and in the next moment she's up and standing on the other side of the coffee table, her arms tellingly crossed over her chest. "Don't…"

"What? Tell the truth?"

"It's…" she seems to struggle finding the right word until she settles on, "…inappropriate."

"That doesn't make it less true," I insist, trying not to scoff.

"Nicky—"

I quickly press on before she can stop me. "I know she talked to you. She talked to me as well. She knew, well before I was willing to acknowledge it, and possibly right from the start, that my head may have been invested but my heart wasn't."

"How can you say that?"

Both dogs startle awake at Taz's loud outburst and Stitch whimpers confused.

"Because you and I both know it's the truth, and so did

Nicky. There's always been something between us. I suspect even your mother knows." Taz claps her hands over her ears and closes her eyes. "Taz…" She doesn't—or pretends not to—hear me. I get up and step in front of her, peeling her hands away from her head. Her eyes open to reveal them filling with tears.

"It's not right. She's been gone less than two months."

"Normally I'd agree with you, but be honest, Taz, you and I both know whatever is going on between us dates back years, not months."

"What about the kids? Jesus, my parents? I can't do this to them again."

"Stop it," I snap when she covers her face with her hands. "This is about you and me. Don't get me wrong; I'm not proposing to flaunt anything in their faces. We haven't even had a chance to discover what we have." I gently pull her hands away and hold them firmly in mine. "All I'm asking is we at least be honest with each other. That we explore this. I've spent nine years hiding in a marriage that was a lie from the start. On both Nicky's and my part. I don't want years of resentment to build up between you and me because of lies and misunderstandings. There's been too much of that already."

I see the war waging behind her eyes, and it's so tempting to use her body to force the outcome, but the last thing I want to do is manipulate her decision. Instead I lift her hands to my mouth and kiss first one, and then the other palm, before dropping them. Then I scoop the dogs up under my arms and take them out for a much-needed piddle.

"WHERE DID THESE COME FROM?"

Clearly shocked, Sarah stops inside the door when she is enthusiastically greeted by Lilo and Stitch.

"They're ours," Spencer quickly informs her. "They come from the farm," he says with a serious face.

"Is that so?" I feel before I see the heat of my mother-in-law's glare before she pointedly ignores the wiggling fur at her feet and walks straight toward the kitchen. "That didn't take long," she says under her breath as she passes me, kids and dogs following her.

I quickly suppress the pang of guilt at her words. I shouldn't be surprised she's aware one of the ongoing disagreements Nicky and I had was around pets. I wanted a dog for the kids, she didn't. I'll admit, for me it was more about fulfilling a childhood dream of my own, while Nicky pointed out that with the clinic next door, the kids would have enough exposure to animals without needing to bring them into the home. It had been a standoff to which there had never been a solution.

"Whose farm?" Ed asks, following slower behind.

"Ken Friar, up on Tom Akers Road."

"Maisy's pups?"

"Actually, Maisy's grandpups. Maisy's been gone a few years. They're her daughter's."

He harrumphs something about time flying and, like the rest of the family, heads into the kitchen.

"I need a stiff one," he announces, to which Sarah's head swings around.

"You know what the doctor said. No more than one with that new medication."

Ed waves his hand dismissively and beelines it for the backyard, where the kids are playing. I step out behind him and help him down into a chair.

"It's a good thing," he says when I fold his walker and set it out of the way.

"What is?"

"That." He points a shaking finger at the kids rolling in the grass with the dogs. "I always wanted to get our Natasha a puppy. Veronica had no interest but Taz, she was the one who would tag along with me on calls every chance she got. Crazy about animals, she was. I always thought she'd be the one to work with me in the clinic."

"I sometimes wondered about that," I confess, taking the seat beside him. "How did Nicky end up working there?"

"Convenience, I reckon. She never was one to venture far from the safety of home if she could help it. Taz, on the other hand, now she was a hard one to hold back. Always seemed to be looking for opportunities to explore. Heck, even as a child she had dreams of seeing the world."

"Guess she got her dream," I observe.

"Hmmm. So did Nicky. All she wanted was a husband, kids, and a home to look after."

I'd known that. Or at least I could probably sense it, which is why I figured the older sister would be perfect for me. She seemed to want the same things out of life I thought I did.

"She had those."

The older man nods. "Still, I can't help wonder if either of them were really happy."

I don't have the heart to agree with him. "Ready for that drink?" I ask instead.

"Any of that Glenfiddich left?"

I grin at the same question he asks every time. "You bet." I head into the kitchen where my mother-in-law is hovering over Taz, who bulges her eyes at me. "Drinks, ladies?"

"Not for me," Sarah answers with a wave of her hand.

"Taz, you?"

"Yes, please." She darts me a quick smile before turning back to the pot she's stirring.

I grab a wineglass from the cupboard and dig her bottle of pinot grigio from the fridge. As I fill the glass, I notice Sarah watching me, her lips pressed together tightly.

Unsure what that is about, I slip Taz's glass on the counter beside her, get Ed his Glenfiddich, and myself a bottle of beer from the fridge, before heading back outside.

"Dinner in fifteen," Taz calls after me, and I raise my hand holding my beer in acknowledgement.

"This is yummy," Spencer says twenty minutes later, his mouth full of chicken.

"It is, Son, but no talking with your mouth full, please."

"Very tasty," Ed agrees, eating Taz's dish with relish.

Even Sofie seems to be enjoying the food, although she's shoved the few beans Taz served her to the side of her plate.

"It's good," my mother-in-law finally admits. "Never quite tasted anything like it, but it's good."

Taz smiles at me across the table, and for a moment the

world settles on its axis. Then Ed shakes things up when he turns to his wife.

"Who'd have thought Taz would inherit your knack for cooking?"

The clatter of Sarah's fork on her plate is loud.

Chapter Fourteen

Taz

"Do they make you wear that?"

Spencer eyes the navy handkerchief I tied around my head to keep my hair out of the way.

Aside from occasionally pulling my dreads in a loose twist on top of my head, I don't fuss with them much. After my first day on Monday, however, when three of the four patients we visited almost blanched at the sight of me, I figured maybe I'd cover them up.

I try not to be offended, after all, this is Eminence. Besides, most of the patients are elderly. I'll have to tuck the dreads out of the way until they get to know me better.

"No. It's not really part of the uniform. It simply keeps my hair from flying in my face when I'm working."

"Oh." Apparently satisfied with my answer, he turns his attention on Stitch, who is pulling on his pant leg. "Can I give him a Cheerio?"

"No. Your dad says people food is not good for them."

"That's right," Rafe's voice sounds behind me as he walks into the kitchen. "Eat up your own food. At this rate we'll be running for the bus again."

"Running is fun," Spencer says, grinning.

"Is not," Sofie, who is not nearly as chatty as her brother, counters.

"All right, guys, let's go," their father orders firmly, nipping any bickering in the bud. Spencer gets up and starts walking away from the table.

"Hey, kid," I call him back. "Bowl in the sink. Do I look like your cleaning lady?"

He puts on the brakes and turns back to the table. After he completes his task, he stops in front of me, looking up. "You actually kinda do."

Before I have a chance to respond, Rafe herds him into the hallway to get on his shoes.

"You could always cut your hair."

I swing around at the sound of Sofie's voice. She adds her bowl to her brother's in the sink while looking at me from under her lashes. I'm still contemplating how to respond to that when Rafe calls her from the hallway.

"Sofie, the bus!"

MY NIECE'S comment has stuck with me all day. It's still playing through my mind when Nathan pulls up to the small single-story house where our last patient for the day lives.

The seventy-two-year-old woman was a last-minute

addition to our schedule. With Type 1 diabetes, she apparently has a wound on her leg that won't heal. Not that uncommon, but definitely something that—if not properly cared for—could result in amputation or even death.

There's a single deep bark from inside the house when Nathan knocks. We can hear shuffling and then the slide of a lock, before the door is pulled open and a familiar face pokes out.

I remember Mrs. Myers. Not particularly fondly, though. She's been a member of my parents' church for as long as I can remember, and one of the town's worst busybodies. I'd noticed her at Nicky's funeral as well, sitting front and center so as not to miss a thing.

I don't think she ever liked me, even growing up. Once when I was maybe twelve, I'd climbed on her fence to snatch a few peaches off her tree and she caught me. You'd think I held her up at gunpoint, the way she was carrying on. Called the police and everything. She never let me live that down.

That's what I mean about Eminence, it's impossible to move past your worst moment.

"Mrs. Myers? We spoke on the phone earlier. Good to see you're moving around a little." Nathan smiles at the sour-looking woman as he gently backs her inside. "We're here to have a look at your leg. This is Natasha, and she'll be one of the nurses looking after you."

"Hi, Mrs. Myers." I try for a smile, even though I'd rather stick a fork in my eye. The thought of having to deal with her three days a week is almost more than I can handle. The only saving grace is the overweight beagle who seems to have taken a shine to me. Or maybe it's just he smells the puppies. Either way, I'm glad at least the dog is happy to see me.

"Natasha." She nods, saying nothing more than my name.

I'm grateful for Nathan's presence, he cranks up the charm the moment he notices the tension, effectively distracting the older woman. He keeps her chatting as I quickly tend to her wound.

It's not until we're ready to leave she addresses me directly. "How is your poor mother doing?"

"She's coping, Mrs. Myers. We all are."

"Still," the woman persists, "she was such a treasure, your sister. I'm sure her passing has left a hole her family will never recover from."

Her family?

I don't want to react—for anyone listening it sounds like she's being sympathetic—but something must've betrayed the jab I heard loud and clear, because Nathan jumps to the rescue.

"We should really get going. Janet will be here tomorrow, Mrs. Myers. She'll help you with your bath as well." Without waiting for a response, he ushers me out the door, closing it behind us.

"It's not that hard to switch a few things on the schedule around," he says when we get in the car, further confirming his insight. "I didn't realize you knew each other."

"Most people who grew up here know each other one way or another."

"Winona has about double the population, but it's true

there too. Anyway, like I said, I'm happy to assign her to one of the others."

It's tempting, but I know it would only be a temporary reprieve. I'm bound to bump into more people like Mrs. Myers or even Sheila Mantle, who think they know who I am. I can't really control that; I'll simply have to find a way to deal with it.

"I'll be fine," I tell Nathan with more confidence than I feel.

I HAVE HALF an hour before the kids come off the bus, so the moment I get home; I dart upstairs for a quick shower.

I pull a shower cap over my head before I hop under the stream. This is one of the luxuries I most missed while working in the field: water pressure. Sure, we had showers, but often those would be no more than a rainwater cistern, a simple pulley system, and gravity.

Wrapped in a towel, I wipe the condensation from the bathroom mirror, pull off the shower cap, and watch my dreadlocks bounce free. I take a moment to study my reflection. The familiar face starting to show some of the strain of the past months. The olive skin already a shade or two lighter than when I arrived. My eyes land on my dreads.

For some reason, they look out of place, even though they've been part of me for many years. A symbol of my independent and adventurous spirit. They were rarely given a second glance until I came home. Here they're looked at as an oddity, not so much a symbol of independence as one of nonconformity. It sets me apart in a way that almost underlines people's opinion of me.

I pull open the top drawer of the vanity and pull out a pair of scissors. I only hesitate for a second before I firmly grab one of my dreads and cut half of it off.

"What the fuck?" I jump at Rafe's bark and promptly drop the scissors that clatter in the sink. "What are you doing?"

He's standing in the door opening looking murderous. I'm not sure what reaction I thought I'd get, but anger wasn't it. It's unexpected.

"Cutting my hair," I announce much calmer than I feel. With a slightly shaky hand I reach for the scissors.

"Like hell you are." He's almost growling as he makes a grab for my wrist, twisting the scissors from my hold with his other hand.

"My hair, my decision." I lift my chin defiantly.

"Why?" The question is asked in a much softer tone and momentarily throws me. "Taz?" he prompts, "Why would you do that?"

"They don't fit here," I finally concede, shrugging my shoulders. "It throws people off."

"Fuck people." He takes a step closer and picks a lock off my shoulder, rubbing it between his fingers. I'm suddenly very aware of the fact I'm standing here buck naked but for a flimsy towel. "They suit you. They're a part of you. Since when do you care what others think?"

Even if I had a response to that, I wouldn't be able to answer him. Not with his mouth just inches from mine. All I can do is watch his clear blue eyes go dark as the night, when his lips close over mine.

Rafe

SHE TASTES LIKE SHE LOOKS.

Like spice, sunlight, and pure honey.

My arm wraps around the small of her back, pulling her body into mine. Kissing Taz is like diving in a cool stream after a long, hot day.

Refreshing, free, unbridled, and all-consuming.

Every nerve end is vibrating as her fingers slide into my hair.

Her body suddenly freezes as the sound of a horn penetrates my awareness.

"The bus," she hisses, as she rips her mouth from mine.

"*Shit*. The kids."

"Go." Taz almost shoves me out of the bathroom, closing the door in my face.

I'm out of breath by the time I reach the waiting school bus and mumble my apologies when the driver shoots me an annoyed look.

"Sorry, guys," I tell the kids when they come off the bus. Spencer seems happy to see me, but Sofie is not pleased and darts past me, heading up the driveway.

"Mrs. Ryan says we only have seven more days of school." My son grabs my hand and skips beside me, chattering away.

"Aren't you gonna miss school?"

"No, because Mrs. Ryan says we're coming back after the summer."

My son is pretty easygoing, generally happy, and obviously enamored with his kindergarten teacher. I'm actually surprised at how well he seems to be adjusting, other than the occasional bad dream during the night.

My little girl, on the other hand, appears to be struggling and I'm not sure how to help her. I watch as she disappears inside the house and hope Taz had enough time to get some clothes on.

Fuck me. Just the thought of her, soft and naked against me, her lips hot under mine.

I'd come home a little early, hoping I could catch her before she started on dinner and found her upstairs hacking at her hair instead. It pissed me off. Why in hell she would suddenly want to get rid of something that's so uniquely her? I have no idea. The implication she was doing it to better blend in hit me hard. I may well have been a contributing factor, but that would end right then and there.

So I kissed her.

No doubt in my mind while my mouth was on hers, but seeing Sofie's closed-off face is a sobering dose of reality. We need to keep whatever is happening between Taz and me between us for now. We'll have to be discreet because there's no way in hell I'll be able to shove that particular genie back in its bottle. Not after tasting her.

I almost trip over the schoolbag Spencer tosses in front of my feet when I walk in the door. Before I have a chance to call him on it, he throws himself on the living room floor where Sofie is already playing with the dogs. Neither pays me any attention, so I head straight for the kitchen. There I find Taz with her head in the fridge, her jeans-covered ass sticking out, making for an enticing picture.

"Hey."

I realize my mistake too late as I see her body jerk and hear a distinct thud.

"*Shit.*" She backs out of the fridge rubbing the back of her head where she must've banged it.

"Let me see." I immediately close the distance and start probing her scalp, but she bats my hands away.

"Stop. I'm fine. I have a hard head." She shuts the fridge and turns to face me, not quite looking me in the eye. "I was trying to find something to make for dinner."

"About that. I was going to suggest we take the kids to that Mexican place on the north side of town. Dos Rios?"

"Mexican?" Her face lights up. "Since when is there a Mexican restaurant in Eminence?"

"Not sure. I think it opened maybe five, six years ago."

"Do they serve margaritas?" she asks wearing a grin. "I haven't had a good margarita in forever."

"Pretty sure they do."

"Then I'm game. Should I change?" She looks down at the worn bib overalls and faded T-shirt she's wearing.

"No," I assure her, thinking of the Western saloon-style log building that houses the restaurant. The inside is colorful but with utilitarian furniture, which makes it a great place to eat with the kids. There's nothing to break. "It's nothing fancy, but the food is excellent. The kids love it. It'll give us an opportunity to talk to them."

"About?" The smile on her face is replaced with a look of concern.

"Relax. I mean summer vacation. I got a call from Mom this afternoon. Apparently Dad is responding well to the new meds, and they're talking about taking the RV down to your cousin's farm in Kentucky. They want to take the kids."

"For how long?"

"She's not sure, but she thinks maybe ten days, depending how the kids do being away from home."

"What do you think?" she asks carefully. "It's ultimately your decision."

"I think if the kids want to go, it might be good for them. Fun, even. Your cousin has kids only a little older than Sofie, and there's tons to do there for them."

I considered Sofie, hoping some time away from the everyday reminders might help her. I won't share the next thought I had was the time alone it would give me with Taz.

"When would they go?"

I fight to keep the grin off my face when I answer, "The weekend after next."

Chapter Fifteen

Taz

IT'S surprising how many people are out and about on a weeknight for such a small town. You won't see that many come July or August, they'll all be hiding out inside. Eminence has the reputation being the hottest place in Missouri during those months.

The quaint little restaurant looks like something from the early settler days. A simple log façade, Dos Rios painted over the entrance with hitching posts on either side, makes it feel like we stepped through a time warp.

The kids aim straight for a booth opening up by the window and I follow behind, feeling the brush of Rafe's hand in the small of my back. Already, in the few hours since he scorched me with that kiss, he's found more reasons to touch me than in the previous months. It both excites and terrifies me. Especially with the many curious heads in the busy restaurant turning to watch our entrance.

I try to beat Spencer to the seat next to his sister, but I'm too slow and therefore relegated to the window seat on the opposite side of the booth. Rafe seems pleased as he slides in beside me, effectively boxing me in.

"A margarita, please," I order, when the waitress stops by the table for our order of drinks. I'm not normally a big drinker but I have a feeling I'm going to need the reinforcements tonight. When she leaves us with the menus and toddles off to fetch our drinks, I cautiously peek around Rafe's bulk to take in the restaurant before quickly averting my eyes to study the menu. As I feared, we seem to be drawing quite a bit of attention.

"Thirsty?" Rafe mutters under his breath, when I gulp down half my drink the moment the waitress sets it in front of me and turns to the kids to take their orders.

I ignore him and in as even a voice as I can manage, with his leg pressing against mine under the table, I place my order of enchiladas rojos.

Looking across the table at Sofie, I'm pleased to note she seems a little more animated tonight.

"I'm starving," Spencer announces dramatically.

"They have to cook the food first, dummy," his sister educates him.

"No name-calling, Pipsqueak," Rafe quickly intervenes. "While we wait for dinner, we have summer vacation to discuss anyway."

Sofie's eyes dart between her father and me with worried anticipation.

"Not camp," I reassure her.

"No," Rafe confirms. "I think this'll be more fun than that. Grandma and Grandpa are going on a little road trip to

Kentucky with the RV, and they'd love for you guys to come with them."

"Yay! Do we get to sleep in the RV?"

"I think that's the plan, Spencer," I contribute with a grin at his enthusiasm. Sofie, on the other hand, is not so easy to please.

"What's in Kentucky?" She aims the question at me.

"A farm. We have a cousin who owns a horse farm there. He also has kids about your age."

"Dad, have we ever been to Kentucky?" Spencer asks.

"We've never been anywhere," Sofie bumbles under her breath.

It doesn't go unnoticed by Rafe and he immediately has an answer ready. "You're right, which is why this is going to be a great trip."

"Kentucky is very pretty," I add.

"And we get to sleep in the RV!" It's pretty clear Spencer is on board. "Auntie Taz, do they got dogs?"

Before I have a chance to answer, Sofie announces, "We can't go. Who's going to look after Lilo and Stitch?"

"Your aunt and I will," her father says firmly, as the waitress walks up with our plates.

Rafe is right; the food is amazing.

During dinner it's mostly Spencer doing the talking. He needs to be reminded a few times not to talk with his mouth full, but it's obvious his excitement is slowly rubbing off on his sister.

My delicious drink, the excellent food, and the general good mood at the table has me finally relaxing in my seat. The rest of the restaurant simply fades into the background.

"I hope you don't mind..." My head snaps up to find

none other than Sheila Mantle—I mean Quinn—standing beside our table, a predatory gleam in her eyes. "...for interrupting your cozy family gathering. I simply had to come say hello."

Notwithstanding her toothy smile, I can virtually see the venom dripping from her mouth. *Simply had to* my ass. I didn't trust her in high school when she was leading not only the cheering squad, but also the snarling pack of Eminence High's own mean girls, and I certainly don't trust her now. I'm pretty sure she's never forgiven me for adding Nair to the conditioner in her locker after she had my sister kicked out of cheerleading when I was fourteen.

I never had any interest in it myself, but Nicky had worked hard to make the senior team. It hadn't taken my sister long to catch the eye of Brady Quinn, quarterback for our school football team and object of Sheila's obsession. Sheila, not pleased with this development, had launched a campaign to discredit poor Nicky, who ended up getting caught with a baggie of pot in her locker and was promptly dismissed from the team.

It didn't take much for me to figure out who had been responsible. High school seniors don't tend to pay much attention to gangly fourteen-year-old girls, which is how I was able to overhear them talking in the girls' bathroom, confirming what I already suspected.

I'd been found out and suspended for the Nair incident. The first serious mark on my 'rap sheet' I owed to this snake.

I carefully retract my claws and instead smile my brightest smile. "Sheila, how lovely of you. I'm sure you've met Rafe? Rafe, this is—"

"Mrs. Quinn," he finishes, grinding his teeth.

"Oh, don't be silly. It's Sheila, remember?" she titters, and my eyes almost roll out of my head. "Nicky was on the parent-teacher board with me. We were the best of friends in high school."

The poor kids, clearly picking up on the weird vibes around the table, are suddenly subdued at the mention of their mother. Their eyes furtively bounce from one to the other as their father mumbles something unidentifiable.

"Sheila." An impatient voice sounds behind her, and I almost burst out laughing when I see the podgy, balding man appear behind her. Time has not been kind to Brady Quinn, who looks more like a tired, middle-aged car salesman than the fit, handsome jock he once was. "Let them eat their meal in peace, will ya?"

The smiling teeth disappear, replaced by thin lips pressed into a tight line. Two deep red spots form on Sheila's cheeks as she swings around. "I'm paying my respects," she hisses at her husband, who looks exasperated.

"Funeral woulda been a good place for that, not a family restaurant. Now let's go." He takes her arm and nods at Rafe. "Enjoy your meal."

"She was Mommy's friend?" Sofie asks incredulously, when all four of us watch through the window as Sheila angrily waves her hands in her husband's face after being virtually dragged out to the parking lot.

"No, she wasn't," I state firmly, drawing a raised eyebrow from Rafe. "Well, she wasn't. Your mom was much too sweet to be friends with...*that* woman."

"You're going to have to eat your dinner, guys, if you

want churros for dessert," Rafe quickly distracts the kids, who immediately start shoveling food in their mouths. Then he leans toward me and whispers, "Close your mouth, your fangs are showing."

Rafe

I LINGER outside Spencer's bedroom after reading him his story.

Soft voices drift into the hallway from my little girl's partially open door.

Sofie surprised me when she asked Taz to tuck her in. She hadn't done that before.

I sneak a little closer when I hear my daughter's soft giggle.

"Her hair fell out?"

I have to strain to hear Taz's whispered response.

"Sheila had a bald spot for the rest of the year."

"Did you get in trouble?"

"I was suspended for a week, but it was well worth it."

Another fit of giggles escapes and a warm feeling settles in my chest at the sound. Both heads swing to the door when I push it open.

"Daddy, did you know Mommy was a cheerleader?"

I hadn't known actually, but it suited her.

"It doesn't surprise me," I tell my daughter honestly as I approach her bed, leaning past Taz to kiss Sofie good-night. "Don't make it too long, Pipsqueak. It's a school night after all, you need your sleep."

As I walk out of the room I hear her ask Taz, "Will I like it? The farm in Kentucky?"

"I'm pretty sure you will. I think Grandma probably has some pictures she can show you."

I'm no longer able to hear what is said when I make my way downstairs. The dogs are waiting by the back door, although for one of them it's clearly too late.

By the time Taz comes down, Lilo and Stitch are back inside, I've cleaned up their accident, and a glass of wine is waiting for her on the counter.

"She wants to go," she announces, smiling as she picks up her drink. "I actually think she's excited about it. She just needed a little time to get used to the idea."

"Good." I tap my bottle against her glass and smile back. "Now, do I want to know what this business about hair falling out was that she apparently thought so hilarious?"

Taz takes a quick sip of her wine, peeking at me through her lashes. "Probably not," she finally admits, clearly not ready to share that particular story with me.

In the silence that follows I find myself staring at her, contemplating what ten days alone in this house with her might be like. A long stretch of time by ourselves without discerning eyes to stifle this…thing…growing between us. Nothing holding us back from familiarizing ourselves with the other. Freedom to discover what it is that has me respond so strongly whenever she's near.

Images tumble through my mind of those big brown eyes turning to liquid as I slowly peel away her clothes, right here in the kitchen. Exposing that tempting body I've only been able to guess at, and listening to her breath hitch as I leisurely explore.

Inadvertently my eyes slide down and catch the hint of an erect nipple peeking out from behind the bib of her overalls, against the thin-worn fabric of her shirt.

"Shouldn't you call Mom back?" she blurts out suddenly.

My eyes shoot up to find her face flushed and her teeth nervously biting that lush bottom lip. Fuck, I want to kiss her again, but I'm not sure kissing will be enough. I'm afraid if I even touch her, I'll lose all control. With the kids upstairs in their beds, there is no way I dare take that chance.

So instead of doing what my body is begging for, I close my eyes and sigh deeply. "Probably."

I pull my phone from my pocket and dial Sarah and Ed's number.

"And?" Sarah says answering the phone. Clearly she's been waiting for my call.

"Spencer is about to burst out of his skin at the prospect of sleeping in the RV."

"I knew he'd like it. What about my granddaughter?"

I sneak a peek at Taz before I answer. "A little more reserved, but Taz talked to her when she was tucking her in, and apparently she's warming up to the idea." I wait out a pregnant pause before prompting, "Mom?"

"She talked to Taz?"

"She did. I even heard her giggle. Haven't heard that in a long time."

I share a smile with Taz, who doesn't bother hiding this conversation has her full attention.

"That's…" Sarah falls silent again as she seems to struggle to find the right word, before finally settling on, "…good."

"Yes. Anyway, Taz mentioned you might have some pictures to show the kids? Of the farm? I think it might help if they had an idea what to expect."

Taz's eyes narrow, and realizing I just gave away I was listening in; I shrug my shoulders.

"I do, actually. I think I have an album in the guest room somewhere. I'll dig them up when I'm getting the room ready for Taz."

It's my turn to pause as I try to wrap my head around her comment and look questioningly at Taz. "Why does she need your guest room?"

"Well," she huffs. "She can look after our place. It's not like you need her there without the kids to look after."

Chapter Sixteen

Rafe

"YOU DON'T UNDERSTAND," Taz hisses at me, so the kids won't hear over their Saturday morning cartoons.

We're arguing. Again.

We've done little else in the last week and a half whenever we find ourselves alone. The subject is the same every time.

Ever since I informed her Sarah is expecting her to stay at their house, Taz has been in a state. I think it's ridiculous for her to move to her parents' house while they're gone.

I've tried pointing out it makes more sense to stop by a few times to water the two and a half plants they own and take in the mail, when there are two puppies to look after here, but she's worried the neighbors will know if she's not there every day and report to her mother.

Then I suggested to simply let them know beforehand she's staying here for the dogs, but she's convinced her mother will see right through her. When I remind her it's common sense, she gets mad and tells me I don't understand. Like now.

I bang my head against the kitchen cupboard, frustrated, before turning to face her.

"Here's what I understand," I tell her in a low voice. "You have been in a state of panic for well over a week, over something that has an easy solution. Every day that has passed only made it harder to fix. Now, do you want to stay at their house? Water their plants? Run from me?" Her eyes flare at that. "Because if that is what you want, you should probably go. But if not, then I don't get why—for someone who's never been afraid of confrontation—you're suddenly allowing yourself to be manipulated into this ridiculous scenario."

I can tell she's pissed. She's glaring and trying to stare me down, but I'm determined to have this out today, before they leave in the morning, so I don't give an inch.

"I want to stay here," she finally shares, but before I can ask her if that was so hard to admit, she adds, "but I can't tell her that."

"Why?" I don't bother keeping the exasperation from my voice.

"Because she's already suspicious. She wouldn't have forced this arrangement if she wasn't. Anything I come up with at this point simply plays into what she already believes of me. I'm stuck between a rock and a hard place."

I'm starting to get the picture. This is about more than just the current predicament.

"Natasha, we've done nothing wrong," I quickly reassure her. "*You've* done nothing wrong. Not now, and not back then." I can tell from the way she averts her eyes I hit the nail on the head.

"I can't tell her, Rafe."

I round the island and cup her face in my hands, tilting it up. "Then I will. Let it be on me. You've carried the blame for things you were never guilty of long enough. I'm calling her."

"No, Rafe…"

I press a kiss to her forehead and pull out my phone.

"Rafe—" I silence her by pressing my fingers against her lips.

"Mom? Hi. Listen, I finally had a chance to discuss things with Taz, and she's going to be staying here. We have our hands full training these two pups, so it makes more sense this way. We'll make sure your mail and plants are taken care of though."

I can read the nervous anticipation on Taz's face as I listen to her mom.

"Well, if you're sure. I thought it might be easier for you."

"Positive. It makes far more sense for her to stay right here at home."

I choose my words for the express purpose of letting Sarah know the lay of the land. This is her home now. Taz drops her forehead to my chest and I slip my hand under her heavy hair, resting it in her neck.

"Okay then," Sarah says in my ear. "Are you dropping the kids off tomorrow morning or should we swing by?"

"Maybe it makes more sense to swing by, that way we can load their stuff straight into the RV."

"Sounds good. See you around ten, okay?"

"Ten is fine. See you then."

I drop the phone down on the counter and rub my other hand along Taz's spine as she lifts her face up. "Everything okay?"

I grin down at her. "Everything's fine."

"WHAT DO we need rubber boots for? They're ugly."

Taz turns around in her seat at Sofie's snippy question. "You'll be glad for them when you get to the farm. Trust me on this."

I pull into an empty spot and before I even turn off the engine, Taz is already out of the truck and claiming a shopping cart someone left in the middle of the parking lot.

The boots are only one of the reasons she wanted to go to the Walmart in Mountain View today. A store I would normally not be caught dead in—in fact, I don't think I've ever been to this one—but after finally settling our argument this morning, I'm not about to rock the boat again.

According to Taz, the kids will need the before-mentioned rubber boots, some rough and tumble clothes, and a few other things. The woman has an entire fucking list. I expect we'll be here for a while.

I'm lost the moment I walk into the cavernous store, but Taz seems to know exactly where she's going, pushing that cart with purpose as the kids and I follow a little slower behind.

Halfway through what is turning out to be more of a sprint than a marathon, Spencer announces he's tired and I lift him on my shoulders. Luckily, Sofie's no longer complaining, in fact, she seems to enjoy picking clothes for her and her brother a little too much. I shoot off a silent thanks we don't have Walmart in Eminence, because I can see this becoming her new hobby.

"Good thing you seem to know what you're doing," I mention, as Taz tosses sunscreen and toothpaste on top of the pile of clothes in the cart. The kids now down the aisle picking out new toothbrushes. "I would've been lost. I take it you like shopping?"

She looks over her shoulder to make sure the kids are out of earshot before leaning close and hissing. "I fucking hate it—a colonoscopy is more appealing to me—but if it has to get done, might as well get it done quickly and efficiently."

"So noted."

I grin as she swings the cart around and goes to collect the kids, who seem to have made their selections, before aiming for the cash register. *Yes.*

"I forgot something," Taz announces when the cashier is scanning the last few items. "Why don't you go ahead and load up the car, I'll be right behind you."

"I'll come with you," Sofie offers, but Taz shakes her head, bending close to my daughter.

"Honey, I'm afraid your dad will get lost. One of us has to be in charge here."

Sofie snickers and I wonder when I became the butt of jokes.

Taz

. . .

"You looked like twins."

Sofie drags her finger over the picture.

She's snuggled up beside me on the couch, where we've been flipping through some of the old albums Mom dropped off earlier in the week. Spencer lost interest after about five minutes and is currently running off the pizza dinner with the dogs and Rafe outside.

It's been a hectic day, with the shopping trip to Mountain View, a week's worth of laundry, and getting the kids packed for their trip. Pizza had been Rafe's idea and was loudly approved of. It was my niece who noticed the stack of albums still sitting untouched in the living room.

"We did look alike, although, I was always a bit shorter than your mom."

She flips another page and I smile at the next picture. Nicky and I were in our Sunday best—I can't have been much older than Sofie is now—and already our personalities were shining through. Nicky looked impeccable, her hair still in the pretty bow Mom had fastened that morning before church, and her dress crisp and clean. I—on the other hand—am grinning widely at the camera, my own bow drooping somewhere around my ear, my face grimy, and mud dripping from the bottom of my dress. I remember Dad laughing and grabbing for the camera even as Mom was having a conniption fit when she saw me.

"What happened to you?" Sofie asks.

"I remember we were going to church. Grandma had asked us to wait outside by the car. I think it was a bunny or something that darted under the fence. I tried to go after it, but I got stuck, so Grandpa had to pull me out. I was a mess, as you can see."

I can feel her eyes studying me as I let the bittersweet memories play out in my mind. "Did you always want to be different?" she suddenly asks, and I turn to look at her, a little taken aback by the question. I take a moment to think before I answer.

"No, I don't think I did. Not back then. I just…was. Growing up, I remember I wanted nothing more than to be like your mom. I looked up to her. It took me a very long time to figure out I had to be my own person."

"Is that why you left?"

"How did you get so smart?" I tug her against me and rest my chin on her head. "It's probably part of the reason."

"Didn't you miss Mom?"

I squeeze my eyes shut and inhale the scent of Sofie's clean hair. She smells like Nicky and suddenly tears burn behind my eyelids. "Very much," I confess. "But she was starting a whole new life with your dad, and you on the way. I had to make a life of my own."

Sofie is quiet for a moment before she asks softly, "Are you going back? To your life in Africa?"

I twist in my seat, lift her chin with a finger, and touch her nose with mine. "No, honey. I'm staying," I tell her firmly. "I'm not sure what the future looks like, but I know I want you and your brother in my life. I want to see you grow up, knowing your mom would be so proud of you every step of the way."

I slip my arm back around her, resting my cheek against her head. With my other hand, I flip another page in the album.

A picture of Nicky and me in front of a few grazing horses, a large red barn in the background, with our arms wrapped tightly around each other.

"That's the farm, behind us."

"I miss her," Sofie says with a sniffle.

I press a kiss to her hair before echoing, "I miss her too."

I hadn't noticed anyone coming in, but apparently they did. Rafe is suddenly crouching down in front of his daughter, while Spencer leans against his father's back. Rafe's face is soft as he brushes the pad of his thumb over her cheek.

"Oh, Pipsqueak, all you have to do is look in the mirror to see she's always right there with you."

As Sofie flings herself in her father's arms, I get up, leaving room for him to sit and tuck his children close. I disappear into the kitchen, distractedly cleaning up the remnants of dinner while trying to get my own tears under control.

The kids' excitement about their upcoming trip is notably subdued when we get them ready for bed twenty minutes later.

"I have something for you," I tell Sofie, as I take my turn tucking her in.

"What?"

I hand her one of the packages I quickly wrapped in the laundry room this afternoon. I already gave Spencer his, which held an exploration kit with binoculars, a flashlight, and a magnifying glass.

It takes Sofie two seconds to rip the paper off her point-and-click digital camera.

"I thought you might like to take pictures of your trip, so when you come home you can show your dad and me all the fun stuff you guys have done."

The wobbly smile on her face is thank you enough, but she still throws her arms around my neck. "Thank you."

"You're welcome, honey. Now get some sleep, tomorrow's an exciting day."

I kiss her cheek and move toward the door.

"Auntie Taz?" she calls out, as I'm about to duck into the hallway.

"Yeah?"

"I love you."

I drop my forehead against the doorpost and take a deep breath in through my nose.

"Love you too, sweetheart."

With a soft click I pull her door shut.

———

"Do we have everything?"

Dad's leaning against the side of the RV, using only his cane today. Mom is rummaging around inside, tucking away the kids' stuff.

"I think so, Grandpa," Spencer is quick to answer.

"Then let's start saying goodbye, my boy. We'll be leaving soon."

Spencer immediately turns to me, wrapping his arms around my waist. "Give Lilo and Stitch lots of snuggles, okay?" he mutters against my stomach.

"You bet, honey. Snuggles every day." I bend down and

kiss the top of his head. "You have lots of fun and make sure you listen to Grandpa and Grandma."

"Okay!" He's already turning to his father.

Sofie is next, squeezing me tight. "I'll miss you."

"Miss you too, sweetheart. Remember you can call your dad or me any time—Grandma's got a phone—but you'll probably be too busy having fun. Don't forget to take us some pictures." I notice Mom coming down the steps, observing us closely. "Say goodbye to your dad, honey," I whisper, before reluctantly letting her go.

I take a deep breath in and walk up to my mother, leaning in to kiss her cheek. "Say hi for me in Kentucky."

"Will do."

I'm about to turn to Dad when I'm suddenly pulled into a tight hug. "Mom," I manage, wrapping my own arms around her.

"I'll take good care of them," she mumbles before abruptly letting me go.

Dad is grinning when I get to him. "Keep your eyes on the road, Dad."

"You do know your mother is driving, right?" he points out, wrapping an arm around me.

"Oh, I know. Why do you think I'm asking you?"

Dad is still chuckling as he hoists himself up in the passenger seat. He immediately rolls the window down and leans out. "We'll be fine, Baby Girl."

I'm swallowing down that lump long after the taillights disappear down the driveway.

Dad hasn't called me that in decades.

Chapter Seventeen

Rafe

"I'm off to grab some groceries."

I hit the button to mute the TV and have to twist my neck to see Taz standing at the bottom of the stairs, trying hard to avoid looking at me.

As soon as the RV had disappeared from view, she'd beelined it into the house and I heard her moving around upstairs when I walked in. I had one foot on the stairway to go up after her when I heard the pups scratching at the back door, so I took them out first.

When I'd come back in and things were quiet, I told myself maybe she was taking a nap. That was an hour and a half ago. Looking at her now, I'm wondering if maybe she was just avoiding me.

"I'll come."

"You don't have to," she says immediately, but I'm already getting up and turning off the TV.

She's silent until we're buckled in my truck and I start the engine. Then she mumbles something unintelligible.

"What was that?"

"Nothing," is her curt answer and I glance over. Her hands are clasped together in her lap and her mouth is tight. I leave the truck in park and turn in my seat.

"Taz..." Her eyes slide to me when I call her name. "You can relax, we're only getting groceries."

"It's Sunday."

"Yes, I'm aware of that," I confirm, mildly puzzled.

"It's after twelve."

"I know that." So far I'm not seeing the light.

She rolls her eyes up and sighs. "Church is out and everyone's going to be at the grocery store," she finally says, and her meaning starts dawning on me.

"So what? It's not like this is the first time we've gone to the store together. Besides, we saw half the town when we went out for dinner last week," I point out.

"Yes, but we had the kids with us before. Now it's just...us." She looks down at her hands in her lap and I reach over, covering them with one of mine.

"Since when does it matter to you what anyone thinks?" I ask in a gentle tone. "Taz?" I prompt her and her eyes come up to meet mine.

"It doesn't," she admits. "Not really."

"Then what is it? I know something's going on in that head of yours. Talk to me."

She pulls her hands free. "Fine, I'm scared, okay? Of this..." she waves one back and forth, "...between us. Of crossing that line and if something goes wrong, never being able to go back to how we are now."

"Why would you assume we wouldn't work out?" I challenge her, knowing we're getting to the heart of her concerns, and wanting it all out there.

She throws both hands up. "Oh, I don't know: our differences, the kids, Nicky, my parents, there are so many potential pitfalls in this scenario. Do you really want me to list them all?"

"I'm well aware of the risks, but—" I don't get to finish my thought.

"Rafe, what if we're not nearly as compatible as we think we are?"

I bark out a laugh as I hook a hand behind her neck and pull her close, our faces inches apart. "Bullshit," I whisper, right before I take her mouth. Her hand comes up and slides around my neck, fingers tangling in my hair, only further proving my point. When I lift my head, she slowly blinks her eyes open. "The sooner we get those groceries, the sooner we can be back home," I point out.

I let her go, turn back in my seat, and put the truck in gear.

We're almost down the driveway when she surprises me.

"Promise me, no matter what happens, I won't lose the kids. That's what scares me most of all," she whispers, and I blindly grab for her hand.

"Never."

———

SHE WAS RIGHT; looks like most of the town gets groceries after church on Sunday.

I took over driving the cart when Taz was wielding it almost like a battering ram, carving a path through the busy aisles. Ten minutes into this ordeal and my cheeks are hurting from smiling at the curious greetings—ranging from mild to overt—we receive along the way.

We're almost home free, working our way down the last aisle, when a woman comes trotting up the other end, waving her hand.

"Jesus," she pants, out of breath when she reaches us. "Been chasing you around the store, but this place is mayhem."

"Hey, Meredith." Taz smiles the first genuine smile of the day at the sight of the woman, who barely spares me a glance.

"I think I found it," she announces, handing Taz the can in her hand. "Is this what you were looking for? Palm nut concentrate?"

"Yes! I can't believe you carried it after all. Look," Taz says, showing the can to me. I have no fucking clue what they're on about, but I give her what I hope is an encouraging nod.

"I actually had to order it," the woman clarifies. "A box of twenty-four cans. I hope that dish you cook is good and you do it often, because I don't think there's much call for the stuff in this town."

Taz grins at her before turning to me. "Any objections to a regular diet of that Moambe Chicken I made when Mom and Dad were over for dinner?"

"Fuck no," I answer instantly and her smile widens.

"Oh," she suddenly swings back to the other woman. "Meredith, this is Rafe—Rafe, this is Meredith."

"Nice to meet you," the friendly brunette says before focusing her attention back on Taz. "Now that we've got introductions out of the way, am I getting an invitation for next time you make that...whatever chicken? I'm getting sick of my own cooking and Buck, my husband, would eat the ass out of a rhinoceros as long as you put in front of him."

"I'm sorry," Taz apologizes grinning. "I don't think I have a recipe for rhinoceros, but I'd love to have you over for Moambe Chicken. If that's okay with you," she suddenly adds, throwing a tentative glance my way.

"Of course it is."

After the two girls exchange phone numbers, Taz and I make our way over to the lineup at the cash register.

"Sorry for putting you on the spot, I probably should've checked with you first," she says in front of me.

I lean down so my head is next to hers. "I thought I'd made it clear; it's your home too."

I can't help notice her little shiver when my lips brush the shell of her ear.

Two excited pups greet us when we walk in the house, and Taz seems eager to take them out back for a little relief. To say she's been tense on the way home is an understatement.

While she's looking after the dogs, I haul the rest of the groceries into the house and put them away. When she still hasn't come in once that task is complete, I head outside.

She's sitting on the bottom step, her arms folded protectively around her knees, while watching Lilo, who appears to be chasing something in the grass. Stitch is lying at her feet, his little tail wagging when he sees me.

Taz doesn't move when I make my way down the steps and take a seat right behind her, stretching my legs on either side of her. Sliding both hands under that heavy mane of hers, I feel the tension in her shoulders and neck. Without saying a word, I start working on the knots until her body relaxes under my hands.

"Thanks." She tilts her head back to smile up at me. "I feel like Jell-O now."

"Perfect," I mumble, even as I open my mouth over hers.

Taz

Is it possible to taste desire?

I swear, when Rafe slides his tongue in my mouth it's all I can taste.

No tentative probe, or dominant claim, but a confident, purposeful message I instinctively recognize in the deep bold strokes.

I turn my body slightly so my back is braced against one of his thighs, reaching up to curl my fingers around his neck. A soft growl against my mouth is his response.

With one hand he cups the back of my head, while sliding the other down the stretched column of my neck to spread wide and possessively on my chest. I almost whimper, wanting to feel his touch reach my breast, but Rafe doesn't appear to be in any hurry.

When he finally lifts his head, I look up into his eyes—

dark indigo with want—and a deep satisfaction settles over me.

That look is for me. His need is for me.

"God, you're beautiful." The words just fall from my mouth and he almost looks surprised.

"That's supposed to be my line," he rumbles with a soft smile, as he bends his head toward me.

Unfortunately Stitch picks that moment to tug the rubber flip-flop off my foot and takes off running, his sister on his heels. I jump up and give chase, to Rafe's great hilarity. He laughs when I dive to rescue my footwear from those sharp little teeth, and end up on my face in the grass.

The little bugger is fast, every now and then stopping to fiercely shake his newfound toy, before darting off again. Lilo happily follows him, ears flopping and tongue lolling, content to toddle behind.

When I finally give up and lie back on the grass, listening to Rafe's chuckle, Stitch runs over and drops his trophy on my stomach.

"You're a little turd," I scold him. It makes no impression at all, his little body is wiggling with excitement as he tries to lick my face.

"All right, enough of that," Rafe announces.

I twist my head and watch as he walks up, extending a hand. "Jealous?" I tease, and he grins at me as he pulls me to my feet.

"I can take him. I just don't want to taste puppy slobber when I kiss you again."

Instantly the playful, lighthearted interlude is gone, the air suddenly heavy with anticipation.

While I shove my foot in my soggy flip-flop, Rafe

scoops up both pups, cradling them in one arm. He grabs my hand and almost drags me behind him up the steps and inside. He heads straight for the living room, almost distractedly setting the dogs on their feet before pulling me down on the couch with him.

My breath is choppy as he deftly settles me on my back, his bigger body looming over me.

"You're driving me crazy," he mumbles, bending down as his lips settle against my neck, kissing the rapid pulse of my heart.

"I didn't do anything," I protest hoarsely.

"You're breathing."

Uncertain what to say, I stay silent and focus instead on the weight of his body pinning me down.

Delicious.

Arousing.

I shift restlessly underneath him as my hands explore from his wide shoulders down to the rise of his rather spectacular ass. I've looked plenty, but there's nothing like the intimate pleasure of feeling the clench of muscle under your hands.

"Fuck, you feel good," he mutters, his lips sliding down my chest, as his hand pulls at the droopy neck of my ancient shirt, clearing the way.

"Rafe…" I inhale sharply when my breast pops free of its confines and I feel the warm heat of his mouth close over the tip.

Months—no, years—of build-up converged in this moment. I feel like I'll burst out of my skin when he presses his hips between mine, grinding the hard evidence of his own passion against the already damp apex of my thighs.

His hand roughly yanks on my shirt to free my other breast, tearing the worn material in the process. I don't care. He can rip every stitch of clothing from my body in this moment and I wouldn't even blink.

I'm too busy feeling.

A groan vibrates against my skin when he switches attention to the other side, a hand sliding down the back of my pants to squeeze the ample flesh of my butt cheek. My toes curl as I tilt my hips for better friction.

"God...*please.*"

The moment the plea leaves my lips, he rolls away, letting go of my nipple with a soft plop, before softly blowing on the wetness his mouth leaves behind. He props himself up on an elbow and looks down on me.

"Beautiful," he murmurs, his free hand whispering over my naked skin, leaving goosebumps in their wake.

His eyes find mine as he brushes his palm down my belly, sliding his fingers under the waistband of my jeans, and I belatedly realize my lack of grooming in that area. It doesn't seem to faze him when his fingertips encounter the damp curls. In fact, the blue of his eyes impossibly deepen a shade as he brushes the turgid little bundle of nerves hidden there.

My body arches off the couch, my mouth falling open, at the charge his touch sets off. So sensitized it's like I can feel every ridge of his fingerprint as he rolls my clit with his pad.

Hungry for a deeper connection, I hook a hand around his neck and pull his mouth down on mine. The moment his tongue darts between my lips, the heel of his hand presses down on my sweet spot as a long digit slides inside me, followed by a second one.

Primed for months, it's all it takes for me to fly apart, fragmenting into a million little pieces.

My ears still echo with the rush of my own blood, when I faintly detect the sound of a ringing phone.

The next instant I feel Rafe shift before hearing him answer with a curt, "Hello?"

Chapter Eighteen

Rafe

MAGNIFICENT.

The way her body unapologetically asked for what it needed.

Full abandonment on her face as she careened over the ledge of her climax. The memory of that kept playing over and over, keeping me awake most of the night.

Unfortunately, Sarah's untimely call to inform us they'd arrived safely at their stop for the night put an instant chill in the air. I talked briefly to each of the children, who wanted to talk to Taz as well. When I went in search of her, she was in the kitchen chopping vegetables. Her clothes were back in place, and aside from the tear in her shirt collar, you never would've guessed she came apart underneath me just minutes ago.

When I handed her the phone and she glanced at me, her eyes were guarded.

I took over dinner prep, listening with half an ear to her side of the conversation with the kids. When she finally put the phone down, I could tell by the way she immediately went about getting dinner ready, without affording me another look, she needed some distance.

I took it as a good sign when I tucked her in the crook of my arm as we watched a bit of TV after dinner, and yet I didn't stop her when she tilted her face up and kissed the underside of my jaw, announcing she was going to bed.

No need to rush things—or so I'd convinced myself— but in the lonely hours of the night, sporting blue balls I couldn't recall having since my adolescent years, I wished I'd pushed a little harder. I much rather would've had her end the day in my bed, or me in hers.

In hindsight I wonder if I made a mistake, giving her space.

When I glance at the clock, I note it's already four in the morning. I'm going to have to do something, if I want any chance of getting some sleep.

I toss back the covers and get out of bed, aiming for the bathroom. Maybe taking matters in my own hands in the shower will do the trick, but at the last minute I turn and head for the hallway.

Her back is to me when I ease open her door. I don't give myself time to think before carefully sliding under the covers behind her. She doesn't stir until I wrap an arm around her, fitting myself closely to her back.

"Rafe?"

"I can't sleep," I confess when she turns her head. "I can't stop thinking about you in a different bed when I want you in mine."

My hand slips under the tank top she's wearing and finds the soft swell of her breast, plucking her nipple between my fingers. The little hitch in her voice has me press my hips against her ass. For a moment she freezes at the feel of me, but then snuggles her butt firmly against my erection.

I take it as the invitation I hope it's intended as and drop my mouth to her neck, while sliding my hand down her belly, and into her panties, where I find her already wet. In seconds I have both of us stripped naked. With a hand behind her knee, I lift her top leg and slide my straining cock between the lush globes of her ass.

"Say yes," I whisper hoarsely against her neck, as she takes in a sharp breath at the feel of me probing her entrance. "Please."

"Yes."

A deep groan escapes me as I slide inside her, sinking deep into the tight, warm heat. With only my hand for company for longer than I care to admit, the feel of her soft, pliant skin against me and the snug fit of her body almost has me come on the spot. I press my face into her neck and wrap her tightly in my arms, holding her still while I try to hold on to my control.

"Please move," she moans, wiggling in my hold.

"Sweets, I move now it'll all be over. Give me your mouth."

She twists her head on the pillow and I don't waste any time taking her plump lips in a hungry kiss. Slipping a hand between her legs, I strum her clit until she whimpers down my throat. Then I move, with short, fierce strokes, my slick fingers keeping up their friction.

"God, Rafe…" she mumbles, as she rips her mouth from mine and shoves her face in the pillow, her body going taut against me.

"Let go," I growl into her neck, my hips furiously pumping as I feel the first ripples of her release triggering my own.

Taz's heart is pounding against my hand and matches the racing of my own, as we both try to catch our breath. My nose is buried in her dreadlocks and my arms hold her close as I feel myself softening and slipping from her body.

"You are perfection," I whisper, feeling her jar in response. "Let me look at you."

She doesn't resist when I roll her on her back. Her shining brown eyes speak volumes as they focus on mine. I don't need to hear words to know she's as affected as I am at what just happened.

"Beautiful," I murmur, feathering my fingers over her flushed face and swollen lips. She arches her neck as I trace its length and down her chest.

Her breasts are full, with dark plum nipples, and I can't resist leaning down to taste first one and then the other. Taz shivers in response and her hand comes up to trace my face.

Time doesn't matter while we leisurely explore, getting familiar with the tastes and textures of each other's bodies. When I position myself between her spread thighs this time, our eyes are locked and unguarded, every emotion exposed as we make love.

"WE DIDN'T USE ANYTHING."

Taz sets down the coffee pot and turns to face me. "I know."

"I haven't...I mean, not since..." I run a frustrated hand through my hair at my bumbled attempt. "There hasn't been anyone else for a long time, but still I should've—"

"It's okay," she interrupts, the tug of a smile on her mouth. "I've always been careful."

I note she doesn't say there hasn't been anyone and I feel that in my gut. I have no right—fuck, I know I don't—but the thought of her with someone else...

"Stop that," she snaps, closing the distance between us. She puts a hand in the middle of my chest and lifts her face up to me. "If we start looking back instead of moving forward, we don't stand a chance."

She's right. Of course she is.

I stroke her chin with the backs of my fingers. "Point taken." My eyes scan her face before I get us back on topic. "What about pregnancy?"

Taz lowers her gaze as a blush deepens on her cheeks. "What about it?" she whispers.

"Taz..."

Her eyes snap back to mine. "Don't worry about it, okay? I should still be covered by my last Depo injection."

"Well, that's good, right?" I try, not fully understanding her snippy tone. But I clue in when she turns away again, biting her lower lip. "Sweets..." With my index finger under her chin, I coax her to look at me. "It's not that I wouldn't be happy to find out you were pregnant with my child. I'd be over the fucking moon. What I *am* saying is we might want to time it better. Get everyone used to the fact there is an *us*, before we think about adding siblings and grandchildren."

Taz

"Before you go, Charlton could do with a bath."

I try not to roll my eyes at Mrs. Myers' request. Monday it was a walk he needed, and if not for the dog's adorable face when she mentioned the magic word, I would've refused her.

Looks like I set myself up for more extracurricular tasks.

"Mrs. Myers, looking after Charlton is not really part of my job description," I politely remind her, as I bite the inside of my cheek.

"Well, forgive me," she fires back tartly. "I thought, having been raised in a church-going family like yours, you would've at least picked up some basic sense of charity for those less fortunate. If your sister were here, she would've—"

I raise my hand to cut her off, taking a deep breath in. "Mrs. Myers," I force myself to say calmly, when I feel all but calm. "I will give Charlton a bath today, but I suggest for future reference you perhaps could find a mobile groomer who is able to come to your house." Before she has a chance to answer, I scoop up the overweight dog and carry him upstairs to the ancient bathroom.

It's a good thing Mrs. Myers is my last appointment for

the day, because bathing Charlton proves not to be as easy as the dog's laid-back demeanor might've promised. It was a twenty-minute struggle with the surprisingly agile beagle. By the time a fresh smelling Charlton hobbles down the stairs and takes up his spot at his mistress' feet for a nap, my entire front is soaked, my forearm is throbbing with an imprint of the old dog's surprisingly powerful jaws, and my patience has worn thin.

"Now that wasn't too bad, was it?" the old hag taunts as I silently grab my things.

I freeze at her words. It's the last straw.

"Mrs. Myers, it's that I'm a nice person, and my parents raised me well, or else I would be tempted to file a personal injury suit." I shove the arm that bears the clear markings of Charlton's chompers in her face. "Now I'm sore, I'm soaked, and I'm half an hour late getting home, so if you'll excuse me." Without another word I walk out of her house.

By the time I've stopped by the walk-in clinic for a tetanus shot—the dog broke skin—called Nathan to give him a report, and pull into our driveway, I've cooled off a little.

Meredith called me earlier in the week, and I'd planned to pick up a few things for the dinner party we arranged for tomorrow. It's a good thing I'll have the day off so I can do it in the morning. I'm not in the mood for a public appearance right now.

Rafe is already busy in the kitchen and looks up when I walk in.

The last few days we've fallen into a natural groove with easy touches and sweet affection. The last two nights we've become intimately acquainted with every inch of each other's body, and have fallen asleep sated in each other's arms in my room. I still have to pinch myself in the mornings to make sure I'm not dreaming. It's been a little surreal to say the least.

"What the hell?" Rafe is stalking toward, me taking in my appearance, complete with cleaned and bandaged arm, courtesy of the clinic. "What happened to you?"

"Mrs. Myers," I inform him, but at his confused expression I quickly add, "I guess technically Mrs. Myers' dog."

"Charlton?" I don't blame him for the disbelief in his voice. If I hadn't experienced it, I wouldn't have believed the docile mutt capable.

"Apparently he's not a fan of baths."

His eyes squint. "Care to tell me why you'd be giving her dog a bath? I'm sure that's not part of your normal work routine."

"Well no, but she kinda guilted me into it."

"How is that?" He reaches for my arm and starts unwinding the bandage. I let him.

"Oh, I don't know. Something about not being charitable like my family." I purposely stick to more general terms, not wanting to bring up my sister. It doesn't matter, I can tell from the way he looks at me, he's reading enough between the lines.

"I'm thinking it's high time Mrs. Myers and I have a heart-to-heart. The woman is relentless in her pursuit of free services. She's been living off this family's 'charity' much too long already." I hiss when he probes the two tears in my skin from the dog's canines and the colorful bruising forming around it. "That old boy got you good. Your tetanus up-to-date?"

"Already got my shot. Look…" I quickly pull my arm back, "…I don't want to make a fuss. I already called Nathan to report it."

"Good. So he'll take her off your roster?"

"Well…" Rafe lifts an eyebrow. "He offered, but I said no," I admit.

"Why would you want to go back there?"

I can't blame him for his incredulity; I doubted my own sanity a few times. "It's not that I want to, it's I feel I have to." His other eyebrow shoots up, so I try to explain. "People already have a hard time putting their trust in me. How would it look if at the first hint of trouble, I give up? If I'm going to make a life here, I need to start changing their perception of me. I need to prove I'm better than what they see."

"They don't have a clue who you are." Rafe's voice is gruff as his arms close tightly around me and I snuggle into his chest.

"Then it's about time they find out." I lift up my face and kiss the underside of his jaw. "Besides, I don't like the idea of letting that woman win."

Chapter Nineteen

Rafe

"WHICH ONE OF you was it this time?"

I take the last few stairs to find Taz standing in the front hallway, a mangled flip-flop in her hands and snippets of rubber littering the floor into the living room. Stitch and Lilo are nowhere to be found.

"I see the kids have been busy."

"I swear, I turn my back for a second and they get into trouble." She marches right past me into the kitchen and dumps the mangled footwear in the garbage. "My favorite ones too."

I walk up behind her, slip my arms around her waist, and kiss her neck. "I'll buy you new ones."

Turning around she grabs my shirt and drops her forehead to my chest. "How long does this phase last?"

The dogs have newly discovered all the creative ways

they can use their teeth. Throw pillows, remote, table leg, but by far their favorite chew toy is footwear.

"You don't wanna know," I assure her. "I'll pick them up some appropriate chew toys, maybe a couple of bones. We can teach them not to attack the furniture, but we'll also have to make sure we don't leave anything tempting in their path."

"Good thing they're quick studies," she mumbles.

They are. We've only had one 'accident' in the past few days, and they willingly go in their shared crate at night.

"I can take them with me for the day," I offer, looking down in her upturned face.

"Aren't you out on calls today?"

"They can stay in the truck, or maybe Lisa won't mind keeping them at the office for a bit."

She shakes her head. "No, I can handle them. I'll simply crate them when I go to get groceries." Right. Taz's new friend, Meredith, and her husband are coming for dinner. "Want some coffee?"

"Mmm." I drop a kiss on her mouth and let her go before stepping into the laundry room to grab the broom.

The dogs are under the coffee table, either asleep or doing a good job at pretending to be. I leave them be while I clean up the mess they made.

"Did you talk to Nathan?" I ask when she hands me my cup.

"Oh yeah, I forgot to mention that last night."

Probably because I barely let her come up for air. I grin at the memory of eating sandwiches in bed for dinner at around ten or so. Buck naked. If it were up to me, Taz would never wear clothes at home, but with the kids coming home next week, that's not an option. In fact, we'll probably have to get used to *not* touching each other all the time again. I love my kids and miss them, but that's one part I'm not looking forward to.

"And?"

"He's looked at the schedule and says if I can pick up a few extra shifts before and after, I can probably have most, if not all, of the last week of July."

Taz had been immediately on board when we discussed taking the kids camping, it had been a matter of being able to take time off so soon after starting her new job. I find myself getting even more excited at the prospect of spending time in the outdoors with the kids and her, now I know we can start planning.

"I'll tell Lisa to keep that week clear. I have an intern starting next week, in time for when the kids get back, so we should be covered." I notice a pensive look steal over Taz's face. "What's wrong?"

She seems startled at my question and shakes her head. "Nothing really. I've just been thinking about logistics. I mean, I get that things will go back the way they were once the kids are back, but what about when we go camping? You said you have a tent, but maybe we should get a second one?"

I don't need to ask why she's suggesting it. Hell, I've been wondering how to introduce our changed relationships to the kids myself, but I'd hoped perhaps the camping trip would be a good time to ease them into it.

I step close to her and put my hands on her hips. "First of all, things can't go back the way they were. It would be an impossibility." I quickly press a finger to her lips when I see she's about to protest. "Hear me out. I don't plan on flaunting us in front of anyone, but if you think I can go any stretch of time without touching you, you're nuts. We'll be careful, but don't ask me to go cold turkey. Not now that I've become addicted." She shows a pleased little smile in response. "As for camping, the tent I have is big, and having only the one makes it perfectly justifiable for us all to sleep in one space, including the dogs. The kids likely won't even question it."

"What about after? When we get home?"

"One step at a time, Sweets." I lean down and give her a hard kiss on the lips. "I've gotta run, but call me if you need me."

Tagging my mug, I pick up my phone and my keys and make for the back door. I've barely stepped outside when I hear Taz's voice behind me.

"Drop that, Stitch! Bad dog!"

I'm still grinning when I walk into the clinic.

"Do I wanna know?" Lisa questions me right away.

"The pups are teething and keeping Taz busy."

"You know," she says, leaning her chair back as she scrutinizes me. "You have been unusually upbeat this week. Almost nauseatingly giddy at times, if you must know the truth. Anything I missed?"

I meet her raised eyebrow with one of my own, but since I still have a grin on my face it's not nearly as effective. "Can you book me off last week of July? The intern can maybe cover the walk-in clinic, and for emergencies we can always call on Rick Moore."

"So Taz got the week off?"

The way she asks the question leaves me no doubt she

has a pretty good idea of what has me in a good mood. "Yup."

"I'll make it happen."

"Much appreciated. Oh, and, Lisa? Can you get me Mrs. Myers' phone number?"

Taz

I'M NOT sure why I'm so nervous about tonight.

I've had butterflies in my stomach all morning while getting the house clean. Not that it was dirty, but with the dogs being their rambunctious selves, there's bound to be slobber and hair somewhere. Scrubbing the laundry room and the fridge may have been a little over the top, though.

It's my own fault I'm running a bit late getting to Express Liquor in Winona. They carry a decent selection and I make sure to stock up a little. This means I have my arms full as I half-run out of the store, wanting to get home so I can get started on dinner, and barrel right into someone, dropping half my load on the pavement.

"*Shit!* I'm so sorry," I exclaim, first looking at the disaster at my feet before I glance up to find Kathleen in front of me.

"Planning a party?" she asks sardonically, looking from the mess on the ground to the remaining bottles I'm hanging onto for dear life.

"Sort of, and stocking up," I explain.

"Party for two?"

"What? No. I..." Belated I realize how this might come across to Kathleen. I've all but avoided her this past week, letting a couple of calls go to voicemail. She knows me too well and I've been afraid she'd cotton on to the change in my relationship with Rafe too easily. I'm not ready to let reality—and the inevitable judgments it comes with—into our intimate bubble.

"Aren't the kids in Kentucky?" she persists, and I find myself fidgeting.

"Well, yes, but—"

"It's funny, because I was just talking about you this morning," she says, as a Liquor Express employee comes rushing out with a broom and a dustpan and starts cleaning up the shards of glass. The young girl refuses my help with a smile and I turn back to Kathleen.

"Who were you talking to?" I ask, a little apprehensive.

"Mrs. Myers. She roped me into taking her damn dog for a walk in the mornings, and today I got an earful."

"About what?" My feigned ignorance doesn't fly as Kathleen makes it clear by tilting her head. "Fine. Her damn dog bit me yesterday. Apparently sweet as pie until you stick him in the tub, then he becomes a snarling heap of fur."

"So that's what happened. All she told me was that you threatened her yesterday, and that you apparently turned that nice Dr. Thomas—her words, not mine—against her. He called her this morning and got her all in a tizzy."

I roll my eyes heavenward. "Lord, give me patience." To Kathleen I say, "I told Rafe not to interfere. And I didn't threaten her, technically. I merely told her if I wasn't such a nice person I might be tempted to sue."

My friend apparently finds that funny, because she busts out laughing. When she calms down, she asks, "What I'm surprised at is, with all this happening, you haven't thought to call me. Or maybe return one of the messages I left?"

"I'm sorry. Things have been a bit…hectic."

"I'm sure that's as good word for it as any," she mumbles, and I don't even want to ask what she means by that. I can venture a guess. Like I said, Kathleen knows me well. "But, uh, getting back to what started all this, what's with all the booze?"

I realize she won't let that go, so I do my best to mitigate the hurt feelings I'm afraid will follow. "For tonight's dinner, to which I hope you and Brent can come? I'm making a traditional Congo dish."

"Who else will be there?"

Busted.

"Do you know Meredith and her husband, Andrew? She's a manager at the—"

"I know Meredith," she cuts me off, and the flash of hurt in her eyes fills me with guilt. "I'm not sure about Brent, but I'm due for a night away from the kids. Count me in."

I'M STILL TRYING to catch up for the time I lost when Rafe walks in at five thirty. The guests will be here at six, and if I was nervous before, I'm near tears now: I just discovered a pee puddle on the living room carpet.

"What do you need from me?" Rafe says with one glance at my face.

"Accident on the living room carpet, and beer and wine that's been sitting in my car all afternoon should probably come in and be refrigerated."

He tags me behind the neck and kisses me hard on the mouth before disappearing into the laundry room where I hear him fill a bucket with water. I blink away tears. I don't have time for those.

At ten to six, with the table set, the food staying warm in the oven, appetizers on the counter so the dogs can't get at them, and wine chilling in the fridge, I run upstairs to change. By the time I get back down, Rafe is opening the door to Meredith, her husband, Andrew—a dark, brawny giant who dwarfs her—and Kathleen.

It soon becomes clear the two women know each other as they chat away, keeping me company in the kitchen, while Rafe keeps Andrew engaged with beer, conversation, and the dogs, in the backyard.

I'm actually starting to relax a little by the time we sit down for dinner. The dogs are safely tucked in their crate, gnawing on the bones Rafe brought home for them.

"I didn't know you could cook like this," Kathleen shares, already halfway through the food on her plate.

"This is great," Andrew agrees, helping himself to a second serving.

"You learn fast in the field." I smile at Kathleen but it's Meredith who responds.

"The field?"

"Taz was a nurse for Doctors Without Borders until

earlier this year. She worked in Central Africa for years," Rafe answers for me.

Meredith looks a little confused from Rafe to me and back again. "Oh. I thought…" She shakes her head before continuing, "I must've gotten my wires crossed."

"What did you think?" Kathleen prompts, and a feeling of dread grows in the pit of my stomach. Meredith shifts a little uncomfortably in her seat.

"She thought you were married," Andrew fills in, pointing his fork at Rafe and then me, before pinning his wife with a glare. "What are you kicking me for?"

At the same time I feel Kathleen's eyes on me, and I do my best to keep a poker face. "Not married, but probably should've been," she declares, her eyes never wavering, before calmly turning to Meredith. "I'm pretty sure they've secretly been in love for almost a decade, but Rafe had already committed to Taz's sister."

I sit in stunned silence as Rafe's hand finds mine under the table, linking our fingers.

Meredith's eyes grow larger as my friend explains my return to Eminence and Nicky's passing.

"That's so sad—and beautiful—at the same time," Meredith says, her eyes suspiciously shiny as she turns to us.

"It's…confusing," I'm finally able to respond. "It's also complicated."

"We'll get it sorted out," Rafe says in a confident tone, giving my hand a squeeze. "We're trying to be discreet out of consideration for everyone it impacts. Especially the children." In a few words he manages to clearly get the message across we're trying to keep a low profile for now.

"So noted," Andrew acknowledges, reaching over the table to fill his plate for the third time. "You guys are done eating, right?"

"Andrew!" Meredith admonishes him, but he seems unfazed.

"What? You know heavy subjects make me hungry."

Rafe starts chuckling beside me, and pretty soon the whole table is laughing, as Kathleen gets up to grab the next bottle of wine.

Chapter Twenty

Rafe

"I RODE A HORSE TODAY!"

I have to hold the phone away from my ear at Spencer's spirited volume. He's loud enough Taz, who just comes walking into the living room, smiles at hearing his enthusiastic declaration.

"That's great, Son." I wave her over to come sit next to me on the couch, but she opts for one of the chairs. "Does the horse have a name?" I ask, a little distracted as I try to gauge Taz's mood.

She seems a little distant today, but that may be the aftermath of an evening filled with good food, good company, and way too much alcohol. She'd stumbled upstairs right after our guests left and was passed out by the time I got there, after taking care of the dogs and locking down the house.

"Coco!" Spencer yells. "And Sofie's horse is Moonbeam. Mine was brown, but hers was black with white spots on its back. Grandpa says we can go again tomorrow, but first we have to help feed the aminals."

"Animals," I correct him with a smile. It's one of those words he's always struggled with. Cinnamon is another he can't seem to wrap his mouth around.

"That's what I said—*aminals*—and Sofie made lots and lots of pictures to show you. Daddy? Did you know that fish eat worms? Grandpa stuck one on my hook and I catched a big one. I've gotta go find some more worms now."

I hear the clatter of a phone being dropped on a hard surface, followed by running footsteps and finally the slam of a door. Clearly my son is done with the conversation but forgot to end the call.

I'm about to hang up when I hear a rustle and then Sofie's soft voice.

"Daddy?"

"Hey, Pipsqueak." I see Taz's eyes warm at the use of my name for Sofie. "Sounds like you had fun today."

"Yeah, but my horse's name is Sunbeam, and Uncle Steve says he's an Appaloosa."

"Make sure you take a picture of him so I can see."

"I already have. Daddy?"

"Yeah?"

"I miss you," she says in a wobbly voice, and my heart is suddenly in my throat.

"I miss you too, baby, and I can't wait to see you next week. In the meantime, I want you to have fun with your cousins. Are you getting along?"

"Yeah, they're nice. I just don't like sleeping in one bed with Spencer. He farts in his sleep."

I bite down a chuckle. "I don't think he does it on purpose." Before she has a chance to lament her brother's shortcomings, I redirect the conversation. "Only a few more nights and you'll be back in your own bed."

"Grandma says we're leaving Monday morning."

"You probably won't get home until Tuesday, but we'll be here waiting for you."

When I end the call I notice Taz looking; a pensive expression on her face.

"She's homesick," she accurately concludes.

"Why are you sitting all the way over there?"

She seems to ignore my question, and instead pulls her feet up on the chair, wrapping her arms around her legs. "I've been thinking."

That's rarely a good thing, especially when her entire posture screams distance. "About what?"

"Well, in part about last night. What Kathleen said about us." I'm trying to recall exactly what she said, but Taz already continues, "It made this whole thing sound so...I don't know...illicit. Almost tawdry, like some damn soap opera."

"This whole *thing*?" I can't help focus on that rather dismissive term. "You mean our relationship?"

She has the grace to look a little guilty when she confirms with a soft, "Yes."

I lean forward with my elbows on my knees. "Does this feel tawdry to you? What we have going on here? Does it feel cheap to you? Because it sure as fuck doesn't feel cheap to me. Sure, from an outsider's perspective it may appear illicit, but from right here..." I slap a hand on my chest, "...where it matters, all it feels is *right*."

Taz blinks a few times at my words, contemplating them before she speaks.

"Then how come I woke up this morning with you sneaking out of the spare room to have a shower in the master bathroom down the hall, like you have every morning this past week?"

That observation takes the wind out of my sails. Actually, it's the slightly rueful tone she uses that jars me. Of course she's right, I've left her every morning, slipping out of her room to get ready for the day, but only so she could catch a few more winks. "I didn't want to wake you."

Her smile is a little sad. "I appreciate that, but it's not my point. What I'm saying is that you've come to my bed every night, but haven't once invited me into yours, which..." she holds up her hand to stop the protest forming on my lips, "...I get, I do, but at the same time it makes me feel like a guilty secret."

I hear her loud and clear, and I'm kicking myself for not sharing my reasoning behind my trek into her bedroom every night. So much for insisting on clear communication, I'm failing miserably myself.

I'm across the room and in front of her chair in a flash, taking her hands and pulling her to her feet. "Put something on your feet, you're coming with me." I don't let go of her hand when she stops; slipping her feet in the Crocs she keeps by the kitchen door.

"The dogs."

"They can come with."

The sun is already down when we cross the lawn to the

clinic's back entrance, the dogs dancing around our legs. I lead her through the dark hallway to my office and flick on the lights.

"Sit here." I push her down in my desk chair and lean over her to boot up my laptop.

"Rafe, what are—"

"Just give me a second, Sweets."

A few clicks and my amateur drawing fills the screen.

"What is that?" She leans closer, looking at the markings on the scanned sketch. "Is that the upstairs?"

"Yup." I tap on the screen. "There's the master suite."

"I can see that, I see Spencer's room, but what is this here, where Sofie's room's supposed to be."

I lean down and kiss the patch of skin showing at the base of her neck. "I started working on an alternative layout for the upstairs about a month ago." She swivels her head around, looking at me with surprise. "I knew what I wanted, Taz. I didn't know how to make it feasible. This…" I point at my sketch, "…was the one thing I could plan for, the only part I felt I had any control over." I sit down on the edge of the desk and slightly adjust her chair so she's facing me. "I like this house. I like having the clinic right next door. I like that the kids get to grow up in a real family home. Your family home." I pause for a second, making sure I get the words right. "But it's also the house where I shared a life with Nicky, and I fully understand if that were a deal breaker. I thought about ways to make this *your* house. Our house, even."

"Rafe…" Her warm hand comes to rest on my knee. "You don't need to—"

"Oh, but I do," I interrupt her, drawing her attention back

to the screen. "Because I never want you to think you're only a fill-in—someone's guilty secret—and yet you're already feeling it. I didn't say anything because a lot depends on if Sofie would want to move into the master bedroom." I point to the sketch, at the wall between Sofie's and the spare bedroom. "If we take that wall down, we have space enough to make a new master suite, complete with our own bathroom."

"But you'd lose your guest room."

I turn and slide my hands along her face and into her hair. "We wouldn't need one."

Her hands grab on to my wrists when I drop my forehead to hers.

"It's barely been a week," she whispers.

"Not planning on knocking down walls tomorrow, Taz, but it's good to plan for when the time is right. And for the record…"

I drop my mouth to hers for a gentle kiss.

"…It's been nine years."

Taz

"*RAFE…*"

I barely get his name out before I'm pulled out of my chair and find my hips wedged between his knees. His mouth slams down on mine, his tongue spearing between my lips in a bruising kiss.

He reaches around and slaps the laptop shut before

using that same hand to mold my breast, brushing my hard nipple. I moan down his throat in response, and suddenly all control is gone.

My shirt is gone, his is next, and I only have a second to thank the universe I'm wearing yoga pants. He one-handedly shoves them down, taking my panties with them, until they pool at my feet. Then he plants a foot between my legs, and with an arm banded tightly around my midriff pulls me straight out of my pants, and deposits me with my bare ass on his desk.

With a hand flat between my breasts he pushes me down to my back, his eyes that midnight blue as he scans down my body.

"*Christ*, my fucking wet dream spread out like a banquet." His voice is gruff as his hand follows the path of his eyes, fingers trailing through the dark curls between my legs. "Wet."

"Your proximity will do that," I confess, biting my lip on a moan when he lightly brushes the pad of his thumb between my slick folds.

When his hands push my knees wide, I'm sharply aware of the bright light overhead and the hard surface underneath me. So different from the soft shadows of night and the silky feel of bedsheets, which were the scene for each time we've tentatively explored each other these past days.

This is different: raw, revealing, and deliciously decadent.

I feel liberated, unashamed, and almost greedy with need as I prop up on my elbows, pull my heels onto the edge of the desk and let my legs fall open in a blatant invitation.

Rafe's eyes betray his barely contained hunger as he takes in my offer, nostrils flaring. His fingers dig into the soft skin on the inside of my thighs as he leans down using the tip of his nose to brush my curls.

"Fuck," I hear him curse before he drops to his knees and buries his face between my legs.

The moment his tongue laps at me, I fall back to the table and reach down to twist my fingers in his hair. I hold his head while my hips grind against his mouth.

He's voracious, using his teeth to nip at my tender flesh, sending shivers up my spine. I tilt my head back, eyes closed, as my skin feels like it's on fire and the tension coils low between my legs.

The next moment his mouth is gone. I hear the sound of a zipper, the rustling of clothes and then the broad head of Rafe's cock teasing at my opening.

"Look at me." My eyes blink open to find him leaning over me, veins standing out on his forehead and his lips still slick. "Brace," he whispers, before moving his hands behind my knees, pushing them wide, and filling me in one powerful stroke.

I reach up around his neck and pull his head down for a wet, openmouthed kiss as his hips find a rhythm.

"Hook your legs around me," he mutters against my lips, "and hold on."

The moment my legs are wrapped around his hips, he slips an arm under my ass and one behind my back. I barely have time to grab on to his neck as he lifts me up. In two steps he has my back braced to the wall, setting a furious pace as he drives inside me, grunting in my neck.

I'm not even aware of any sounds I make. I'm helpless as our bodies take over with wild abandon until I splinter apart, left breathless, boneless, and senseless.

"This is a first for me," Rafe pants, his face in my hair.

I'm not sure whether he means the wall, the office, or the wild ride we just enjoyed, but I don't really care.

I'll take his first and tuck it away like the treasure it is.

Later, with his large body wrapped around me in bed; he rocks my world again.

"All those fantasies of you I've had over the years pale in comparison to the real thing," he softly mumbles in my hair.

I turn in his arms until our fronts are plastered together and we're nose to nose. "If I wasn't still recovering from that inspired pounding I received, I'd be happy to share some of my fantasies."

His lips pull into a wide, self-satisfied smile. "Inspired, huh?"

I roll my eyes at his smirk. "Of course that's all you'd hear," I mutter, mock-annoyed.

He tightens his arms around me. "I heard every word, but I'm trying not to focus on those fantasies of yours. I'm not twenty-five anymore, I may need a little more time to recuperate before I can even allow myself to wonder what exactly those fantasies might be."

I smile with the knowledge I have the same impact on him as he has on me. "We'll save them for another time." I press my lips to his and he immediately takes over and deepens the kiss. "Rafe…" I mumble.

"I know, I know." He pulls back, tucking one of my dreads behind my ear. "I want to take you on a date tomorrow."

I smile and press my face against his hand. "I'm kind of a sure thing, you know. You don't need to wine and dine me."

"I'm not looking to get you in the sack, I'm looking to show you off."

"Is that wise?" I can't help myself; it's a knee-jerk reaction. The prospect of setting tongues wagging all over Eminence, right before my parents and the kids come home, is not that appealing.

Rafe reads me well. "I thought we'd head to Winona, grab a bite there and maybe do the drive-in? Wouldn't mind making out with you in the truck."

"I haven't been to a drive-in since I went to college." I grin at him. "I'd love to." I snuggle under his chin, drape my arm over his stomach, and hitch my leg up over his. "Show me off, huh?"

His hand lazily trails up and down my spine. "Be proud to," he says, his voice gruff.

I tuck that away safely too, and press a sweet kiss to his chest.

"That earns you a bonus kiss."

Chapter Twenty-One

Taz

"Jesus, you scared the crap out of me. What are you doing here?"

Rafe is off on a call and I'm in the middle of washing sheets when I walk out of the laundry room to find Kathleen standing in the kitchen.

I wince when I see the annoyed look on her face.

"When my best friend decides to ignore my calls after a night of massive revelations, I get worried maybe she's taken off again for parts unknown."

"I'm right here," I softly point out, feeling a bit guilty I didn't take the time to call her back. "I'm sorry I didn't call you back, but yesterday was a busy day. Time kinda got away from me."

"Hmm." She pins me with a glare before finally looking around the kitchen. "Tell me you have coffee. We're gonna need some."

Fortified with two steaming mugs, we sit down at the kitchen table.

"So," she starts, not wasting any time. "Anything you want to tell me?"

"Oh, Kathleen, it's complicated."

"Yeah, you mentioned that the other night, but I don't get what that has to do with me." She actually sounds hurt.

"I thought you'd be upset. Nicky was your friend too."

"You're not giving me much credit; I've always known how you felt about him, Taz. I *know* you. I discovered recently Nicky knew too, and more than that, she believed Rafe returned your feelings. I've spent most of the past ten years pissed at him more than anything."

"Why?"

"Because he's the reason Nicky was unhappy and you ran away to another continent."

"First of all, you can't blame that on him. He was doing the right thing by Nicky, or have you forgotten she was pregnant at the time? As for me leaving; what else would you've had me do? Stay here? Be miserably reminded every day of all the ways I'd been a disappointment to my family? No, thank you."

"You were never a disappointment to me." She grabs my hand over the table and gives it a squeeze. "Or to your sister, for that matter. She blamed herself all these years, you know? She carries responsibility in this whole fucked-up scenario as well. Why do you think she made me promise to get you back to Eminence by whatever means possible? She knew she was running out of time to set things straight."

I take back my hand and silently process this information, blinking with the burn of tears as I wish my sister were here sitting at the kitchen table, having this heart-to-heart with me. "We've made such a mess," I finally lament, shaking my head.

"No one is perfect, Taz," she's quick to respond. "Not you, not Rafe, and as some of us now know, neither was Nicky."

When Kathleen gets up to leave twenty minutes later, my life is still a mess but my heart feels a lot lighter.

By the door she pulls me into a bone-crunching hug.

"No matter what happens, I will always—*always*—have your back. Always."

———

"WHERE ARE WE GOING?"

I turn my eyes on Rafe who just turned west instead of south to Winona.

"Mountain View," he says shooting me a quick glance. "We've got some shopping to do."

"You hate shopping."

"Not this kind of shopping." This time when he glances over he wears a grin.

"Which is?" I prompt him, still confused at this turn of events.

I was expecting a *very* early dinner at Flossie's Apple Barrel—since for some reason Rafe hustled me out of the house at three—and whatever movies they were running at the drive-in this weekend. Heck, I even packed drinks and snacks in a cooler, and packed a blanket so we could watch from the back of his truck.

Apparently somewhere along the line shopping was added to the trip. Something he failed to tell me about.

"Bed shopping," he announces.

"You know," I start prickly, "it would help if you'd elaborate on what is going through your head, because as useful as it would be, I am *not* a mind reader."

He chuckles at my snippy tone as he reaches for my hand and slides his fingers between mine. "I'm buying you a bed."

"I have a bed," I point out.

"It's a queen and the mattress is lumpy."

"It's big enough for me and it's comfy."

"For you, but since I plan on spending time in it we need one bigger."

"Rafe," I get his attention to try and talk some sense into him. "You already have a big bed."

"Taz," he mimics me. "We're getting rid of your bed, *and* my bed, and buying a bed for us."

I remind him of our conversation last night. "I thought you said we'd wait until the time is right?"

"To knock walls down, yes. Right now the time is perfect to pick out a bed we both like, without the kids running interference."

"You're charging ahead," I caution him, but he has an answer for that too.

"I'm *planning* ahead. Big difference."

I give up. He's wearing a smug grin; everything I say seems to bounce off. So I mumble the only thing one can in a situation like this.

"Whatever."

I ignore his soft chuckle as he drives us to Mountain View to shop for a new bed.

We strike out at Anderson Home Furnishings, despite the very gung-ho and borderline harassing sales associate.

I ended up being marched right out the store after the guy—in all his eagerness to make a sale—decided to help me test the bed I was trying.

I felt almost bad for him when Rafe turned around from the mattress he'd been inspecting, and in two long strides stood beside us, growling at the man as he unceremoniously yanked me off the bed. The sales clerk must've recognized his mistake because he didn't even bother to stop us when we walked straight out the door. Actually, Rafe *stalked* and I was almost running to keep up with him, all the time fighting to hold back the fit of giggles threatening to let loose. That would probably not have gone over well.

We get to our next stop in silence. It's not until Rafe pulls into a parking spot out front of JB's Beds that he speaks.

"Don't wander off on your own."

I probably should be insulted, but his comment sparks the bout of hilarity I've been suppressing. I toss my head back and crack up.

I was right, he doesn't think it's amusing, but that doesn't stop the tears of laughter rolling down my cheeks.

"I don't see what's funny."

"You are," I finally manage, hiccupping. "With your generally laid-back attitude, you sure hid that alpha streak well."

"Don't know what you're talking about," he grumbles, getting out of the truck.

That strikes me as funny too, but one look at the dark scowl on his face as he rounds the hood to get to my side, and I swallow it down. Discovering his mile-wide possessive streak is a shockingly pleasant surprise, but I'm smart enough not to poke the bear.

Too much.

Rafe

WELL, that takes care of the date.

I'm more than merely annoyed at this chain of events.

First that snot-nosed punk crawling in bed with my woman. Then bumping in to Sheila fucking Quinn in the parking lot of JB's Beds. I'd lowered Taz from the cab of the truck and pressed her against the side to kiss the laughter from her mouth, when the woman walked out of the salon right next to the mattress store. There was no doubt the queen of the Eminence gossip tree had caught our spirited lip-lock from the shocked expression on her face.

What the fuck are the odds?

To top it off, we discovered after Taz and I managed to agree on a mattress, frame, and headboard, that JB's Beds was cash and carry only. There's no way I'm going to the drive-in with a bed and mattress strapped to the bed of the truck.

"You know," Taz carefully breaks my silent brood. "We

can still go for dinner. We can ask for a table by the window so we can keep an eye on the truck while we eat."

I immediately feel guilty for my foul mood. Taz has taken the events of this afternoon in stride, even the encounter with the gossip queen, merely rolling with the bumps. All I've done is get increasingly frustrated because things weren't going to plan.

I take her hand and by way of apology press my lips to her palm. "After dinner we'll go home, rent a few pay-per-view movies, and test the new mattress on the living room floor. Just the two of us."

The response I get is a wide grin. "That sounds perfect."

Flossie's Apple Barrel is far from romantic gourmet fare, but the stick-to-your-ribs home cooking seems to fit both of us better.

When we get home *just the two of us* turns into four of us. I'd forgotten about Lilo and Stitch, who are thrilled we are home and waste no time trying out their new giant dog bed.

"This isn't exactly what I had in mind," I admit, making Taz snicker again, which she's been doing a lot of.

But this time I flop on my back on the mattress and laugh right along with her.

———

"RAFE?"

I direct my gaze from the scrolling movie credits on the screen down to where Taz's head is resting on my shoulder, her face turned up. "Yeah, Sweets."

"Do you think Sheila is going to spill the beans?"

I bend to press a kiss to her forehead before answering. "I think that's pretty much guaranteed."

"That means Mom and Dad will find out soon."

"Very likely."

"Shit."

I roll us until she's on her back and I'm leaning over her. "Most definitely, but maybe it's better out in the open. Rip off the bandage so to speak." I touch my hand to the side of her face and she leans into it.

"But the kids…"

"We'll make sure they're shielded. At least until we head up to go camping in two weeks. We'll tell them ourselves then."

"Aren't you worried it's too soon?"

My instinct is to evade the question, but I promised honesty. "It probably is, but…" I quickly add, "…these aren't exactly normal circumstances. It's not like they'll be introduced to someone new they have to accept into their lives. You're already in their lives. They already love you. When you think about it, little will change for them."

She seems to think on that for a minute. "I guess that's true. Seeing us being affectionate with each other, or when we start sleeping in the same bed every night, will take getting used to, but kids at this age tend to take their cues from the people they love. If we don't put too much weight on it, they likely won't either."

"We need to make sure certain people don't have a chance to paint what is happening with a negative brush."

"You're talking about Mom and Dad." I hate the sadness in those pretty brown eyes.

"Yeah. I'm not entirely sure how your dad will react, but I'm pretty positive Mom won't be thrilled. We'll have to brace for that."

Now she grins. "I'm always braced around my parents, Rafe. I'm conditioned that way."

"So noted." I grin back and drop a quick kiss on her lips. "Now why don't you head up and I'll let the dogs out before crating them."

"What about the mattress?"

"That's going in your room tomorrow." I get to my feet, not giving her a chance to object. "Go on up. I'll be there soon."

By the time the dogs are safe in their crate, I've locked up the house, and peek around the bedroom door; Taz looks to be asleep. I do my nighttime routine in the master bath, strip down to my boxers, and make my way back to the spare bedroom.

The moment I slide under the covers, though, Taz rolls over to face me, her eyes barely open.

"Rafe?"

"Yes, baby."

"That was a great date," she mumbles, her eyes already drifting shut again.

"The best."

Chapter Twenty-Two

Taz

I PULL the CRV along the curb in front of Mrs. Myers' house and see the curtains in the window move.

My least favorite stop of the day, even though on Friday she was surprisingly subdued. I have a suspicion she'll have plenty to say today. It's been an interesting weekend, some of which I'm sure has filtered through to her. It doesn't take much in this town.

After an interesting day on Saturday, yesterday had been blissfully drama free.

We took the dogs out for a long hike in the woods and while they were sleeping off the morning's exercise, Rafe and I took apart the bed in my room and hauled it downstairs to the truck, before replacing it with the new bed and mattress. It fits, but it's tight.

We drove into town, dropped off the old bed at the thrift store, and picked up groceries for the week ahead. Aside from a few curious glances—which I almost don't notice anymore—that exercise was uneventful, although I'd hoped to run into Meredith, but she was off.

A quiet night, a thorough testing of the new bed, and a good night's rest closed out the weekend.

But now it's back to regular scheduling, which means Mrs. Myers is waiting inside.

"Took you long enough."

I take a minute to take a deep breath and greet the tongue-lolling Charlton first. You'd never know the docile, friendly dog is the same one who tried mauling my arm less than a week ago. He doesn't seem to have anything against me, just to bath time.

"Afternoon, Mrs. Myers." I force a smile for the older woman and set my medical kit on the coffee table and fish out some gloves. "How are you today?"

I barely listen to her laundry list of complaints—only mumbling sympathetically every now and then—while I focus on cleaning her wound, and change the dressing.

"Are you listening?" Her sharp tone draws my attention.

"I'm sorry, what was that?"

"I asked you when your parents will be home? I've missed them at church."

I bet.

"Tomorrow, actually. They left Kentucky this morning." I can almost see her mind churning as she narrows her eyes on me. Before she has a chance to say anything, however, I quickly add, "Which is why I should really get going. Lots of stuff to do before the kids come home." I quickly stuff my things in my bag, but not fast enough.

"You mean your sister's home."

There it is. I thought I might be able to get away without a confrontation, but I guess that was too much to ask. I could ignore her and walk out, but I promised myself I wouldn't give her the satisfaction.

"Actually, it's technically Rafe's home—his name is on the deed—and I guess since I live there on invitation, it's my home too." I force a wide grin—determined to kill with kindness—and toss my bag over my shoulder. "I'll see you on Wednesday, Mrs. Myers. Same time."

I have my hand on the door before she has a chance to hiss her response.

"Shameless." She intends the word to injure, but ironically it does exactly the opposite.

I should be without shame. There's been enough of it loaded on my shoulders, by myself as much as others.

With my shoulders straight and my head held high, I walk out the door, not even giving her the satisfaction of a retort.

I assume Rafe is out on a call since I don't see his truck parked in the driveway when I get home. The house is quiet without the dogs he either has with him, or left at the clinic. With nothing demanding my attention, I head upstairs to try out the Jacuzzi tub in the master bath I've been eyeing for months.

I spend a few minutes filling the tub with sudsy water and adjusting the jets before lowering myself in. I lie back and manage to enjoy it for about two minutes before I get restless. Not wanting to waste the tub full of water, I grab for my phone I left on the ledge.

"What's up?" Kathleen answers on the third ring.

"Nothing much. I'm having a bath." Knowing she would understand.

"You hate baths."

"I know, but I thought maybe the jets would make it more interesting," I confess a little sheepishly. "I'm a little disappointed."

Kathleen laughs at me. "You haven't changed one bit. Still can't sit still long."

"Whatever. What are you doing anyway?" I hear clanging in the background. She accuses me of not being able to sit still, but she's no different.

"Emptying the dishwasher." *See?* "Damn kids, I grabbed for a glass this morning and the cupboard was empty. Thirty-six damn glasses and not a single one on the shelf. Spent an hour going around the house with a tub, collecting plates and cups and cutlery from every nook and cranny. Jesus, some of the plates looked like science experiments—you don't even wanna know."

I stifle a chuckle since she was no different growing up. I clearly remember Kathleen's bedroom looking like the aftermath of a bomb explosion most of the time. Her own mom used to be forever on her case, trying to get her to clean her room and bring down the dirty dishes.

"I remember—" I barely get the word out before she cuts me off.

"Yeah, yeah. Mom would probably have a good laugh at my expense if she could see me now."

Kathleen lost her mother fifteen years ago quite suddenly. "Do you still miss her?" I ask, suddenly serious.

"Every day. People say it gets easier, but I think you simply get used to the pain. Do you miss Nicky?"

"Every day," I echo, trailing my fingers through the disappearing suds. "I can't wrap my head around how it is possible to be happy, and still hurt so much."

"Oh, honey…that's life. That's adulting. Nothing is ever all good or all bad."

"He bought me a bed."

It's silent on the other side. I try to wait her out, my hand reaching for the edge of the tub, holding on tight. "Kathleen?" I finally prompt.

"Wow. Not wasting any time."

I can't quite gauge from her tone whether that's a good thing or not, so I nervously start rambling. "My bed was lumpy and his bed…well…anyway, I know it sounds fast, but it's really not when you think about it. Besides, he has plans."

"I'd say," she interrupts, but I ignore her.

"He showed me his drawings."

"I'm sure he did." This time she chuckles and I take that as a good sign.

"He wants to build a new master suite. When the time is right, of course. Although that might be sooner than we planned now that bitch, Sheila, is probably running off her mouth."

"Stop," Kathleen orders and my mouth snaps shut. "I'm having a hard time following. How does Sheila fit into building a master suite?"

"Not the new bedroom. The new bed," I clarify, noting that the water is getting a little chilly.

"Honey, that's not helping," she notes dryly.

"Hang on, I'm gonna put you on speaker, I've gotta get out of this tub." I put the phone on speaker and set it on the toilet tank while I get out. "So we stopped at JB's Beds in Mountain View…"

"Shopping for a new bed."

"…Obviously. Anyway…" I say pointedly, trying to keep us on track while I dry myself off, "…we're in the parking lot at JB's, and Sheila walks out of the hairdresser's, and *sees* us"

"So? I don't see the problem?"

"Well, seeing as Rafe had me pinned against the side of the truck and had his tongue in my mouth, I'm sure you'd agree that's a pretty significant problem."

"I see."

"Right? I'd bet good money that snippet of news is making its way around Eminence as we speak. Hang on, taking you off speaker." I wrap the towel around me, put the phone to my ear and make my way to the bedroom to get dressed. "My parents and the kids are coming home tomorrow, how long do you figure it'll take before they hear it?"

"You'll have a week's reprieve, at least," she concludes.

She catches me with one foot suspended as I'm putting on clean underwear, almost putting me on my ass. "How do you figure that?"

"Saw her and Brady drive out of town yesterday morning pulling the boat trailer. Sheila usually runs roughshod over the man, but when it comes to his annual fishing trip to Roaring River State Park, he's got an iron will. They're usually gone for a week."

I slump down on the edge of the bed. "Still not a lot of time," I point out.

"Maybe not, but enough to stay ahead of the game."

Rafe

"THERE YOU ARE."

Taz's head whips around already smiling.

I went looking through the entire house before I noticed the front door open a crack. She's on her knees next to one of the large planters, her dreads tied back with a handkerchief, and a smudge of dirt on her cheek. She appears to be pulling weeds.

"I *was* going to cook dinner, but I got a little distracted. Are you okay with grilled cheese and a salad?"

I bend down and kiss her upturned face. "Don't worry about dinner, I'll toss some burgers on the grill. What are you doing?"

"I'm weeding."

"That part I got," I assure her with a grin. "What I'm curious about is what brought that on?"

"Oh." She brushes her forehead with the back of her hand, leaving a fresh streak of dirt. "Well, I was putting clean sheets on Sofie's bed and noticed the picture she has on her dresser: the one with her sitting on the edge of the planter in front of the house."

"I know the one."

"The planters had flowers in them. Gardening was never my thing, it was Nicky's, but I thought maybe it would be nice to put something in these planters for when they get home tomorrow. How hard can it be? I noticed a garden center on the way to Mountain View Saturday; I thought maybe I could pick some up tomorrow morning. Make it look pretty before they get here."

"I'm not sure Spencer will notice but Sofie probably would."

"Yeah?" Her pleased smile lights up her face, but I have a suspicion it won't last.

"Absolutely. In fact, I'm sure she'll love giving you a hand." At her confused expression I rip off the bandage. "Your mom called fifteen minutes ago; they stopped for an early dinner in Dexter. They decided to drive straight through and should be home in a little over an hour."

As I suspected it might, the smile disappears.

"You mean they're coming home? Like...now?" She immediately scrambles to her feet and starts wiping her hands on her well-worn jeans. "But I'm not ready. I—"

I grab her by the shoulders, forcing her to look at me. "Breathe, Taz. The kids just want to come home. They'll be thrilled to see the dogs and sleep in their own beds. There's nothing to be ready for."

Even as I try to reassure her, I can tell the panic is winning. She twists out of my hold and runs inside, tripping over the dogs who've apparently been waiting right behind the door. I follow inside at a more sedate pace, hearing Taz mutter to herself as she tears upstairs. Stitch and Lilo sit at the bottom, staring up with equally woeful expressions.

I'm tempted to go after her, but decide instead to get those burgers on the grill. Maybe it's better to let her do what she thinks she needs to do without interfering.

I get it. Things have changed from when the kids left for Kentucky in a major way. It's been good to have this time alone to find our footing, but that's about to change.

I suspect a good part of her panic has less to do with the kids, and more with her parents, though, and if I'm honest, I'm not exactly looking forward to that confrontation either.

"I can't eat," she announces half an hour later, after having taken one bite of her burger.

She came down a few minutes ago, her face washed and dressed in a navy pair of shorts and some flowery top I'm pretty sure I've seen Nicky wear before. Her hair is tied back at the nape of her neck and she doesn't look like herself, but I wisely keep my mouth shut.

"Eat a little more," I urge her, but her eyes shoot fire in response. I ignore it and take another bite, both dogs sitting in the grass, eyes glued to the food.

"I don't get how you can eat at all," she snaps. "They could be here any minute."

"You're getting worked up over nothing, Taz." I try to be reasonable, but I can tell right away that doesn't exactly go over well.

"Nothing?" She jumps up from the steps where we were sitting. "You won't call it nothing when Mom sniffs out what we've been up to while they were gone." She leans close and hisses, "And trust me she will."

Right. Time to get this under control.

I get up, set my plate next to Taz's on the railing—to the great disappointment of the pups— and put my hands on her shoulders, backing her against the brick.

"If she does, we deal. The state you're in, I'll be surprised if she doesn't cotton on. You need to settle down."

"Don't tell me to settle down!"

I slide my hands up her neck and rest them on either side of her face, leaning in close. "It'll be fine. Whatever happens, we handle it together. You're not alone in this, Sweets. I'm right beside you."

Her face softens a fraction, but she's not quite done yet. "But—"

I don't let her finish and head straight for the last resort, shutting her up with my mouth on hers. Her body immediately goes rigid, but with a little coaxing her lips part, letting me in, and her hands fist in my shirt.

Then the dogs start barking as a voice sounds from inside.

"Daddy! We're home!"

Chapter Twenty-Three

Taz

I FEEL my mother's eyes scrutinizing me as she joins me in the kitchen.

Rafe is upstairs, putting the kids to bed. They've been glued to him ever since they walked in half an hour ago. Spencer announced within minutes of getting home that he was 'starving' so I pulled out some cheese and crackers, which both he and Sofie devoured in no time, regaling us with excited stories all the while. It didn't take long for them to burn off their energy and were half asleep when their dad announced bedtime.

I left Mom and Dad to finish the drinks Rafe poured them, to tidy the kitchen. Hiding out, more accurately. Not just to avoid them, but to come to terms with my father's appearance.

He's not doing well.

I'm a nurse, I understand the stages of Parkinson's, and

it's clear to me sometime over the past week and a bit, Dad has deteriorated. He's been pretty lucky so far, the first stages of the disease having been slow in progressing, but it's obvious things are changing.

His face is almost expressionless. That wasn't the case before. Sure, he had a few tics and twitches, which is common, but those muscular spasms have been replaced with lack of muscle movement altogether. I also noticed his hand missing his glass several times because of the increased tremors. When Mom finally picked it up and put it to his lips, I had to look away.

It's clear this last adjustment in his medication is not working effectively.

Parkinson's may be incurable, but in and of itself it's not necessarily fatal. It's the complications in the more progressed stages of the disease that can be lethal.

"You noticed."

I turn to face Mom as she glances over her shoulder into the living room before stepping closer.

"Hard not to," I admit. "Does he?"

She nods. "I wanted to come home right away, but he insisted on staying until today as planned. I need to take him to see the neurologist in Springfield. I already called for an appointment on Friday."

"When?"

She looks at me questioningly. "Friday. Why?"

"Because I want to come." There isn't even a conscious thought involved when I blurt that out, and I've clearly surprised Mom.

She pauses before she responds. "You want to come?"

"I thought I might be helpful," I scramble, suddenly not

so sure. Still, in for a penny, in for a pound, so I forge on. "I have a decent understanding of the disease and have read up on treatment options since Dad was diagnosed."

She looks disbelieving, which I can't blame her for, all she knows is that I disappeared. She has no idea I've kept up as best I could through Kathleen.

"Have you heard of DBS?" she asks.

"Deep Brain Stimulation? Yes. Is that an option?"

"I don't know. That's what we're hoping to find out on Friday. Maybe it'll be good if you come, half the time I don't understand what his doctor is talking about. Maybe you can interpret for us."

"Be happy to, Mom."

Before things get uncomfortably close to a sappy moment, Rafe walks in, cocking his thumb over his shoulder.

"Dad's half asleep on the couch, want me to get him back in the RV or should I give you a ride home in the Honda? We can drop off the RV tomorrow for you."

"Yeah, I should get him home. If you wouldn't mind driving, that would be great. It would be easier for him to get in."

"Of course."

I touch Mom's arm. "Why don't I give you a hand getting what you need from the trailer?" I offer.

"Sure," is her somewhat hesitant response.

It takes us only a few minutes to move their stuff into the back of the SUV. By the time we're locking the RV back up, Rafe comes walking out, supporting Dad. I'm a little concerned at the jerky way he moves, but fatigue can be a factor there too.

When my father's buckled in the front seat, Rafe holds the back door open for Mom to get in, while turning to me.

"Kids are already asleep. I won't be too long, Sweets."

I freeze when the endearment slips from his mouth and is followed by a sharp hiss. My eyes instantly dart to my mother as her head snaps around, her face showing confusion, as Rafe swings the door shut.

"Wave, Taz," he says under his breath before he jogs around to the driver's side.

I force a smile on my face, raise my hand, and watch them drive off.

Fucking hell.

I TURN my head and look at the alarm clock on my nightstand.

Three in the morning and I've done nothing but stare up at the ceiling since I went to bed almost five hours ago. I went up after quickly letting the dogs out and locking them safely in their crate after Rafe left.

I heard him come home shortly after and listened to him move around downstairs until I heard him come up. His footsteps stopped outside my door and I waited with bated breath, but then they moved away down the hall.

My mind has done nothing but churn on that slip of the tongue, Mom's reaction, Dad's condition, the kids, and no Rafe in my bed. Not that I expected him here; we'd agreed on sleeping in our own rooms. Still, this new bed is massive with only me occupying it.

It would've been nice to ask him if Mom said anything

—gave him any indication she heard what he said—but that's my own fault. I'm the one who panicked and hid in the bedroom.

Stupid.

I check the clock again, three fifteen.

Shit.

There's a rustle in the hallway and I freeze, my eyes focusing on the door. Even in the dark, I can see the handle move before it slowly opens and Rafe's familiar form slips inside. He takes a few steps and I hear a thump, followed by a whispered litany of very creative swearing.

"Rafe?" I shoot up in bed.

"Shit. Did I wake you? Sorry."

I feel the mattress dip when he slides under the covers. He pulls me back down and tucks me with my back to his front, his body curved around me.

"What's going on?"

"I stubbed my toe on the damn bed."

"Yes, I figured that when I heard the cursing. I mean why are you here in the middle of the night? I thought we'd agreed—"

"I can't sleep," he interrupts in a low voice.

"Neither can I," I admit. "I can't get my mind to shut up."

"Wanna talk about it?"

"God, don't get me started. There's that slipup I think my mom heard." I turn in his arms so we're face-to-face. "Did she?"

"Fuck. It slipped out. I was waiting for her to say something, but she just looked at me funny. I figure maybe she's not sure what she heard."

"I hope so. Otherwise it would make the drive to Springfield on Friday very uncomfortable."

"Springfield?"

"Dad has an appointment with the neurologist."

"Yeah, he seemed a lot worse." He strokes the back of his fingers over my cheek. "So you're going with them?"

"That's the plan. I'll see if Kathleen can take the kids for the day."

His smile is warm as he leans in for a soft brush of his lips, then another, before he slants his head and takes my mouth in a sweet, lazy kiss.

"Get some sleep, baby," he mumbles when he finally lifts away, and I turn so we're back to front again.

"What if the kids—"

"I'll be up before them."

I close my eyes and with his breath brushing my shoulder, and the secure weight of his body wrapped around me, I feel myself finally drifting off.

"Rafe?"

"Hmm?"

"Why couldn't you sleep?"

"I missed you."

Rafe

"PULEEZE, CAN WE HAVE A HORSE?"

I look over at Spencer. "Son, we've had this talk."

In fact, we've had this talk every morning over breakfast since the kids got home. The animals vary; he's asked for a goat, a potbelly pig, and this morning's horse is a repeat of Tuesday. What has been consistent, and a bit puzzling, is he always seems to turn to Taz and asks *her*.

I have a sneaky suspicion Sofie is putting her brother up to it. She'll whisper something to him and then intently observes the interaction with special focus on her aunt. This morning is no different.

It's not the only thing I've noticed. Since coming back her behavior toward Taz has changed. Short monosyllabic answers and when I catch her looking at Taz, she seems almost hostile at times.

"Sofie, can I have a word with you?" I tilt my head in the direction of the living room and watch as she gets up from the table and drags her feet out the door.

The clinic will have to wait; my daughter and I need a talk.

"Finish your breakfast, Spencer," I hear Taz tell him when I follow my daughter into the living room.

"I haven't finished *my* breakfast yet," Sofie challenges the moment I walk in.

"You can finish it when we're done."

I ignore the scowl on her face and pull her down on the couch with me, my arm around her shoulders firmly anchoring her in place.

"What's going on with you, Pipsqueak?" I ask gently.

"Nothing."

Yet I can feel her go rigid under my touch at my question.

"It's not nothing. I know my girl." I give her shoulder a

squeeze. "This business with your brother every morning, that has to stop."

She looks at me with those pretty brown eyes, so much like her mother and her aunt, and innocently blinks at me. "I don't know what you mean."

"Not buying, Sofie. I'm not sure what you're trying to do, but it's not fair to Spencer. Are you upset about something? You seem angry. At Aunt Taz, especially. What's going on?"

"Nothing." This time she drops her head as she mumbles the word and I can hear her voice crack.

I move to sit on the coffee table across from her, so I can look her in the eye. Leaning forward, I put my hands on her legs. "Did something happen in Kentucky?" She shakes her head, but I notice a tear rolling down her face. "Did someone say something? Come on, Pipsqueak, I can't help you if you don't talk to me."

"She's just going to leave us too," she hiccups.

"Who is? Aunt Taz?"

"Yes." With that she bursts into tears, sobbing uncontrollably.

I slide to my knees in front of her and pull her shaking body in my arms. "Oh, baby. Aunt Taz isn't leaving. Who told you that?"

Over her shoulder I can see Taz in the door opening, worry sketched on her face. I shake my head and mouth, *"I've got this."*

My little girl is sobbing inconsolably. I move to sit on the couch, pulling her on my lap, and wait patiently for the crying to subside.

"Why would you think Aunt Taz is leaving, Sofie?"

"Be-because I huh-heard Grandma and G-Grandpa fight. Grandma said sh-she wouldn't be able to handle us, that she wasn't gonna stick around once she understood how much work raising kids is."

"Grandma is wrong," I say with enough conviction she lifts her head from my drenched shirt and looks up. I struggle to control the rush of anger at the look of devastation on my daughter's face.

"But..."

Cupping her jaw with both hands I brush my thumbs at the wet on her cheeks. "She's not leaving, Pipsqueak. There's nothing you can do that would make that happen."

"Promise?" she whispers, hope replacing the sadness.

"Cross my heart and hope to... I promise." I hug her close and bury my nose in her soft hair, before loosening my hold so I can look at her sternly. "Now what's with all these barnyard animals?"

She has the good sense to look a little sheepishly from under her eyelashes. "I dunno."

"No? You and I both know you were testing your aunt, Sofie. That stops now, okay? The short snippy tone you're taking with her, the dirty looks, and most of all enlisting your brother to be at his most annoying."

She giggles at that, and I have a hard time keeping the stern look on my face. "Okay, Daddy."

"Good. No more barnyard animals."

I'VE BEEN behind the eight ball since this morning's late start.

I never even had a chance to brief Taz on my conversation with Sofie. Luckily she said she'd drop the kids off at Kathleen's on her way to her parents' place.

My first patient of the day had been a badly injured dog, hit by a car as the young animal took off across the street. The owner walked in, carrying the poor thing in a blanket, and of course I took him straight to the back. Everyone else in the reception area would have to wait.

I managed to patch him up, but I'll have to keep a close eye on him so he's staying the weekend.

Although most were understanding; I had a few disgruntled owners come in with their pets. The last of whom I sent on their way, when my cell phone rings.

"Hey, you," I tell Taz when I see it's her.

"Hi, I wanted to check in with you. Dad's doctor had an emergency and is running behind."

I snort. "That seems to be a theme today. I'm running behind myself."

"Oh shit. I should probably call Kathleen then. At this rate I may not be home in time to pick up the kids and get dinner on the table. We may end up eating on the road. I'm sorry."

"I'll take care of the kids and call Kathleen," I assure her. "You have other things on your mind."

"Okay, I'll let you go. See you tonight."

The last is full of promise and spoken very softly, putting an immediate smile on my face. I drop my voice an octave when I answer.

"Yes, you will."

Lisa is staring at me slack-jawed when I tuck my phone back in my pocket.

"What?"

"I've thought it, I've hoped it, I've sensed it, but until now I wasn't sure. Now I know."

"No clue what you're talking about," I lie, looking at her smug face.

"I bet. Happy for you, Rafe."

Chapter Twenty-Four

Taz

"How are you getting along with the kids?"

I lift my eyes to the rearview mirror, where I find Mom looking back at me from the back seat.

We've been on the road for an hour and this is the first direct question she's asked me. For the most part it's been quiet, with occasional exchanges between her and Dad about day-to-day stuff.

I'm instantly alert at her question.

"We're doing well," I offer carefully. "Spencer is… well, Spencer, so he's pretty easygoing. Sofie has had a few tough moments, but that's to be expected. She's at that age." At my mother's affirming nod I'm encouraged to share a little more. "She's been testing me."

Mom's eyebrows shoot up with more than only passing interest. "What do you mean?"

"Well, since you guys got back, she's been a bit testy

with me. Short, you know?" I chuckle as I tell my parents about Spencer's relentless nagging for a variety of farm animals at his sister's prompting. "It was pretty obvious she was orchestrating it. Rafe clued in to it too. He took her aside this morning for a talk."

"And?"

I glance at my dad, who appears to be following the conversation, wondering if I should repeat what Rafe discovered. With another hour and some in our drive, it might get uncomfortable. Still, I forge ahead, since Mom opened that door, keeping an eye on her in the rearview mirror. "Turns out Sofie is afraid I might be leaving." I catch Mom and Dad sharing a look, and I decide to throw the stick in the proverbial henhouse. "She overheard you two talking about me."

The silence in the car is telling as Mom now stares out the window, her lips firmly pressed together, while Dad twists his head to give her a death stare.

"Well..." Mom finally drawls. "I'm sorry she heard that, but maybe it's better she's prepared."

"Sarah!" Dad suddenly barks, startling me and almost sending me off the road.

"Jesus, Dad, you scared the shit out of me," I admonish him before getting back to the topic at hand. "Mom, can I ask you why you think she should be prepared for me leaving, when I have absolutely no intention to? I know what you think. I know there is stuff we probably should hash out at some point, but does it honestly look like I'm going anywhere? Have I given any indication I want to?"

"You know what they say," she replies instantly and

rather snippily. "The only predictor of future behavior is past behavior."

"Here we go," Dad laments, dropping his head back on the headrest and contemplating the roof.

"Well, it's true. Her whole life she's done nothing but run away. Of course not after first causing trouble."

"I'm right here," I announce sharply, trying hard to keep the car on the road, I'm so pissed. "And let me set the record straight on one thing, Mom. I never ran away from trouble—I left because no matter what I did, I seemed to upset people. I know I wasn't an angel growing up, and I'm sure most of those gray hairs you sport are because of me, but you've never let me live it down. You're still judging me based on things I did as a teenager. I'm thirty-eight years old, Mom. I've done a lot of good things in my life you don't give me credit for, yet you easily hold a grudge for things I'm not even guilty of."

A derisive snort is all I get for a response, followed by another warning, "Sarah," from Dad before he turns to me.

"Been thinking on that a lot lately, Baby Girl, and— without digging up old dirt—I for one am ready to move on from that. Your mom may be dragging her feet, but my time is too short to waste on what's already behind me."

I choke up at my dad's words. I don't like him talking about his time being short, even though I couldn't be happier to hear him calling me his baby girl again. Seems like perhaps I have one parent pleased to have me back.

It's a start.

WE DON'T HAVE to wait long for the neurologist.

Barely five minutes after we take a seat in the waiting room, Dad's name is called. He leads the way into the doctor's office and as I'm about to follow him in, Mom holds me back by the arm.

"I just wanted to say I appreciate you coming along. I'm too nervous to take in any information."

As far as peace pipes go, this is an effective one and I quickly cover her hand on my arm with my own. "Wouldn't have it any other way, Mom." We may not be able to settle all our differences easily, but for the sake of my father, we seem to be on one page.

"I don't believe we've met," a handsome older man of Asian descent says, holding out his hand for me to shake.

"Natasha Boran, I'm Ed and Sarah's youngest daughter." Even as I say it, I wince at the knowledge I'm not only their youngest, but also now their only daughter.

"Right, I believe I met your sister at a previous visit then. I'm Dr. Chen. Should we wait for her to join us?"

Dad sucks in a sharp breath and Mom has a sudden fascination with the tips of her shoes.

"Actually, Dr. Chen," I inform him with a lump in my throat. "Sadly my sister passed away quite suddenly this past April."

The poor doctor's eyes dart between my parents before landing back on me. "I am so sorry to hear that. Right, maybe we should get started then."

"Please," Dad says in a rough voice.

Dr. Chen is all business after that: outlining the decline in Dad's condition, the options going forward, and his own personal recommendations.

Dad pales distinctly when he finds out what DBS actually entails; the battery of tests leading up to it, the many hours of surgery, the electrodes left in his brain, the insertion of an electrical stimulation device under the skin. Of course there are some serious risks attached to the surgery that should be considered as well.

"I can check if there's room today, but otherwise we can schedule a day next week for the preliminary scans and blood work, if you choose to go ahead. We can also schedule a tentative surgical date for you."

Dad swallows hard before nodding, but Mom looks panicked.

"Dr. Chen," I interrupt what feels like a runaway train. "Is it at all possible to take a few minutes for all of us to process this? I understand you have more appointments, so maybe it would be easier if my parents go grab something to eat, talk things over, and perhaps pop in between appointments after lunch?"

"Yes, of course. I'll let my assistant know you'll be back."

With that I let Dad lead the way out of the office again, Mom close behind me. I feel a warm hand in the middle of my back and a soft voice in my ear.

"Thank you, honey."

IT's ALMOST five when we finally walk out of the hospital.

We had a good talk over lunch, with Mom voicing her concerns, me providing some medical insight, and Dad explaining his reasons for wanting to go ahead with the surgery. When Dad mentioned he needed to try everything possible to maximize the time he has left with her, he cemented the decision for Mom. He even had me in tears.

The rest of the afternoon was spent hopping from test to test, and we walk out of the hospital with an appointment for surgery four weeks away. I can tell it's taken a toll on Dad especially.

"I'm taking the back seat," he announces. "That way I can have a snooze while you girls yap."

"Why is it always women who yap?" Mom immediately has her tired hackles up.

"Because you do. Yap, chatter, gossip, babble, jabber. It's what women do." I bite my lip, trying not to laugh at Mom's disgruntled huff. I remember these types of exchanges from when I was young.

"Are you saying men don't?"

"Men confer, huddle, and once in a blue moon shoot the shit, but real men never yap."

My mother's almost ready to blow so I quickly intervene, reaching over to put a hand on her arm.

"Remember, Mom, this comes from a man who still reads the Sunday funnies first."

"And likes his toast cut in perfect triangles," she adds, grinning at me.

"And cries like a baby when his Cardinals get eliminated in the playoffs." I wink at her.

"See? Yapping," Dad contributes, sticking his head between our seats. "I'm having a nap."

Five minutes later the occasional snore drifts from the back.

"He's tired," Mom notes.

"I'd be worried if he wasn't. Heck, I'm tired. Been a long day, Mom."

"Yeah, it has." She suddenly sounds exhausted herself and I reach over to give her hand a squeeze.

"It'll be okay, Mom."

"I hope so, honey. God, I hope so. I don't think I'd survive the alternative."

Rafe

"HAVE YOU HEARD ANYTHING FROM TAZ?"

I've barely got my foot over the threshold at Kathleen and Brent's.

"She called earlier to tell me they're running late. Doing some testing. We'll find out soon enough."

"It's too much, having to deal with this after Nicky's death," she concludes, leading the way to the kitchen where Brent is tossing back a beer at the counter.

"Beer?" he asks, holding up his empty as he walks over to the fridge.

"Sure." Taz won't likely be home soon, and from what I can see through the sliding doors, the kids are having a blast in the pool.

"You wanna stay for burgers?"

I'm frankly shocked Kathleen would ask me. She's never made any bones about letting me know I'm not exactly her favorite person, although I have noticed a slight warming in recent days.

"Well—"

"It'll give the kids a chance to dry up over dinner before you load them in the truck."

"Yeah, if you sure there's enough, we'll stay. Thanks." I nod to Kathleen who grants me a hint of a smile.

Brent hands me a beer, and indicates for me to follow him outside to the deck. Spencer notices me right away.

"Dad! Look what I can do!"

If not for the life vest he's wearing, I'd have a heart attack watching him run down the diving board, straight into the deep end of the pool. Brent chuckles behind me as he fires up the grill.

"That's great, Son." I give him two thumbs-up and he beams. In the meantime, Sofie has pulled herself out of the water and is making her way over. "Hey, Pipsqueak. You having fun too?"

She nods and keeps walking until she has her arms wrapped around me, her wet body drenching my clothes. I bend down and kiss the top of her head. "Do we need to get ready?" she asks.

"Not yet. Kathleen asked us to stay for dinner."

She lifts her face. "What about Aunt Taz?"

I smile down at her. "She's out with Grandma and Grandpa. She'll be home later."

"Can I go back in the water?"

"Sure. Until dinner's ready, okay?"

In a flash she's gone, jumping back in the pool with the other kids.

"Brent?" Kathleen's head pops outside. "Before you toss the burgers on, could you run out and pick me up some mustard? I ran out and I need it to finish the potato salad."

"I can do it," I offer, and she looks me up and down.

"No you can't, you look like someone hosed you down. Besides, you can keep me company." She throws me a sneaky smile before her head disappears inside.

"Warning," Brent mutters under his breath. "My advice? Say as little as possible, you won't need to. Oh, and nod—a lot."

I follow him inside and watch him give his wife a peck before he walks out the door with mild apprehension. When I turn to Kathleen she's staring at me.

"Don't look so panicked," she notes, turning her focus back on the potatoes. "I'm not gonna bite. I just feel I need to clear the air."

I pull out a stool and sit down, taking a fortifying sip from my beer. "Okay."

"I blamed you for a lot of things over the years," she starts. I don't say anything, because frankly I have no idea how to respond to that. Luckily Kathleen needs no prompting. "You made my two friends very unhappy." She lifts her hand when I open my mouth to protest, and I immediately snap it shut. Best to let her get it out so I nod instead, as Brent recommended. "I get now you were doing what you thought was right, but I'm still gonna tell you it was stupid. Not that you were the only one I was pissed at. I was pissed at Taz for disappearing, and I was pissed at Nicky for stepping out on you. But I already loved them so it was easier to blame all of it on you." I shouldn't be surprised she knows about Nicky's indiscretions, but it nevertheless makes me feel like a chump. Still, I only nod. "I just wanted to tell you I'm not pissed anymore," she says, pinning with a hard glance. "That is, unless you fuck up with Taz, then I reserve the right to hunt you down and shoot you."

A pregnant pause follows in which she stares me down, until I finally ask, "Is it okay for me to speak now?"

"Nobody likes a smart-ass, Rafe Thomas," she snaps, turning back to her potato salad, as I fight back a grin.

"Right. First of all, I get it—no need to explain—and if it's any consolation, I agree: I was stupid. Hindsight being twenty-twenty. I also need you to know I don't regret it, because that would mean to regret them." I look outside where my kids are having fun in the water. "Secondly—and the only reason I'm giving you this is because I know you love Taz—I'm not going to hurt her. I'd rather cut off my dick than hurt that woman."

Kathleen's hand comes up again accompanied by a disgusted look on her face. "Fuck me, man. We're about to have dinner; don't be talking about your dick. TMI."

"Best way to illustrate how serious I am about that."

"I get. Move on, please."

"That's it."

"Hardly," she fires back. "What about your in-laws?"

"What about them?"

"They find out what's going on with you two, they're not gonna react well."

"Not news, Kathleen."

"It's gonna be hard on Taz."

"I know that too."

"That relationship is fragile as it is."

"Maybe you should make your point, because I know all this."

"You can't leave her facing them alone again," she finally says, turning serious eyes on me.

"She won't have to," I bite off, more than a little irritated now.

"You say that, but when it comes to—"

My turn to cut her off.

"Listen. She. Won't. Have. To."

Just then Brent walks in, shaking his head at me in warning.

"Dude, what'd I say?"

"What exactly did you tell him, Brent McKinnon?"

Chuckling, I grab my bottle and head outside, leaving them to fight it out.

Kathleen is right though. It's too risky to leave anything to chance, so we need to simply tell Sarah and Ed first chance we get.

"ARE THEY IN BED?" Taz asks when I walk outside and join her on the steps, sliding my legs on either side of her and pulling her back against me.

"Asleep already. Burned out after a day in the pool."

"Good. I hope they had fun."

I kiss the top of her head. "They had a blast. Want to tell me about today?"

"Dad wants the surgery."

"Okay. How do you guys feel about that?"

"Can I tell you tomorrow? I haven't even begun to process it all."

I drop my chin to her shoulder. "Of course. Why don't

we ask them for dinner tomorrow? I'll make ribs; your dad loves those. We can talk about things then."

"Sounds good. I think I may be heading upstairs too. I'm beat."

"Kiss me first."

She tilts her head back and I don't hesitate to cover her mouth with mine, groaning as her taste hits my senses.

I love this woman. Completely. The sounds she makes, the feel of her skin under my touch, the humor in her eyes, her wild hair and ratty clothes. I love her sweet and her bite. The way she can brighten a room simply by being in it, and the way she adores the kids.

Most of all I love how her eyes give me everything she hasn't put in words.

She loves me too; I'm just not sure for how long once she finds out a little honesty is on tomorrow's menu.

Chapter Twenty-Five

Taz

"Can we get ice cream?"

I look at Sofie, who has her nose pressed to the door of the cooler.

Rafe was called out on an emergency this morning so the kids tagged along to the grocery store with me.

"I planned on making an apple crumble for dessert," I tell her.

"Exactly," she points out, "which will taste even better *with* ice cream."

"Ice cream is the best!" Spencer puts in his two cents' worth.

I'm quickly discovering that grocery shopping with children for only a handful of things ends up with a full cart. I'm being tag-teamed and I know it. Still, I grab a container of vanilla ice cream from the cooler and add it to the cart, because there's no denying; apple crumble *does* taste better with a scoop of ice cream.

"Okay, guys. Let's get going, I think we have everything."

"Can we get the puppies a new toy?" Spencer wants to know when we pass through the aisle with the pet food.

"Kid, they've got more toys than you and your sister combined, they don't need more. When we get home you can give them one of those rawhides when you take them out of the crate."

Lilo and Stitch are teething, which means they're chewing on everything. It's been a challenge to keep everything out of the reach of those little sharp chompers.

Meredith comes walking up when we get to the checkout, a big smile on her face.

"This is the brood?" She looks from Sofie to Spencer, who both stare back at her.

"Guys, this is my friend, Meredith."

"You work here?" Spencer asks her, his eyes big when he spots the store logo on her shirt.

"Yup."

"Do you get to eat what you want?"

Meredith bursts out laughing at my nephew's wide-eyed question.

"The perpetually hungry man-child is Spencer," I clarify with a grin. "And this is Sofie."

"Oh my, I can see the family resemblance; you're as pretty as your aunt."

I can't quite tell what is going on behind Sofie's eyes, but it's clear from the way she looks at me the comment gives her thought.

"Anyway," Meredith continues. "I was going to give you a call to see if you'd like to come over for dinner next weekend. I got Andrew a new grill for his birthday a few weeks ago, and he's been eager to show it off. Bring the kids," she adds, ruffling Spencer's hair, "there'll be plenty of food."

"Would love to, but we won't be around. We're heading up to Mark Twain National Forest next weekend."

"We're gonna be sleeping in a tent," Spencer adds excitely. "And I'm going fishing."

"A tent, huh? Well, that sounds like fun." Meredith turns to me, with her eyebrows raised and a smirk on her face.

I pretend not to notice. "Yes, so can we take a rain check on dinner?"

"Sure. We'll do it when you get back. I'll call you— we'll hash out the details."

Grill me is probably more accurate. I hide a grin and shake my head. "Let's hash them out over coffee instead, and we might as well get Kathleen in on that: two birds with one stone."

Sofie has been quiet and it's not until the ride home she says anything.

"Aunt Taz?"

"Yeah, honey."

"Do you think I'm pretty?"

I look in the rearview mirror and take in the expression on her face, wishing I could touch her. "Very much so," I assure her. "The kind of pretty I know will blossom into beautiful."

She turns her face to the window and a little smile tugs

at her mouth. She's quiet again the rest of the way home, but the smile stays.

"Okay, guys. Everyone grab a few bags and bring them straight through to the kitchen, please."

The kids are waiting for me to unlock the front door and barge right through inside, only to freeze a few steps in.

"What's going—" I don't get any farther as I freeze right behind them and take in the devastation that was the living room. "Sofie? I thought you said you locked the dogs' crate."

"I did," she whispers. "I'm sure I did."

We were gone for maybe an hour—tops—and the living room looks like a bomb exploded. Stuffing bulging out of the couch, torn pillows strewn about, their contents spilling everywhere. Snippets of paper, old coffee grounds, ripped plastic bags, and God knows what else. And in the middle of it all, two exhausted pups sleeping right through our return.

"Kids, take the dogs out."

I wait for the kids to hustle the dogs outside and then I sink down on the bottom step of the stairs and drop my head in my hands. Of course this has to happen only a few hours before my parents get here.

I could cry, but that's not going to solve anything. Instead, I take a deep breath in, grab the grocery bags that were dropped by the front door, and proceed to put the stuff away.

An hour later the kids are in their rooms, the dogs in their crate—properly locked this time—and I am tying up the last garbage bag. I open the door to toss it with the other five bags already stacked outside, as Rafe's truck pulls up.

Shit. I'd so hoped to have the worst of it taken care of before he got home.

"What are you up to?"

He walks up in that casual stride, unaware of the destruction still waiting inside. I sure hope we have duct tape, we're gonna need quite a bit of it to temporarily patch things up inside.

"I'm, uh, cleaning up. We had a bit of an incident here."

Rafe looks instantly alarmed. "Kids okay?"

I have to grab his arm to stop him from barging inside without warning.

"Kids are fine. Dogs are fine, although I'm not sure for how long. They got out and...rearranged the furniture."

He pulls up his eyebrow. "Rearranged? How badly."

"Oh, pretty badly. We're gonna need to do some furniture shopping."

"You're shitting me," he mutters, as he walks in the door.

I expect a series of expletives, some yelling maybe, but instead it stays silent, and finally I follow him inside. He has his back to me—beside the couch—standing stock-still. Then his shoulders start shaking.

"Rafe?" I rush up behind him and put my hand on his back, which is when he throws his head back and starts laughing.

Not the reaction I was expecting.

I look at what's left of the living room and back at Rafe, trying to figure out what is so funny.

"Don't look so worried," he finally says, humor still

shining in his eyes as he hooks an arm around my waist. "I don't care. My whole life I've cared. Put too much importance on stuff. Even growing up I held on to what little was mine thinking it would make me happy."

"Rafe..." I slide my hand up his chest and look up in his face.

He tugs me closer, smiling down. "Now I know stuff is just that; stuff. It doesn't make you happy—people do. My kids do. *You* do. I lo—"

"Hello! We're a little early. Why is the front door open?"

Rafe

TAZ JUMPS BACK like she's hit with ten thousand volts.

It doesn't go unnoticed. Sarah glares sharply at Taz, before her eyes come to me.

"What's going on here?"

"Grandma!" Spencer comes running downstairs and barrels straight into her legs, wrapping his arms around. Sarah's eyes drop down as her hand automatically goes to his floppy hair.

"Hey, little man."

"Where's Grandpa?"

"Right here, little buddy." I hadn't even noticed Ed coming in behind his wife.

Taz is still standing frozen and I give her a little nudge when I pass. "Let me find you a place to sit, Dad."

"Lilo and Stitch were bad," my son volunteers. "They ate the living room."

"I can see that," Ed says dryly, taking a look around.

"Why would you leave the dogs alone? Look at the furniture." I look at Sarah apparently focused on Taz, who hasn't said a word yet.

"It was my fault," Sofie says, coming down the stairs, her face drawn. "I thought I locked the crate, but I guess I didn't." Tears immediately pool in her eyes when they catch on me.

Before I have a chance to respond, Taz moves quickly, pulling Sofie in her arms. "It was an accident. A good reminder for everyone to make sure those latches are closed properly when we put the dogs away." She sets Sofie back a little and leans her face close. "Besides, it comes with the unexpected bonus, we get to shop for new furniture now." At that a smile breaks through Sofie's tears.

"Yuck. Shopping is stupid, right, Dad?"

"Let's call it a necessary evil, okay, Son? Now, why don't you two," I look at both my kids, "get Grandma and Grandpa set up outside in the shade with some drinks, while Aunt Taz and I sort out things in here, all right? Let the dogs out too."

"I'm getting the dogs!" Spencer yells already, heading for the dog crate.

Ed shuffles his way to the back door with Sofie on his heels, but Sarah stays put.

"I'll help," she announces, but I put a hand on her arm.

"Thanks, Mom, but we've got this. We won't be long." I can tell she's not pleased, but she still follows when Spencer leads the dogs through the kitchen.

Taz dramatically wipes her brow when they disappear out of view.

"That was too close," she mumbles.

"We need to talk to them, Taz. Before they find out another way."

"I know, but I think we've had enough excitement for today, okay? Let's get this place in some order and start on dinner. We'll go over and talk to them tomorrow. Do you have duct tape?"

She picks up what looks to have been a remote control and puts the pieces by the TV. I'm tempted to push the issue, but decide to leave it for now and instead go in search of tape.

Half an hour later, with the living room taped back together as best we could manage and a start made on dinner, I head outside to light the grill.

"Does Taz need a hand in the kitchen?" Sarah asks when she sees me.

The kids are rolling in the grass with the dogs and Ed looks like he's napping in his chair. "She's wrapping the potatoes to go on the grill. She'll be out shortly." I can feel her eyes on me as I run the steel wire brush over the racks.

"I'm not sure it's wise to encourage her, Rafe." She's come up behind me and speaks in a soft voice. "It'll just be harder for the kids when she eventually moves out."

I bite my tongue. I'd like to tell her she will not be moving out at all, but that would lead to explanations Taz wants to avoid tonight. I don't want to lie either, so I abruptly change the subject as I turn to face her. "Can I get you a glass of port to go with dinner, or would you like something else?"

She stares at me for a long pause before she answers. "Port sounds good."

When I look over at Ed to see if he needs a refresher, I find him awake and keenly observing us. I'm used to him being quiet. I've never considered maybe quiet doesn't equal unaware. "Dad? Ready for another beer?" He holds up his empty bottle in response.

Taz

"STAY AND TALK TO ME."

I'm on my way inside to help clean up when Dad grabs my hand.

The kids are upstairs in the master bedroom watching TV—since we need to replace the remote for the one in the living room—and Mom and Rafe are cleaning up in the kitchen.

I sit back down beside him, but he holds on to my hand.

"How are you settling in? How's the new job?"

"I'm good, Dad. It's nice to have Kathleen back and I've made some new friends." I chuckle at that. "Who'd have thought there were new friends to be made in Eminence?"

"This town isn't that bad, sweetheart," Dad points out with a serious face. "Most people are kind. We look out for each other. No one's ever gone hungry here."

"True," I grudgingly admit. "Although I could do

257

without Mrs. Myers; the woman is a menace." I tell him about her snippy remarks and the dog incident.

"Charlton? He's a pussycat."

"Apparently not when exposed to water. The old hag knew it too."

"She's been sour since Henry died...gosh, damn near thirty years ago. Never got over it, never moved on. There was a time that woman was happy and smiling all the time, but when her husband passed too young, it's like a light went off."

"I never knew her like that," I admit.

"You were too young to remember." He lifts my hand and kisses the back of it, before he continues in a gentle tone. "I know you haven't had an easy time here. Not before you left, and not now, but I hope you stick it out, sweetheart. I understood why you wanted to leave, but I sure like having you back."

"I missed you, Dad." I'm getting all choked up. Talks like this are something else I've missed for too long.

"Me too, Baby Girl," he responds in kind. "You don't have to stop reaching for the sun, though. Grab on to your chance at happiness, Natasha."

Chapter Twenty-Six

Rafe

I WAKE up with Taz's scent up my nostrils.

Last night after her parents left and the kids were asleep, she'd been quiet. Halfway through an episode of *Designated Survivor* she announced she was tired and going to bed.

Earlier I'd watched her talking to her father through the kitchen window. She'd seemed emotional and I kept an eye out, but since it didn't look like they were arguing, I didn't want to interrupt.

The whole night had been uneasy. Sarah had seemed subdued to the point of uncommunicative, and Taz had been on eggshells, which is why I didn't stop her when she went to bed. I finished watching the episode, took the dogs out for a pee before locking up for the night, and followed her upstairs.

"I know you're awake," she mumbles, her head on my

259

chest. She'd curled into me the moment I slipped into bed with her.

"How long have you been up?" I stroke my hand up her back and under her nightshirt.

"A while."

"How come?"

I can feel her shrug. "Trying to anticipate how they're going to react when we tell them."

"Your parents?"

"Hmmm. Mom's going to blow. I'm not sure about Dad, though. He said something last night that made me wonder."

"You looked like you were having an intense conversation."

She lifts her head, her eyes meeting mine. "Not really intense; it was sweet. I haven't had a talk like that with my father in forever. It felt good."

"So those were happy tears I saw?"

She smiles, her eyes soft. "Yeah. He told me to grab hold of happiness. I've been wondering if he was talking about us. About you."

I curl my fingers in her dreads and lift my head so I can reach her mouth for a brief kiss. "I wouldn't put it past him," I whisper against her lips. "I think your dad is more perceptive than he's credited for."

"But if that's the case, why did he seem upset with me when I first got back?"

This time it's my turn to shrug. "Don't forget I was too. Misunderstandings tend to be persistent when you only get one side of the story."

"I guess so," she mumbles, dropping her head down to my chest, my hand resumes stroking her back.

"It'll be okay."

"You keep saying that."

"Because it's true. I'm not saying it'll be easy, but we'll get through. You wanna know how I know that?"

"How?"

"Love."

Her head pops up again and her eyes search my face. "Yeah?"

"Absolutely. It's what connects us all. Nicky, the children, your parents, and us; you and me."

"Are you saying you love me?"

"I'm saying I love everyone, but I'm *in* love with you."

Her eyes go soft and I feel the sudden need to be inside her. A little smile tugs at her lips when I roll her on her back, quickly shed my boxers, and wedge my hips in the cradle of hers.

"Make love to me, Rafe."

"I always do."

I feel her already wet when I pull aside the gusset of her panties and rub my cock along her crease. Our eyes stay locked when I slide deep inside her, her heat closing around me.

"For the record," she whispers on a gasp. "I'm in love with you too."

"Don't hit your fingers."

Spencer is wielding the small mallet like a tennis racket as he tries to hammer a tent peg down.

The kids are helping me set up the tent in the backyard to make sure the mice haven't eaten any holes in the fabric. It's been packed away for quite a few years. The sleeping bags are hanging on the laundry line to air out, and Taz is inside making a list of things to bring.

Our campground is only about two hours away, but you still don't want to have to drive back home for something you forgot. I would've liked to venture out a little farther but staying a bit closer to home this time makes sense. Ed's health is a bit unstable, the dogs are still pretty young, and this'll be our first trip together. In addition, we plan to have a talk with the kids, which—especially in Sofie's case—is at best unpredictable. Better not to get trapped a day's drive away in case things go south.

"Sofie, don't let Stitch pull on the tent flap like that. He'll tear it." Still a little shaken by the dog's rampage yesterday, she's quick to pull him away.

"Is this good, Dad?" Spencer calls out and I walk over to inspect the peg he managed to get halfway into the ground.

"Well done, Son. You can be my helper next week when we set it up at the campsite."

"Sofie! I get to be Daddy's helper!"

"So what?"

Ignoring the familiar ensuing bickering I inspect the tent, not finding any holes. I pick up Lilo, who seems to have found a place to nap inside, and close the zipper for the bugs.

"Guys, let's grab something to eat, okay? We're dropping you off at Kathleen's for a few hours in the pool after lunch."

With the dogs in their crate for a nap and the kids having a sandwich at the table, I walk inside to check on Taz who said she'd be *right out.*

"Watcha doing?" I find her curled up in one of the club chairs; her laptop perched on her knees. I sit down on the armrest and look at the screen. She starts to close the lid, but I stop her and point at one of the couches, a dark tan, leather sectional. "I like that one."

"So much for the surprise," she mutters under her breath.

"Surprise?"

She tilts her head back to look at me. "Your birthday is in a few weeks, I thought…never mind. It was a stupid idea."

"Not stupid at all. I can imagine a lot of fun things we could do on that couch."

"The kids," she hisses in warning.

"Are busy eating their lunch."

I tilt her chin up and lean down for a kiss. I plunder her mouth, fueled by images of Taz bent over the armrest of the leather couch, her lush ass in the air and my cock sliding in and out of her, slick with her juices.

A sharp intake of breath functions like a bucket of ice water on my libido.

Fuck.

Taz

. . .

"I DIDN'T WANT to believe it."

Mom is standing in the open front door, looking at us with hurt in her eyes.

"Mom…" I scramble to my feet, setting the laptop on the table, but Mom holds up her hand, pressing her eyes closed.

"I didn't want to believe it," she repeats. "Not from that nasty cow, Sheila. Never could stand the woman. But when Mrs. Myers hinted at the same thing this morning in church I started wondering. I'd noticed a change—a word, a touch —but I convinced myself it couldn't be. No way you would betray Nicky's memory like that." She looks up, her face marred with disappointment. "Now I know they were both telling the truth. How could you?"

"Grandma?"

My head swings around to find Sofie standing in the doorway to the kitchen, looking confused.

"Why don't you drop the kids off at Kathleen's." My voice is flat, almost resigned, as I turn back to my mother.

"I'm not lea—" Rafe starts to object, but I cut him off.

"Please, Rafe. The kids."

I wait for a tense minute, my eyes focused on my mother's, until finally I hear Rafe gathering up the kids, mumbling to them in a hushed voice.

"She's barely cold in her grave," Mom says in a low voice the moment the door closes behind them. "I'm almost glad she doesn't have to know how her own sister didn't waste any time moving in on her family."

"Mom, you don't know—"

"I don't?" Her voice is shrill as anger starts to trump disappointment. "I know plenty. I know how you threw yourself into Rafe's arms when your sister was pregnant with his child. I know how you tried to put a wedge in their marriage three years after that, when she was expecting Spencer. I know you cared so little about us you stayed away for years—*years*. I thought you'd changed. Thought maybe this time you came back for the right reasons, but boy, was I wrong."

Tears burn my eyes as every word she says slices like the crack of a whip, but I swallow them down.

"I came back because I love my sister and she wanted me here. I came back because I hoped, maybe, I could make up for time lost with you and Dad. With the kids. I never intended to...to..."

"Take her family? I can't even stand to look at you."

"That's enough, Sarah."

Her head whips around at the sound of my dad's voice. "How did you get here?"

"Hitched a ride with Kathleen after church. After you took off like a bat out of hell when Cynthia Myers did what she does best; stir the pot. Dammit, Sarah."

"Do you know what your precious *Baby Girl* did, Ed?" I flinch at the way she spits out his nickname for me, like it's something dirty. "She finally got her claws into Rafe. Her sister's husband. The love of Nicky's life."

I sink back down in my chair and drop my head in my hands. There's no way I'll ever be able to change her perception, and I will not betray my sister by speaking ill of her in an effort to clear my own name. I won't do it.

"Bullshit," Dad barks, surprising me. "He was no more

the love of her life as she was his. You'd have to be blind not to see that, Sarah."

"You knew about this?" she snaps incredulously. "This…" she agitatedly waves her hand, "…sordid affair? Oh my God, those poor children."

I keep my head down so I don't see Rafe coming in, but I hear him.

"The only reason the kids are upset is because you came in here making a scene," he says sharply. "As for Taz and me, we were coming over to talk to you after we dropped the kids off at Kathleen's. Luckily she drove up with Dad so I was able to send the kids with her. They shouldn't have to witness their grandmother tearing apart their aunt."

"You're blaming this on me?"

"This scene? Hell yes," Rafe says in a surprisingly controlled voice. "The past nine years? No. We are all to blame for those."

"Amen." I almost start giggling at Dad's solemn voice. I feel like I've landed in the middle of a horrible daytime soap opera.

"Now sit down, I'll get us some drinks, and maybe we can have a normal conversation."

I look up to find Mom doing as instructed, I imagine a little stunned at Rafe's uncharacteristic confrontation. Dad sits down beside her on the duct-taped couch and winks at me. I bite off a smile.

Rafe walks in with the Glenfiddich, the bottle of port, and four tumblers. Mom doesn't say a word when he hands her a generous glass of port. When the rest of us have a glass of whiskey, Rafe sits back down on my armrest, his warm hand resting in my neck.

"It's not right," Mom mutters, shaking her head at Rafe as tears well up in her eyes. "You belong to Nicky."

"Mom, I love you like the mother I never had, but I never belonged to Nicky. I loved her, but not the way I should've. What's more, she didn't love me like that either."

"Don't you dare say that about my daughter!"

"Hush, Sarah, let the man speak."

I stay silent; knowing anything I say will only inflame the situation like it always did in the past when Mom and I had a disagreement. Maybe it's a sign I've grown up.

Rafe takes a deep breath in as he gives my neck a little squeeze. "Nicky wanted this for us. I never told her how I felt about Taz, even nine years ago, but somehow she knew. We both thought we were doing the right thing, getting married, and we tried. Both of us did. This is something I never intended to share with either of you, but given the circumstances I think I should. We were filing for divorce right before Nicky had her heart attack."

"Convenient. You say that now." Mom is desperately hanging on to her vision of Rafe and Nicky's marriage and part of me understands. She's already lost a daughter. I recognize it's pain that has her lashing out. At Rafe this time.

"Mom," he responds gently. "I can show you the paper-work. It was by mutual agreement. We'd been living in separate bedrooms for nearly a year."

She sniffles and Dad fishes out his linen handkerchief,

handing it to her. "Can you blame her? You may as well have cheated on her."

I can take her taking potshots at me, but she's blaming the wrong person and I can't let that stand. "Rafe wasn't the one cheating," I tell her as gently as I can. "No one is perfect. Not even Nicky. She told me the last time I was here—when she was pregnant with Spencer—she had been seeing someone. Mom," I plead for her to look at me. "It was an impossible situation from the start. That's why I left. It seemed an easier solution for everyone."

She stares at me, and I hurt at the pain in her expression. "I can't…" she starts, letting her words trail off as she shakes her head. "I need to go." She suddenly jumps to her feet and heads for the door.

"Sarah, hold on." Dad struggles to stand up. "You'd better not drive off and leave me stranded twice in one day."

"Mom…" It's no use, she's already outside, and Rafe rushes to give Dad a hand.

A few minutes later he comes back inside.

"Maybe she shouldn't be driving," I suggest, a little late.

"Your dad insists they'll be fine."

"I'm sorry. I didn't want them to know—I knew how much that would hurt—but I couldn't let her blame you for something you didn't do."

He walks up and pulls me close; my arms automatically slip around his waist. "I know. Sometimes you need to let the wound bleed clean before it can heal."

"I think maybe we're all bleeding a little," I suggest, snuggling closer.

"Yeah, it may take some time, but we'll eventually heal. Even your Mom."

He tugs my head back by the hair and presses a hard kiss to my lips.

"What did you tell the kids?"

"That you and Grandma had something to work out. They didn't ask any more."

"We have to warn my parents."

"I already did. They don't want to hurt the kids any more than we do."

Chapter Twenty-Seven

Rafe

"Give him one tonight with dinner, and make sure you finish the full course. He should start feeling better in twenty-four to forty-eight hours."

I scratch the docile malamute's big head before handing over the antibiotics to its owner. The dog was brought in with an infected wound to one of his hind legs. The owner hadn't noticed it under the thick fur until the dog started licking it and his paw became swollen.

I walk with them to the reception area where I leave them in Lisa's hands before turning to see who's next.

"Mrs. Myers," I try not to show my irritation when I greet her.

Taz mentioned a few days ago she was relieved the woman was taken off her roster of visits. It doesn't surprise me, as soon as she's back on her feet, I find her back in my clinic with poor Charlton.

"Dr. Thomas."

"Why don't you come back to the exam room and tell me what brings Charlton in today." I lead the way to the back and show her into the room.

Then I leave her to fetch Jason, my intern who's in the back monitoring the two animals we spayed this morning. I like the guy. He's good with the animals, personable with their owners, and seems to have a steady hand and a good head on his shoulders. He should do fine with Rick Moore's support while I'm on vacation.

He's had a chance over the past few weeks to meet most of my regular patients, except for Charlton.

"I'd like you to step in with me. Mrs. Myers and her dog are what we'd call frequent flyers. Charlton's a beagle and has a myriad of health issues, most related to his morbid obesity. We've tried for years to get him to lose the weight, but it's impossible without his owner's cooperation."

"All right," he agrees, closing the door to the crate of the tabby scheduled to be picked up later this afternoon.

The moment I close the door behind us, and finish introducing Jason, Mrs. Myers starts talking.

"He's not eating."

"When was the last time he had anything?" I ask, lifting the overweight dog onto the table and notice its labored breathing.

"He ate a little of his dinner Monday night, but nothing since."

It's Friday morning now. "Has he been drinking?" I notice a tremor in the dog's legs as I palpate his abdomen, as if he has trouble standing.

"Not as much as usual."

I fit my stethoscope in my ears and listen to the elevated and highly irregular heart rate, as Charlton sinks down on his butt. The poor dog's heart is failing. I want to yell at the woman for not heeding my warnings these past years. Beagles can live a healthy twelve to fifteen years, but Charlton—at only nine years old—is at his end. Frustrated I yank the stethoscope off and gesture for Jason to have a listen. I've tried to explain how dangerous obesity is in dogs. Urged her to keep the dog on a strict diet.

I wait for Jason to finish his examination. When he looks at me and faintly shakes his head, I know he's come to the same conclusion I have.

"Mrs. Myers, Charlton is not well. In fact, his heart is failing." I try to keep my tone gentle. In spite of her disregard for my warnings over the years, there's no denying the woman loves her dog, as tears fill her eyes.

"Can you fix him?" her voice whispers and suddenly I see her for what she is; a lonely old woman, scared to death of losing another loved one.

My heart goes out to her, even as I prepare to break hers.

"He's suffering, Mrs. Myers. His heart is not pumping effectively, and he has trouble breathing. I can't fix him, but I can end his pain."

"You mean put him to sleep? Now?"

———

"RAFE."

Sarah's voice is curt when she answers the phone. We

haven't seen Taz's parents since last Sunday, although I spoke to Ed earlier this week when he called. He mentioned Sarah would need some time, but they wanted to see the kids before we left to go camping. They're supposed to take them for dinner tonight.

"Mom, I need your help."

"Are the kids okay?"

"Yes. It's not the kids; it's Cynthia Myers. Or more accurately, her dog. Heart failure. She's agreed for me to euthanize him, but I'm worried about her."

"Give me ten minutes," she snaps, hanging up immediately.

We've given Mrs. Myers some privacy with Charlton. Jason's looking after a cat with a torn ear someone just brought in, and I get a head start on my notes while I wait for Sarah to get here. I hear her come in as promised ten minutes later, and listen to the muted voices in the exam room next door for a few moments before I go in.

I hate euthanizing, but when an animal is beyond help, it's the only thing left I can do for them. Still, it makes me feel like shit when I watch heartbroken owners leave.

Sarah has an arm around Mrs. Myers as they walk to her car.

"Don't worry about your car, Mrs. Myers," I tell her as I follow them out. "If you'll leave me your keys, we'll drop it off later."

Without a word she pulls them from her purse and hands them to me. Sarah helps her into the passenger seat and makes sure she's buckled up before closing the door and turning to me.

"Thanks for calling."

"Thank you for coming. I thought she could use a friend."

She nods, letting her eyes drift to the house. "I'd still like to pick up the kids from Kathleen's for dinner as planned, but maybe Cynthia will want to tag along, if that's okay."

"Of course. Mom…" I reach for her but she turns away and quickly rounds the car.

I watch her get in and start the car. I'm still standing in the same spot when Taz pulls in minutes later.

"Was that Mom?" Taz asks the moment she gets out of the SUV.

"Yeah. With Mrs. Myers. I just had to put Charlton down."

"Oh no, what happened?" She puts a hand on my arm and I automatically reach for her, pulling her close. She tilts her head back to look up at me.

"The inevitable. His heart gave up."

She snuggles closer. "She must be devastated. That dog was like a child to her."

"I know. That's why I called your mom."

We stand there for a moment, arms around each other. "Are you done for the day?" she finally asks, stepping out of my hold.

"I have to go back and arrange for Charlton's body to be picked up, and get Jason to help me drop off Mrs. Myers car before I hand off the clinic to him."

"Okay. I'll go finish laundry and start packing the kids' stuff. Why don't you pick up some pizza on your way through town for dinner? We can start loading up some things after we eat."

I tag her behind the neck and press a kiss to her lips. "It's a plan." I watch as she walks away and call her name right before she disappears inside. "Taz?"

"Yeah?" She stops and turns, her eyebrows raised.

"I love you."

Taz

I'M STILL WEARING the same smile when I finish putting clean sheets on the last bed.

This way I won't have to worry about washing them when we get back next week. I'm sure we'll be bringing back enough laundry as it is.

It's funny how easily Rafe and I have settled into our changed relationship. It feels natural: right. Even with the need to watch ourselves around the kids, the significance of those seemingly casual touches, the easy glances, and the frequent warm smiles, sustain me.

Still, I look forward not having to be secretive. It does make me nervous, though. Don't get me wrong, I couldn't care less what people in town might think, but I do care about my family. The kids especially. Rafe wants to talk to them early on in our trip, so we have the whole week to let them get used to the idea. I don't disagree; I'm just worried if they don't react favorably, this whole trip could be ruined.

I hear my phone ringing downstairs and grab the kids' duffel bags before running downstairs. Tossing them toward the front door, I quickly snatch up the phone from the coffee table before it stops ringing.

"Hello?"

"Tomorrow night. Salty's on the river for girls' night," Meredith says without introduction. "Kathleen is on board."

I smile. "I bet she is, but we're leaving tomorrow to go camping, remember?"

"Shit. I forgot. When are you back?"

"Next Saturday. Probably early afternoon."

"Good, we'll make it next Saturday then."

I'm about to protest when it occurs to me I might be ready for a little girl time by then. "It's a plan."

"We're telling the kids this weekend," I blurt out.

"Nervous?" Meredith asks immediately, and I'm reminded how wonderful it is to have friends who seem to get you without explanation. Even Meredith, who I haven't known all that long.

"Honestly? Shitting my pants. Rafe and I; things are pretty good, even though we have to be very careful. If this does not go well, it could seriously complicate things."

I'm not sure what I'm expecting, but it's not Meredith cracking up.

"Oh, my God, you're funny," she finally informs me, still chuckling. "Complicate things? Honey, from what I hear your situation is about as complicated as it's gonna get. Shee-it, girl."

"Kathleen told you about my parents, huh?"

"Sure did, and I gotta tell you, it's not half as bad as I expected it could be. Besides, it sounds like your man did pretty good throwing down for you like that. From what she tells me, he's as close to them as if they were his own. He sure put it all on the line for you."

She's right. As far as my parents go, he stands to lose as much as I do.

"He loves me." I can't stop the smile sounding in my voice.

"I hate to tell you, but that's no secret, honey. I could see it in the way he looked at you the first time I met him. Why do you think I assumed y'all were married? He looks at you the way Andrew does at me when he thinks I don't notice. Like he's still wondering after years how the hell he got so lucky."

"It's soon." I can't help trying to talk myself down from the high her words give me.

"It is what it is. Soon, late, it all depends on how you choose to look at things. Who the hell cares anyway? I meant what I said before, there's something so tragically beautiful in your story. Anyone who can't see the cataclysmic perfection of you two together is not worth your time."

"Thanks, Meredith," I tell her softly, thinking my sister would've appreciated that way of describing our messy lives. "Nicky would've liked you."

There's a brief pause before she responds. "Of course. What's not to like?"

"Next Saturday," I confirm with a grin.

"Pick you up at eight and prepare to get hammered. Andrew is designated driver, he'll come pick our sorry carcasses up."

I've barely hung up the phone when I hear the front

door and the dogs run for it as Rafe walks in, carrying a pizza box.

"Hey, honey," I greet him, taking the box from his hands so he can say hello to the dogs.

In the kitchen I pull off a few sheets of paper towel—not bothering with plates—and grab a few beers from the fridge. I'm washing my hands at the sink when two strong arms slip around me from behind.

"I like that," Rafe rumbles in my neck. "You calling me *honey*."

A charge ripples over my skin as one of his hands comes up under my shirt to cup my breast, and the other slips down the front of my lounge pants. "The kids," I remind him, even as I press back into his body.

"They won't be home for at least another hour. After that I won't be able to do this for a whole week." His fingers stroke leisurely along my folds, as he plucks at my nipple with his other hand.

"Pizza will get cold," I point out, almost breathless with arousal when his thumb finds my clit.

"I'd rather have you hot," he whispers, before laving my neck with his lips and tongue. "And wet," he adds, slipping two digits inside me.

"Rafe…" I whimper helplessly, as he gives me my first orgasm in front of the kitchen sink.

The second with my ass on the counter and his mouth on my pussy. The third with my ass in the air, bent over the kitchen table as he pounds in me from behind.

It takes us ten minutes to collect the various items of clothing Lilo and Stitch have dragged all over the house.

We've finished cleaning up and are about to sit down with cold pizza, when the front door opens.

As usual, Spencer is the first one to come barreling inside with his sister following at a more sedate pace.

"Hey, Daddy, hey, Aunt Taz. Guess what?"

"I give up," I joke, but Spencer's already well into his story about Grandpa giving him his lucky fishing hat to take on our trip.

As Spencer is proudly showing his dad, I notice Mom staying in the hallway, Sofie by her side. "Won't you come in?" I ask, getting up to join her there.

"No, I should get back to your father. I just wanted to wish you a good trip." She watches as I absentmindedly stroke Sofie's braids.

"Thanks, Mom. I'll have my phone, though. Anything happens, call, okay? We'll only be a couple of hours from here."

Her eyes dart over my shoulder and I can sense Rafe closing in. "Lisa also offered to be on standby for whatever you need," he adds, and I see Mom nod.

She seems to swallow hard as she takes us in; Sofie with her back to my front, my arms loosely crossed over her chest, and Rafe behind me, not touching, but close.

Then she nods again, "I will," and walks out the door.

Chapter Twenty-Eight

Rafe

"WHO'S COMING with me to gather wood for tonight's fire?"

"Me!"

I chuckle when, of course, Spencer is the first to raise his hand. We did pick up some firewood on the way, but it's barely enough to last us the first night.

"Daddy, are there snakes here?"

"Pipsqueak, there's snakes everywhere. Even in Eminence. You used to bring me snakes all the time."

"They're gross." She shivers dramatically.

"Why don't you help me get our beds ready, Sofie?" Taz suggests. "No snakes in the tent."

She only hesitates for a moment before she darts inside the tent.

"Looks like it's just you and me, Son."

The campground is basic: remote and private sites, a picnic table and firepit, a central shower building with bathrooms—not much else. But, it has a ton of hiking trails, and it borders a river teeming with trout. Maybe this afternoon we can do some fishing.

I dreamed of trips like this when I was growing up. Imagined parents who could teach me basic survival skills. I'd seen a movie once of a family on a camping trip: the father and mother showing the kids how to make a shelter, build a fire, and catch fish. I was never that lucky, but when I was old enough I taught myself, and was determined to pass it on to any kids of my own.

Sofie had been an adventurous toddler, and Spencer barely a year old, the only time we ever took them camping. What should've been a week ended up being a three-day trip. Nicky had been miserable, Spencer had been cranky, and the only person having fun had been Sofie.

In hindsight, it probably hadn't been a good idea to go camping with a baby and we never tried again, but now—at five—Spencer seems to be soaking it up.

"This one, Dad?"

He holds up a small branch of dead wood.

"That's good kindling to start the fire, Son. Find me more pieces like that."

By the time we head back to the campsite, he has his arms full of branches and I'm dragging an entire dead tree behind me.

"What are you doing?" I ask Sofie, who's standing underneath a tree on the far side of the small clearing, looking up.

"Aunt Taz is tying ropes."

Spencer drops his bundle by the firepit and rushes over to stand beside his sister, peering up into the tree. "Cool! Can I come up, Aunt Taz?"

Sure enough, when I join them and tilt my head back, I can see Taz straddling a thick branch about ten feet up, affixing a rope to the trunk. "You break something you'll ruin the trip, you know that, right?" I call up.

Her response is a wide grin aimed down at me. "I'm not gonna fall. Our Congolese drivers didn't nickname me *Makaku* for nothing."

"What does that mean? *Maka*–whatever," Sofie asks.

Taz loops a second rope around the branch she's sitting on before climbing down with more confidence than I feel. "*Makaku*—monkey," she explains with a smile when she has two feet firmly back on the ground. "Best way to get fresh fruit in the Congo is to get it right from the tree; bananas, mangoes."

"No fruit up there," I point out.

"Nope, but a rope between this tree and that one over there," she points to one about fifteen feet away, "will keep our food safe."

"Why do you have to hang it in a tree?" Spencer asks, and this time it's his sister who answers.

"So the bears and the mountain lions can't get at it. Right, Aunt Taz?"

"Bears?" he looks around with a worried look.

"Don't worry," I quickly reassure him. "They don't like people much, so they tend to stay away unless we leave food lying around. They don't mind an easy meal."

I watch as Taz hands one end of the rope she looped over the branch to Sofie. "Hold on, honey." The other end she ties to the emergency tarp I had in the back of the truck. "Spencer? Do we have more tent pegs? Would you mind grabbing those?"

Eager to help, he runs off to look for them.

"The food would've been safe in the truck," I whisper, sidling up to Taz.

"I know, but where's the fun in that?" she mumbles under her breath, before making her way over to the second tree.

I grin as she loops another coil of rope diagonally across her torso, and easily climbs up.

Grabbing a beer and a chair, I sit down and enjoy watching her show the kids how to build a cover with the large tarp. This is even better than in my childhood dreams.

"You're amazing, you know that?"

The kids are out of earshot, manning the two fishing poles at the edge of the river. It had been a bit of a struggle getting them to wear their life vests, but once they realized there wouldn't be any fishing at all unless they put them on, they quickly complied.

Taz and I are keeping an eye from in the folding chairs we dragged to the water's edge.

She turns her head my way, smiling. "How so?"

Instead of answering I reach for her hand, bring it up to my mouth, and kiss her palm. "You just are."

I smile at her and turn my eyes back to the kids, in time to see Sofie with her back to the water, watching us. Before

I have a chance to react, she throws down her fishing rod and takes off running toward the trees.

"Sofie!"

I shoot out of my chair and hightail it after her, trusting Taz will stay with Spencer.

She's fast, darting through the woods, but with my much longer legs I have no trouble catching up with her. She's crying when I finally hook her around the waist and swing her, struggling, up in my arms. I sit down with her on an overturned log and hold her until the crying subsides into sniffles.

"Sofie…Pipsqueak," I start gently.

"Why?" Her pitiful plea cuts me deep. "Don't you love Mom?"

"I do, and I always will. Your mom gave me the two most precious things in this world. You and your brother."

"Then why—"

"Because I love your aunt, Taz, too," I persist, even though I have no idea how to explain to an eight-year-old the difference. "If I could bring your mother back, believe me, I would in a heartbeat. I realize it's difficult to understand, but as much as we miss your mom, I know she would want us all to be happy. She asked Aunt Taz to come home, so she could spend time with her before she died, but also so your aunt could look after us after Mom was gone."

"I heard you fighting."

I freeze at her softly spoken words. "Fighting?"

"You and Mom."

"When was that?" I'm trying to think back to any particular argument, but realize sadly there were plenty more than one occasion when she could've heard.

Sofie remembers, though. "Right before you started sleeping in the spare bedroom."

Jesus.

Goes to show kids are far more perceptive than you give them credit for. That was almost a year and a half ago, and we thought we were hiding our marital discord so well.

"I'm sorry you heard us fight, baby."

"You were really mad at Mommy."

Fuck me.

I lift Sofie off my lap and set her on her feet between my legs so we're eye to eye. "Listen to me; your mom and I would get mad at each other sometimes, just like you and your brother do from time to time. That doesn't mean you don't love him anymore, right? He'll always be your brother. People get angry—they fight—sometimes over things they can't change. I could get angry with Mom, but I still loved her because she'll always be the mother of my children. That doesn't change, not even now she's gone."

"Are you gonna marry her?"

Sonofabitch.

She's not holding back a thing. I guess I should be grateful for that, but I wish she'd save that question for a next time.

"Probably." I opt for honesty. "There's no rush with that, though."

She nods, staring at the toes of her sneakers, and I wonder what other questions are brewing. She surprises me. "I tried to hate her; Aunt Taz." Her eyes meet mine shyly. "I didn't want her, I wanted Mom—but it didn't work."

"She's hard to hate, much easier to love."

"I know," Sofie whispers.

Taz

THANK God I'm not queasy, although shoving my hand down the throat of that big fish Spencer just pulled out of the water is not my idea of fun.

"Can you feel it?"

My fingers brush the metal. "I can. Give me a sec."

The poor fish is barely flopping on the grass while I try to remove the hook from its gullet. Spencer wants to throw it back, but I'm not so sure it'll survive.

I give a sharp yank in an attempt to dislodge the thing, and wince when I feel it give away. I don't want to think about the damage I may have done.

"Hey, kiddo?"

"Yeah?"

"I don't think our friend here is gonna make it."

Spencer bends down over the now motionless fish and pokes it with a grubby finger. "Can we eat him?"

I bite down a grin at the pragmatic five-year-old. "Sure. It's big enough to feed the four of us." That is, if there are actually gonna be four for dinner.

Spencer had been so distracted by the fish he hooked, he barely noticed his sister running off, Rafe close behind. I tried hard not to think about them while I helped my nephew land his first fish.

"I got a fish!" I hear Spencer yell. When I look up, I see

Rafe and his daughter walking toward us, holding hands. I blow out a relieved breath and keep an anxious eye on Sofie as they approach, but she's focused on the now dead fish her brother can barely lift up.

"Your first fish, that's great, Son," Rafe compliments with a quick wink in my direction.

"We're gonna cook it for dinner."

"I'm gonna have to clean it first," I announce, getting to my feet.

"I can do it."

I grin at Rafe. "Not my first time for that either. You can build a fire while I take care of the fish."

He hands me the hunting knife he carries in the sheath on his belt before he turns to the firepit. The kids decide the fire is more interesting than my scaling of the fish until Sofie sees me gutting it. Thus leads to a brief biology lesson while I clean and wash the trout, both kids listening with rapt attention.

Dinner consists of the corn we picked up at a road stand on our way here, a few baking potatoes we'd brought from home, and Spencer's fish.

"Why does it taste so much better?" Sofie asks, taking another bite from the large cob.

"Nothing beats food cooked over a wood fire," I tell her. "Wait until we make bacon and pancakes tomorrow morning."

"Can I help?" she asks, and I have to swallow a lump in my throat before I can answer.

"Absolutely."

"Hey, Son?"

I'm not sure whether Rafe was waiting to gauge his

daughter's reaction to me, but the moment I hear him call on Spencer, I know what he's going to say.

"Yeah, Dad?"

"Your aunt, Taz, and I...well, we really like each other," he says clumsily, and I almost laugh.

"I know," Spencer says matter-of-factly, shoving another bite of his trout in his mouth.

Rafe tries again. "What I mean is, we're a couple. We—"

"What your dad is trying to say," I jump in, trying to clarify, "is that—"

"They're gonna get married," Sofie announces, surprising the hell out of me.

Shocked, I look over at Rafe, who merely shrugs.

"I know that," he tells his sister agitatedly. "They practice all the time. Kissing and stuff."

My mouth drops open as their father throws his head back and bursts out laughing. I glance over at Sofie, who is watching her father closely, the hint of a smile on her lips.

"The only thing I don't know," Spencer adds. "Is Auntie Taz still our auntie?"

That sobers the mood and I quickly grapple for an answer.

"That won't change, buddy. My sister will always be your mom, so that makes me your aunt."

"It'll be weird, though," Sofie points out. "If you and Dad are together and we still call you Auntie."

"I see what you mean," I agree.

"What if you just call her Taz?" Rafe suggests. "Leave off the Auntie. Unless you have a better idea?" He looks at me and I shake my head.

Sofie startles me with a soft snicker. "We can always call you *Makaku*."

Spencer finds his sister's idea hilarious, and the two dissolve in giggles while their father and I smile at each other over their heads.

It's all going to work out.

Chapter Twenty-Nine

Taz

"Auntie...I mean Taz?"

"Yes, honey?"

"Do you think Mom sees us?"

I turn my head and glance at Sofie's profile.

We're lying on a blanket by the waterside, staring up at the endless stars above. Spencer is already sleeping in the tent and Rafe is having a beer by the fire, the dogs sleeping at his feet.

"I'd like to think so. I would imagine she's always around, so she can see you and your brother grow up."

I turn back to the stars and a silence stretches between us, but not uncomfortably so.

"Would she be mad?"

"Because of your dad and me? I don't think so, Sofie. Your mom and I talked quite a bit before she died." I hesitate, trying to figure out the best way to word this without going into details that shouldn't be shared with an eight-year-old. "Sweetheart, she asked me to look after you and your brother, and I'd like to think maybe she was hoping this might happen."

She doesn't respond immediately, and I sneak a glance to find her still staring up into the night sky.

"Daddy says he loves you."

"I love him too."

"He says he also loves Mom."

"As do I. That never goes away."

"Isn't that kinda weird?"

I try to keep my face impassive, even though I want to smile. That question makes my niece sound like a typical preteen. "Nope. I don't think there's a limit to how many people we can love." I sense Sofie's eyes on me and turn to face her. "Your heart doesn't run out of space, honey. It has endless room for love."

She looks at me with sad eyes before returning her focus to the stars above, and I do the same.

"Do you think she's lonely?"

Her tremulous little voice has me reach over to find her hand, and I curl my fingers around it. "How could she be? She has all of us."

Not much later Sofie announces the bugs are getting bad, and I walk with her to the bathrooms so she can brush her teeth and do her business before turning in.

"Night, Daddy." She bends down to kiss Rafe good-night, but he pulls her down on his lap, hugging her tight.

"I'll tuck you in," he rumbles before setting her back on her feet and walking her to the tent.

"Stay," I order Lilo and Stitch, who grudgingly lie back down, but in no time are back asleep.

It's been a busy day for the pups, first sniffing and exploring the campsite, and after that decimating a large tree branch they'd pulled from the underbrush. Neither of them seems inclined to wander too far away, which is a relief.

Sitting down by the fire, I toss another log on when I hear Sofie's voice from behind me.

"Night, Taz."

I twist my neck and see her head poking out of the tent. "Night, honey. Sleep sweet."

Bullfrogs strike up a chorus by the water's edge, blending with the buzz of the cicadas, and the soft hum of voices in the tent. It's oddly peaceful and I breathe in deep, filling my lungs with fresh air and a whiff of woodsmoke. The perfect way to end an eventful day.

I'm well aware it could've ended much differently. Having Sofie open up to me earlier was an unexpected gift. If there was ever a time I could feel Nicky's presence it was then, under the millions of stars dotting the night sky.

Staring into the flames, I'm lost in thought and don't notice Rafe walking up until a warm hand slides under my dreads, giving my neck a squeeze.

"I'm grabbing another beer. Want some wine?"

"I'll have a beer too."

Rafe leans over me and I tilt my head back for the kiss I know is coming. It's short but sweet and ends sooner than I'd like. It doesn't take long before he's back, pressing a bottle in my hands and taking the seat beside me, propping his feet up on the edge of the firepit.

"Thank you," he mumbles, reaching over to take my hand in his.

"For what?"

"I heard you and Sofie talking. You managed to find the exact right things to say to her. I know it's short-sighted to think there won't be snags along the way, but she's in a better place than I expected her to be."

"Spencer was a bit of a surprise, wasn't he?" I share with a grin. I'm sure the easy acceptance by the little boy went a long way to making his sister more receptive to the idea of her father and me together.

"Life should be pretty simple at five. Sleep, eat, play, and as long as the people you care about are happy, you are too." There's a wistful tone to his words.

"How old were you when you ended up in the foster system?"

"A toddler. I don't really remember anything from before. Apparently my mother overdosed on heroin, and I was found wandering around the parking lot of a seedy motel in nothing more than a dirty diaper."

I tighten my grip on his hand. "Did you ever try to find out more? Maybe find your father?"

"Nothing to discover. My mother is still listed as a Jane Doe: no papers, no name, and no record of my birth anywhere. I didn't have a name."

"Who gave you one?" I look at his profile, lit by the flames, showing the dark shadows and deep angles of his handsome features.

"I have no idea. I'm guessing someone with CPS where I ended up."

I didn't think there was more for me to discover about

Rafe, and although he may not seem to know much about his own background, it goes a long way to explaining the choices he made.

"You're amazing," I echo his words to me from earlier today.

He turns to me, his clear blue eyes smiling. "You're stealing my line."

"Nah, it fits you better," I tell him. "I was blessed with a family to grow up in—a place I belonged—and only now am I learning to appreciate that. But you…you didn't have any of that. You had to claim yourself a place in this world —create a family to belong to—and you did that without any guidance. That's amazing."

Other than the tight grip of his hand on mine he has no response, but it's enough to put a smile on my face as I stare into the dying fire.

I'm not sure how long we sit there, but eventually we get up, tidy up the campsite and toss sand on the fire. We crawl into the tent, only to find the kids huddled together in the center, leaving room on either side of them. The dogs go into their crate we set up at the foot end without coaxing and curl up together.

When I've settled into my sleeping bag next to Sofie, I turn on my side to find Rafe propped up on an elbow. His eyes drift over the sleeping forms of his children before they find mine.

"I'm blessed," he whispers.

Rafe

. . .

"It's cold!"

I glance over to where Spencer just joined Taz and Sofie in the water. The dogs are barking excitedly, neither getting more than their paws wet.

Both kids are wearing life vests, regardless of their complaints. They may be fine swimming in a pool, but the river, with its unpredictable currents, is another story.

We're all sporting a tan after a week with near perfect weather. A week that's gone by much too soon. I'm going to miss the easy routine we've fallen into. It didn't take Taz long to coax the kids into the water, despite Sofie's fears of creatures touching her under the surface. Every morning while I built a fire to make coffee and cook breakfast, the three of them would splash around in the river until it was time to eat.

We'd spend most mornings exploring the many trails, and on two occasions drove into Potosi to replenish our supplies. The afternoons we generally lazed around the campsite, and even with the leisurely pace of our days, we inevitably ended up in bed early.

The plan for today is to have a good breakfast, clean up, pack up, and head home. Sadly. Back to the daily grind. I've already decided that next year we'll do two weeks.

"Five minutes, guys!"

"Okay!" Taz calls back.

I turn the bacon and flip the pancakes as Stitch trots up, drawn by the smell of food. "No bacon for you, bud. You've had your breakfast." Not deterred, he flops down on his belly, his head resting on his front paws as he follows every move closely. Waiting for something to drop.

Sofie is the first out of the water, which is perfect, because there's something I've been meaning to talk to her about.

"Almost ready?" she asks, dropping her soaked life vest on the ground.

"Yes, hang that on the tree to dry, will you? And grab the orange juice from the cooler on your way back, please."

Even though she grumbles under her breath, she does as I ask before sitting down at the picnic table. She's had some moments this past week, but nothing more than an occasional sharp look or roll of the eyes when she caught Taz and I touching. We've been careful with public displays of affection, but I've held her hand on hikes, and occasionally kissed the top of her head, much like I do with the kids.

"I wanted to ask you something," I start, my back to her as I pour more batter into the pan, trying to be as casual as I can. "How would you like having a bathroom of your own?" When I turn to look I see her eyes have gone big.

"Really? Like…how? Are we moving?"

"No. We're not moving. We're thinking of making some changes upstairs. Starting with you maybe moving into the master bedroom. We could look at painting it a different color; maybe get new curtains. And the best part is, it comes with the big bed."

"Can I have sleepovers?" she asks immediately, and I bite off a grin.

"Sure, every now and then, but you'll have to wait until the work is finished."

"Are you going to sleep in my old room?"

I note she's already calling it her 'old' room, which I guess means she's on board with the plan. So far.

"Actually, that's the next part. I want to turn your room and the spare bedroom into one bigger bedroom with a bathroom for Taz and me."

She seems to ponder on that while I flip the last pancakes. "But what happens if you guys have a baby? Where is it gonna go?"

I almost drop the spatula from my hand. I hadn't even considered that possibility.

"We're having a baby?" Spencer asks, as he too drops his life vest in a puddle on the ground.

From the corner of my eye I see Taz—who was coming up right behind him—freezing on the spot. "There's no baby," I inform my son, and by default Taz, "but if you pick up that life vest and hang it to dry the way you know you're supposed to, I'll fill you in on what your sister and I were talking about."

I note Taz keeps glancing at Sofie, as I catch both her and Spencer up on the conversation. Of course my son loses interest the moment I set his breakfast in front of him, but I seem to have Taz's attention.

"So what about the baby?" Sofie persists.

It would appear my girl has got her jaws in something and is shaking it like the little terrier she can be.

"Honey, there's no baby," Taz tries.

"But what if there is? Lisa Brinkman is in my class and her mom just had another baby."

Great. Now she's glommed on to the idea of a little brother or sister.

"Let's stick with the four of us for now, okay?" I

suggest, hoping that ends the topic, but my daughter clearly isn't done yet.

"I'm just saying…"

"Enough, Sofie."

It's not until after we finish breakfast, clean up, and send the kids to pack the toys in their backpacks, that I get Taz alone for a minute.

"Do you get the sense her head has been busy this past week?"

She snorts as I take the folding chairs from her and fit them in the back of the truck. "So I gather. I'm not sure if that makes me happy or concerned."

"How's that?" I ask, taking the cooler she hands me.

"Well, I guess it's good she's thinking of us as a family, but she may be creating expectations we can't live up to."

That statement gives me pause. "You're saying you don't want children? More children," I correct myself, jumping down from the truck bed.

"I didn't say that. I mean, you have two beautiful kids, I assumed…"

I grab her lightly by the shoulders and lean down so I'm eye to eye. "Don't assume. Just because I haven't really had a chance to think about more children doesn't mean I wouldn't want them. Tell me what you're thinking."

She grabs on to my wrists with her hands and takes in a deep breath. "I might…some day."

"Some day?" I tease, grinning at her responding eye roll.

"Yeah," she taunts me right back. "If I find the right guy."

She squeals when I bend down and put my shoulder in

her stomach, lifting her off her feet. The dogs start jumping up and barking as I carry her toward the water.

"Rafe! Set me down!"

"What are you doing?" Sofie wants to know. Alerted by the dogs, she and her brother come crawling out of the tent when I march past.

"I think Taz needs another dip. The heat's already gone to her head."

The kids giggle and follow behind me while Taz continues to struggle against my hold.

"I just put on dry clothes, don't you dare, Rafe Thomas!"

I stop right at the river's edge.

"Give me a good reason not to toss you in, Natasha Boran."

"All right, all right—I already have the right guy."

I slowly let her slide down my front until her feet touch the ground, but I don't let go of her. "And?"

Her indignant huff only makes me chuckle, and she finally gives in. "And I love you."

"A good start, but not what I'm after."

She bulges her eyes at me before darting a glance at the kids, who are following our interaction closely.

"And…the rest is up for discussion."

I grin down at her before planting a quick hard kiss on her lips.

"Ewww," comes from the peanut gallery.

Chapter Thirty

Taz

"Jesus. I need another drink."

Kathleen wipes her eyes with her cocktail napkin.

"Do us another round, yeah," Meredith instructs the waitress, who's been keeping an eye on our table with no small amount of interest. I can't blame her; three teary-eyed women sniffling in their drinks in the middle of a bar draw attention.

I just finished telling them about my talk with Sofie under the stars.

"I don't want to get hammered," I warn Meredith, who waves me off.

"Told you, Andrew is picking us up."

"Yeah," Kathleen pipes up. "Besides, last time we got sloshed together was about ten years ago; the night before you took off for Africa. Except then it was to drown your misery. Now we're celebrating, so drink up."

I remember that night. I'd been staying with Kathleen in an attempt to avoid everyone after Mom walked in on Rafe and me in the kitchen. I'd been so hurt—felt so betrayed—I was licking my wounds.

Tonight is much different. I know I'll be going home to Rafe and that makes all the difference.

"Can I remind you, I spent a week with a very hot guy in a tent, separated by two kids?"

"Ahhh," Meredith is the first to clue in. "Someone's hoping for some nookie tonight."

"Now I really need that drink. Where the hell is that waitress?" Kathleen grumbles, looking toward the bar. "I could do without you putting images of Rafe Thomas—naked—in my head, thank you very much."

Meredith snickers and I join in.

"Just to say, there's worse things to visualize than Rafe naked," I point out.

"Agreed," Meredith adds, her eyes sparkling with humor. "Shit, I wouldn't say no to a picture, should you be willing to share some-a-that."

Kathleen shoves her fingers in her ears. "La-la-la-la-la, I can't hear you."

I elbow her sharply. "Stop that. How long are you gonna keep him in the doghouse?"

"Until I know for sure he's not gonna fuck up again."

"He won't," I assure her. "And neither will I. I'm happy, Kathleen. Really happy. Can you be happy *for* me?"

"I am. I'm cautiously happy for you."

"Whatever," Meredith flaps her hand, "I still think your story is like a bittersweet fairy tale with a very happy ending. The only thing that would make it better is if you guys had a baby."

When I don't react, both girls turn their eyes on me.

"Christ, tell me you're not preggers," Kathleen says far too loud, as the waitress walks up with our drinks. "Did you have to press the grapes yourself?" she grumbles, as our wine glasses are set in front of us.

"Don't mind her," I tell the waitress, making a mental note to tip her generously later.

From the corner of my eye I see the very unwelcome figure of Sheila slink by, curiosity plain on her face as she peers over on her way to the ladies' room. *Fuck*. With my luck she overheard our conversation, which would mean more food for the Eminence gossip mill to grind.

I turn back to the table. "For the record; no, I'm not pregnant." Too bad the gossip queen is out of hearing, but I can at least set my friends straight. Kathleen dramatically pats her forehead with the napkin she still has in her hand. "For now," I tease, chuckling as I see her eyes go big.

Still grinning, I tell them about Sofie's reaction to the proposed renovations this morning, and the resulting exchanges.

"The kid makes a good point. You don't want to spend money knocking down walls and reconfiguring your bedrooms now, only to have to do it again when you get pregnant. That would be stupid," Meredith lays out.

"I know. That's what Rafe's doing tonight; tweaking the design he sketched."

"That boy is not wasting any time," Kathleen mutters, right before she takes a swig of her wine.

"The way I see it," Meredith responds soberly, "too much has been wasted already."

"Good point."

The moment the words leave my mouth, Meredith pulls out her phone and taps the screen. "Andrew? Can you come get us?"

"Already?" Kathleen whines when she ends the call. "I'm just getting my buzz on."

Meredith leans over and puts a hand on her arm. "You have another ten minutes before he gets here; make good use of it." I'm smiling when she turns to me. "Our girl needs to get laid."

Kathleen whimpers, "Jesus, have mercy," and tosses back her drink.

"You're early."

Rafe sets me back after welcoming me with a long, deliciously wet kiss.

"Meredith insists I get laid."

He chuckles, grabbing my hips to tug me closer. "Are you drunk?"

"I didn't get a chance," I pout, making him laugh harder. "I wanted to, especially after Sheila showed her face at the bar."

Rafe's expression immediately turns serious. "Did she give you any trouble?"

"No, not necessarily," I admit, "but that doesn't mean she won't."

"What do you mean?"

"Well," I drawl, a little hesitant to broach that subject, "she may have overheard us talking."

"About?"

"Just girl talk, you know? Meredith said something about a baby making our story even more of a fairy tale. Then Kathleen overreacted and asked if I was pregnant. Loudly."

The arms around me tighten. "And?"

"And judging by the way Sheila eyed me, I'd guess she heard that."

"You're not, though."

"No. I'm not."

"So what's the problem?"

I let out a deep sigh. "Mom and Dad are going to church in the morning. We're supposed to have dinner over there tomorrow."

Mom's call this afternoon to invite us had been a surprise. A pleasant one. The conversation was a little stilted, but I figure it will take more time for us to find a new normal. Regardless, I'm happy for the conciliatory gesture. Except if Sheila's gonna stir the pot again, which I have no doubt she will, it means more fireworks at dinner. I'm about done with all the upheaval.

"I see," Rafe acknowledges. "I'll take care of it. Now," a lecherous grin spreads on his face, "I believe you mentioned something about getting laid?"

My body instantly responds, tingling in all the right places. I roll my hips against his, my belly brushing his already hard cock pushing against his fly.

"The kids?"

"Asleep about five minutes after I put them to bed."

"Mmm…" I hum, smirking as I look up into his indigo eyes, dark with lust. "I think I'm gonna head upstairs, get ready for bed."

"Be up as soon as I take care of the dogs. Don't you dare fall asleep on me." To emphasize his words he lays a long, heated kiss on me before letting me go.

I run upstairs, two at a time, heading straight for the bathroom to freshen up. I wish I had something sexy to wear; a flimsy nightie or some lace underwear, but sadly all I own is plain cotton. Functional, but not exactly high on appeal. In the end, I slip between the sheets stark naked. My skin is the sexiest thing I own.

When I hear him coming up the stairs, I roll over on my side, my back to the door, and pretend to be asleep. The door opens and I'm having a hard time trying to stay still as I hear a very quiet, but definitely heartfelt, "*Fuck.*"

I tense with the rustle of clothes and the clink of a belt buckle hitting the floor, and I stop breathing when I feel the mattress dip with his weight.

"A little tip," his deep voice suddenly sounds right by my ear, as a hand slides over my hip and down between my legs, where he finds me wet already. "Don't rub your thighs together when you pretend to be asleep."

Grinning, I turn around and lift my leg over his hips, happy to discover he's not wearing a stitch either. "I'll make note of that," I whisper, pushing up so I'm straddling him.

His hands slide from my hips up to cup my breasts. "Although I'm not complaining about all this skin. You're so fucking beautiful."

I brace myself on his chest, lean down, and kiss him. As I rock my hips against him, I slick his length with the wetness between my legs, and catch his growl down my throat.

"You're killing me, Sweets," he groans, ripping his mouth from mine as his fingers press into my waist. "Ride me."

"Yippy-ki-yay," I whisper before filling myself with his cock.

Rafe

THE MOMENT we walk into the house, I can tell word has gotten around Eminence.

Ed seems uneasy as he lets us in and Sarah is banging pots and pans around in the kitchen.

"Sarah! The kids are here," he yells, as Spencer attaches himself to his leg.

"I can hear that, Ed," comes her snippy reply. I look over to find Taz's wide eyes on mine.

"Grandma!" My son lets go of his grandfather and barrels toward the kitchen.

"Hey, my beautiful boy," I hear her coo. "Did you have a good time?"

Spencer doesn't let an invitation to talk go by, and happily launches into a play-by-play of the past week. Sofie wanders into the kitchen as well.

"Wanna pour us a drink, Rafe? Beer for me." Ed sinks

down in his easy chair, patting the armrest of the couch beside him. "Come sit by me, Baby Girl."

"Beer for me too. How are you doing, Dad? Been feeling okay?" Taz asks, taking her father's hand in hers.

"Hanging in. Getting a little nervous about the surgery."

I leave them talking and slip into the kitchen where I find Sarah examining the single dread Sofie asked Taz to twist in her hair a few days ago.

"You're okay with this?" she asks me sharply.

"I am. Sofie asked for it, and I told her she could have one small one."

"My hair is too short," Spencer volunteers. He'd wanted a dreadlock as well.

"Anyway…" I lean down and kiss Sarah's cheek, "… hello to you, Mom. I'm getting drinks, can I get you one?"

At least she looks duly chastised. "Yes, please. I'll have my port."

I pour her drink first, setting her glass next to the stove where she is lifting a lid from the Dutch oven. Then I pull three beers from the fridge and hand one each to the kids. "Can you drop these off for Grandpa and Taz, please? I'll be right in. Try not to spill." I wait until the kids are gone before stepping up beside Sarah, putting my arm around her tense shoulders as I peek into the pan. My mouth waters when I recognize her braised pork chops and onions.

"Kids seem to have had a good time," she says stiffly.

"We all did. It was a great week."

She grunts in response. I let go and turn, leaning my butt against the counter, and crossing my arms over my chest.

"We're not pregnant." Her eyes dart my way. "We're not having a baby. Yet."

"Jesus, Rafe," Taz snaps from the doorway. "That's how you're taking care of it?" She grabs a roll of paper towel from the counter and turns to Sarah. "Mom, I know the gossip mill must've been buzzing, seeing as Sheila seemed very interested in our girls' night out at Salty's yesterday, but please don't believe everything she says."

"I'm not ready for that," Sarah mumbles, her voice wobbling.

Taz shoves the paper towels at me. "Spencer spilled some beer in the living room."

"Got it." I take the roll and head out of the kitchen, knowing when I've been dismissed. A quick glance back shows Taz slipping her arm around her mother's shoulders.

"Everything okay in there?" Ed asks when I bend down to mop up the spill.

"It's all good." I throw him a quick smile before asking, "Where are the kids?"

"I wasn't sure if you wanted them within earshot, so told them they could watch TV in our bedroom."

"That's fine, Dad. Thanks. But there's nothing for them to hear; you're not going to be a grandfather again for a while yet. One step at a time, yeah?"

"That woman oughta have her lips stapled together," he grumbles, shaking his head.

"Don't tempt me," I warn him on a chuckle. "If Sheila Quinn doesn't have shit to stir, she creates some."

I take the wet towels into the kitchen to find Taz and her mom in much the same position, talking softly. When I toss them in the garbage, she winks at me over her mom's shoulder and I quickly make myself scarce again.

Dad seems pensive when I sit down on the couch and take a swig of my beer.

"You know…" His eyes sparkle when he turns them on me. "…I can't figure out whether to be glad or disappointed."

Chapter Thirty-One

Taz

"How is Mrs. Myers?" I ask Mom when she walks through the back door.

The past few weeks have been a little crazy driving back and forth to Springfield for Dad's surgery and the follow-up procedures, and getting the kids ready to go back to school. Poor Rafe's birthday got lost in the shuffle, so we're having a do-over today.

Mom and I have spent a lot of time in each other's company since the non-pregnancy debacle. The long hours at the hospital, waiting for news on Dad, allowed for some good talks that went a long way to bettering our relationship. It's still a work in progress, but I think we each have a better understanding of the other. Of our inherent differences at the root of all our past problems.

I've come to the conclusion, had I not left all those years ago, we likely would've worked those issues out along the way. We've covered a lot of ground these past few weeks, most of it by simply spending time in each other's company.

Today Rafe is scheduled to be out all day doing his quarterly visits, courtesy of Lisa. I enlisted her help to make sure he'd be gone. The new leather sectional the kids and I picked out for the living room is scheduled to be delivered around noon, and I want to have it set up before he comes home. The thing is big enough to seat all of us comfortably, and then some. It may be a weird birthday gift, but as Sofie pointed out with her eight-year-old wisdom, her dad would like nothing better than to be able to snuggle up with all of us at once.

She's right.

"Happy as a clam with her new cat," Mom answers, tying on her apron and unloading the rest of the contents of the tote bag she brought in. "That was nice thing for Rafe to do."

The family who owned the young cat discovered their daughter was allergic and had asked Rafe if he knew anyone who'd want to adopt it. He thought of Mrs. Myers.

"It was," I confirm. "A cat is probably a better fit for her than a dog."

"Let's hope she doesn't send it to an early grave as well," Mom grumbles. "She was letting it lick butter off a plate when I got there this morning."

"Rafe says cats are more likely to stop eating when they're full." I start putting ingredients on the counter while I wait for the fresh pot of coffee to brew.

"Fingers crossed," she says, while greasing the cake pans she brought. "Kids off to school okay?"

"Yup. They both love their new teachers and are eager to go. It's funny, I remember hating school at Sofie's age. Nicky used to love school too."

"You just had trouble sitting still," Mom says, smiling wistfully. "You were always more interested in learning through exploration than from books."

We work in silence for a while, surprisingly in sync as we put together the batter for Rafe's favorite; Black Forest cake. When Mom slides the pans in the oven, I pour us a coffee.

"Dad still doing okay?" I ask when we sit down at the kitchen table while waiting for the cakes to bake.

"He is. I still can't quite believe that since the last appointment this past week, he hardly has any tremor left. He certainly walks a lot steadier. According to him, his mind is less muddled too, although I suspect that may be wishful thinking. It's not like his mind was ever that clear."

I chuckle along with her, amazed and thrilled with the easy camaraderie we've developed. I never would've thought Mom and I could be like this. I still catch her observing when Rafe and I are in the room, but I figure she needs time to adjust to the idea of us together. We, in turn, try to be respectful in the way we interact. I'm sure it'll take my parents a little longer to adjust than it did the kids.

"Did I hear him mention something about the Florida Keys the other day in the doctor's office?"

Mom rolls her eyes. "Now that he's doing better, he's determined to drive the RV down right after Christmas and spend the winter down there."

I smile at her. "So he's not done traveling yet after all. Are you okay with that?"

"Considering his first choice was Alaska during that same time period, I'd say absolutely. I'd rather be roasting on a beach somewhere than get frostbite traipsing through the wilderness."

The doorbell rings just as Mom pulls the pans from the oven, and I run to open the front door to the delivery guys.

After the kids left on the bus and Rafe drove off, Lisa helped me move the old couch out. Good thing both of us have decent upper body strength, because that thing was heavy. It's out behind the garage for now, until we can haul it to the dump. Lisa ended up taking Lilo and Stitch over to the clinic for the day, so they wouldn't be underfoot, and I pushed the other furniture out of the way to make room.

"Looks good," Mom says, admiring the couch as I close the front door. "I'm sure Rafe will love it."

I sit down, running my hands over the tan leather. "Come try it," I encourage Mom, who sinks down beside me.

"Comfy."

"Right?"

"It's big," she notes.

"I know. It'll fit us all."

I'm surprised when she blindly grabs my hand, her eyes staring off in the distance.

"With room to grow," she says softly.

MOM and I have finished putting together some appetizers when I hear Rafe's truck door slam shut. The kids are already opening the front door by the time I come out of the kitchen.

"Happy birthday, Daddy!" Spencer yells at his customary volume and latches himself onto one of Rafe's long legs. Sofie takes up the other side with her arms wrapping around his hips.

"I already had my birthday, guys," he corrects them, somewhat bemused. His eyes find me, before drifting over my shoulder into the living room, taking in the balloons and streamers the kids helped us put up after school.

"We got you a new couch," Sofie shares and he glances down, stroking a hand over her hair.

"I see that, Pipsqueak."

His eyes come back to me as he untangles himself from the kids and steps up to me, wrapping an arm around the small of my back, tugging me close.

"Happy birthday," I barely get the words out, as his mouth is already closing over mine.

His kiss has my bare toes curl on the cool hardwood under my feet, and is barely appropriate in front of the kids. When he lifts his head I'm almost swaying on my feet. "Thank you, Sweets," he mumbles, and I have to grab on to his shoulders for stability.

A soft chuckle belonging to my dad behind me slams me crudely back to earth.

Fuck—my parents. So much for being careful.

However, when I turn, Dad is wearing a grin, but it's my Mom's soft eyes that hit me.

Rafe

To say I was surprised when I walked in the door would be an understatement.

Not only had my birthday already passed, but I never really considered it a big deal, simply another year older.

I've certainly never had anyone go to this kind of trouble before. Of course, we've always made sure the kids' birthdays were special, but adult birthdays were usually just marked with a card, a cake, and maybe a small gift. Taz definitely raised the bar this year.

I don't doubt this is all her doing, and I'm moved at her efforts to make it special. What's even better is she managed to involve everyone, including her mother.

I'd been even more surprised when Meredith and Andrew, Brent and Kathleen with the kids, and even Lisa and her partner, Beth, showed up fifteen minutes later.

Dinner had been served buffet style, with bodies all over the house and yard. All to the great delight of Lilo and Stitch, who were in constant motion looking for attention or spilled food.

"What's this I hear from Kathleen, you're thinking of renovating the upstairs?" Brent asks, when we're having coffee and cake.

I wince when I see Ed's head snap up. Shit. I haven't had a chance to inform my in-laws of my plans yet. It was their house for decades before I bought it, and I would've liked to have broached the subject with a little more care.

"Thinking about it," I confirm. "Just playing around with the layout."

"Got something to show us?" Ed pipes up, and I scrutinize him for any disapproval, but all I see is curiosity.

"I'll grab the sketch," Taz says from behind me, putting her cool hand to my neck.

I showed her my new plans a few days ago. I turn to watch her walk from the kitchen and catch Sarah's eyes, who's standing by the sink and clearly overheard the exchange. She seems to catch herself and busies herself refilling coffee cups.

A few minutes later, all of us are bent over the rough drawings Taz put in the middle of the dining table.

"Of course I'll get an architect to see if this is even feasible and do up a proper plan," I offer apologetically, "but this is the gist of it."

"I like it," Brent announces, looking at the original layout versus the proposed one. "It's a more economic use of space. Other than the plumbing that needs to be relayed —which is a good-sized job—it's a matter of relocating walls and doors to end up with the same number of bedrooms but an additional bathroom."

"When do you want to start the work?" Ed asks.

"I would first have to get drawings done, get some quotes for the work. I don't think it'll be before the winter."

"Do you need it?" The question comes from Sarah who has been looking over her husband's shoulder. "The extra bathroom, I mean? It seems like a lot of money you'll have to fork out to end up with the exact same number of bedrooms." She pulls the sketch toward her and points. "If you wanted to do something new with the master suite, all you have to do is move the wall of the walk-in closet farther into the room so it has an extra window. If you add a door straight out to the landing, it could be a home office, or at some point a perfect nursery."

I feel Taz's fingers dig into my shoulder, and I'm pretty shocked myself.

"And you'd still have an extra bedroom to fill," Kathleen adds, grinning ear to ear.

"Sounds like common sense to me," Andrew volunteers, as he cuts off another piece of cake, ignoring Meredith's hissed, *"Andrew!"*

"Except, Sofie's already been promised her own bathroom." Taz's soft reminder draws my attention to my daughter, who I hadn't noticed coming in from outside.

It warms my heart when Sofie smiles at Taz brightly before sharing, "I'd rather have a baby sister than a bathroom."

"Brother!" Spencer, who heard his sister, argues.

"Sister," Sofie insists. "'Cause I don't wanna share a bathroom with *two* stinky brothers."

Before the two continue their bickering, Sarah intervenes. "If Andrew doesn't mind sharing; anyone else for another piece of cake?"

Taz and Kathleen dissolve in giggles as Meredith elbows her husband in the ribs, causing him to blurt out, "Ouch! What the hell'd'ya do that for?"

"SO WHAT DO YOU THINK?"

It's long after everyone's left and both the kids and the dogs are asleep. Taz is tucked to my side on my kickass new couch and we're watching the last hour of *Live PD*.

I immediately know what she's referring to.

"I should ask you that question."

"Mom's suggestion makes sense."

"It does," I confirm.

"But even if it didn't," Taz continues, "the mere fact she suggested it, makes me think that's exactly what we should do."

"Are you sure?"

"Positive."

I bend down and kiss her softly, grabbing a handful of her dreadlocks to hold her head in place when I pull back. I touch my forehead to hers.

"I don't think of the years behind us as time wasted anymore, it only makes me appreciate what I'm building with you even more. I could not in my wildest dreams have imagined it could get this good. You make my life beautiful, Natasha."

Epilogue

December

Rafe

"SO…MRS. THOMAS."

I grin as I drag my mouth down over the soft swell of her belly, her skin pebbling into goosebumps.

"Yes, Mr. Thomas," she returns in a breathless voice, as I hook my fingers under the elastic of her pretty lace panties. Taz's wedding gift to me, which I'm only now getting to unwrap.

She's wearing my wedding gift in her dreadlocks, spread out over the pillow. Tiny, shimmering, colorful gemstones I had a jewelry designer in Springfield rush order from the Congo and set in small, platinum clips to fasten around the tight twists in her hair. Ten in total: one for every year I've loved her. I intend to add one for every year to follow.

She took my breath away; the hair charms matching the retro-style silk turquoise dress, with large dark pink tropical flowers and leaves she was wearing. When Sarah started crying as Taz came down the stairs this afternoon, looking absolutely stunning, I clued in to the significance of that dress. I'd seen glimpses of it over the years, packed away with Nicky's wedding dress in our closet.

The beautiful way she managed to include her sister in our wedding is a testament to the person she is. Something I know her parents, Sarah in particular, has come to recognize these past months.

Taz still grieves the loss of her sister at times. We all do. But along with the grief, our love for Nicky has become something we all share. The kids talk about her freely, as do the rest of us, making her still very much a part of our lives, and as Taz made clear today, of our futures.

I think Nicky would be happy for us today.

I asked Taz to marry me a little over eight weeks ago, right after we christened our brand-new master suite. I'd had the simple diamond solitaire ring a lot longer, but out of respect to her, her parents, and her sister, wanted to wait a full six months after Nicky's passing. The first night we spent in our new bedroom seemed like the appropriate time.

We both agreed we'd be happiest with a small ceremony, with only our family and good friends in attendance. The only exception had been Mrs. Myers, who Taz had taken under her wing; despite the less than friendly reception the woman had given my wife when she first returned to Eminence.

Taz truly has a heart without limitations. Occasionally I'll catch her mumbling, *"bonus kiss,"* as she presses her lips to the old woman's cheek, something she usually reserves for the kids, her parents, and for me.

She is teaching me to make every moment count, not to focus too much on a future so we don't forget to appreciate what we have today, and my life is better for it.

"I like your gift for me," I mumble, my lips pressing right above her neatly trimmed pubic hair.

"That was just the wrapping," she says, emotion heavy in her voice. "But you're getting warm." I lift my eyes to find her looking down at me, her eyes filling with tears. "It's still tiny, about the size of a raspberry."

I push up and scramble to my knees, placing my hands on either side as I lean over her. "No way," I manage, my voice cracking.

The smile she gives me is blinding. "Oh yeah. Eight weeks as of yesterday."

My mind is trying to catch up. "What about the Depo injection?"

"That only lasts so long. I honestly didn't think about it with everything we had going on. Are you upset?" A note of apprehension creeps in her voice.

"Are you nuts?" I crawl back down her body and cover her belly with kisses, mumbling, *"Fuck me,"* to myself.

She giggles through her tears.

"You did that already, thoroughly, about eight weeks ago."

August

Taz

"MAMA TAZ? Can I put her to bed?"

Mom and Dad came over with dinner, something they've been doing quite a bit since the little one was born two months ago.

They'd both been here when I delivered our daughter in the master bedroom upstairs, in the care of a pair of wonderful midwives. That was my choice.

I've been able to see firsthand the difference between a clinical birth in a hospital, and the many natural births I attended in Africa. Although often living under less than optimal circumstances, one thing most of the mothers delivering at home had in common: being in control of their own delivery, and surrounded by supportive families, seemed to be an empowering experience.

I was adamant, but Rafe had taken some convincing. My parents had been mortified, and objected loudly, but were quick to change their tune when after only six hours of labor, Veronica April Thomas was born. Both cried when Rafe introduced her, and they stayed for an entire week after, sleeping in the spare bedroom.

It was a wonderful week with Mom and Dad running the household, giving Rafe and me lots of time to get acquainted with our new daughter.

"How about we do it together?" I tell Sofie.

She's wonderful with the baby, but I'm not comfortable

letting her carry her sister up to the nursery alone yet. She's had a lot of practice the past two months since our little peanut's birth and expertly lifts her onto her shoulder, but still I place my hand over Sofie's smaller one on the baby's butt and walk beside her up the stairs.

It was Spencer who started calling me Mama, or Mama Taz, even before Nicky was born. He picked it up from Rafe, who would refer to me as Mama whenever he was holding one of many his one-sided conversations with our little girl in my belly. Sofie had not been far behind.

The first time they called me that I bawled like a baby. Both because, well, hormones, but also because somehow these kids found a way to honor me, and their mother at the same time.

I love my kids. All three of them. To think a year and a half ago, kids were not even remotely on my radar, and here I am, mothering three of them.

"First we need to get her in a clean diaper, honey," I remind Sofie when we walk into the nursery.

"You can do that."

I grin at her immediate response. The interest in diaper changes wore off quickly after Nicky had her first blowout. It had been spectacular, going all the way up her onesie and soaked all the way to the surface. If I'm being honest, the event freaked me out as well. Rafe was the only one— apparently having had plenty of experience with Spencer doing the same thing as an infant—who kept his cool. He swiftly stripped Nicky down to her skin while instructing me to fill the trough sink in our bathroom. Spencer had been fascinated, but Sofie swore off changing Nicky's diaper from then on.

She does burp her like a champ and can get her baby sister settled down in a heartbeat when she's fussy.

"All done. Want to put her pj's on?"

"Yeah."

Of course, the moment Sofie is done and tries to put her down in the bassinet, Nicky wakes up and starts crying.

"I'm thinking she needs a little fill up. Why don't we move this to the big bed?"

I don't know how long it's been when Rafe walks into the bedroom. By now both Sofie and Spencer are sprawled on the king-sized bed beside me, watching TV, while Nicky is dozing off at the breast, nursing sporadically.

I smile up at him as he sits down on the edge of the mattress by my hip.

"What?" I prompt him, when he takes in the scene in bed, and then his eyes land on me.

Before he speaks, he leans over me, kisses his baby daughter's downy head, and then my lips.

"Bonus kisses."

Also By Freya Barker

Click here to see all my books!

Standalones:

WHEN HOPE ENDS

VICTIM OF CIRCUMSTANCE

BONUS KISSES

Arrow's Edge MC Series:

EDGE OF REASON

EDGE OF DARKNESS

EDGE OF TOMORROW

PASS Series:

HIT & RUN

LIFE & LIMB

LOCK & LOAD (2021)

On Call Series:

BURNING FOR AUTUMN

COVERING OLLIE

TRACKING TAHLULA

ABSOLVING BLUE

REVEALING ANNIE

CLEAN LINES

UPPER HAND

LIKE ARROWS

HEAD START

Acknowledgments

As always there are a great number of people without whom this book would not have been possible, but for Bonus Kisses my amazing family deserves honorable mention. Without them there would be no story.

I'm so grateful for my siblings. We all have our individual lives but at a moment's notice we will pull together in a united front.

I've already talked about my mother, but she bears mentioning again. It is because of her strength, her creativity, her wisdom, and her love that we are who we are today.

And then, of course, there are the usual suspects. The people who keep me on track, correct my mistakes, support my endeavors, and promote my words. I consider every one of these people my friend;

My editor, Karen Hrdlicka, and alpha reader and proofreader, Joanne Thompson;

My agent, Stephanie Phillips of SBR Media;

My publicists, Debra Presley and Drue Hoffman and my PA Krystal Weiss of Buoni Amici Press;

My beta team—Deb Blake, Pam Buchanan, and Petra Gleason;

Every single blog and early reviewer supporting my work;

And my readers who motivate me and lift me up.

I love you all!

Freya

About the Author

USA Today bestselling author Freya Barker loves writing about ordinary people with extraordinary stories.

Driven to make her books about 'real' people; she creates characters who are perhaps less than perfect, each struggling to find their own slice of happy, but just as deserving of romance, thrills and chills in their lives.

Recipient of the ReadFREE.ly 2019 Best Book We've Read All Year Award for "Covering Ollie, the 2015 RomCon "Reader's Choice" Award for Best First Book, "Slim To None", and Finalist for the 2017 Kindle Book Award with "From Dust", and Finalist for the 2020 Kindle Book Award with "When Hope Ends", Freya continues to add to her rapidly growing collection of published novels as she spins story after story with an endless supply of bruised and dented characters, vying for attention!

https://www.freyabarker.com

If you'd like to stay up to date on the latest news and
upcoming new releases, sign up for my newsletter:
https://www.subscribepage.com/Freya_Newsletter

CPSIA information can be obtained
at www.ICGtesting.com
Printed in the USA
LVHW050712041220
673103LV00003B/286

9 781988 733562